turn me on

turn me on

Cherie Jeffrey

 NEW AMERICAN LIBRARY

New American Library
Published by New American Library, a division of
Penguin Group (USA) Inc., 375 Hudson Street,
New York, New York 10014, USA
Penguin Group (Canada), 90 Eglinton Avenue East, Suite 700, Toronto,
Ontario M4P 2Y3, Canada (a division of Pearson Penguin Canada Inc.)
Penguin Books Ltd., 80 Strand, London WC2R 0RL, England
Penguin Ireland, 25 St. Stephen's Green, Dublin 2,
Ireland (a division of Penguin Books Ltd.)
Penguin Group (Australia), 250 Camberwell Road, Camberwell, Victoria 3124,
Australia (a division of Pearson Australia Group Pty. Ltd.)
Penguin Books India Pvt. Ltd., 11 Community Centre, Panchsheel Park,
New Delhi - 110 017, India
Penguin Group (NZ), 67 Apollo Drive, Rosedale, North Shore 0745,
Auckland, New Zealand (a division of Pearson New Zealand Ltd.)
Penguin Books (South Africa) (Pty.) Ltd., 24 Sturdee Avenue,
Rosebank, Johannesburg 2196, South Africa

Penguin Books Ltd., Registered Offices:
80 Strand, London WC2R 0RL, England

First published by New American Library,
a division of Penguin Group (USA) Inc.

First Printing, July 2007
1 3 5 7 9 10 8 6 4 2

NAL REGISTERED TRADEMARK—MARCA REGISTRADA

LIBRARY OF CONGRESS CATALOGING-IN-PUBLICATION DATA
Jeffrey, Cherie.
Turn me on / Cherie Jeffrey.
p. cm.
ISBN: 978-0-451-21768-4
1. Vibrators (Massage)—Fiction. 2. Women inventors—Fiction I. Title.
PS3552.E54574T87 2007
813'.6—dc22   2006101914

Set in Bembo
Designed by Spring Hoteling

Printed in the United States of America

To the real Irma and the real Roz (in alphabetical order)

Acknowledgments

Thanks to Anne Bohner at NAL for seeing the possibilities, and to Lydia Wills at Paradigm for making the possibilities into realities, over and over. Also to our indefatigable assistant Ryan Berger, Lindy Funaki for her sharp eyes, and Didi Herald, Patricia Foster, Drue Wagner-Mees, and Ava DuPree for reading early versions of this novel and offering sage wisdom. Roxyanne Young did the official Web site for this novel, www.turnmeoninc.com.

One

Annie Albright thought of herself as an ordinary girl—with an asterisk.

She was definitely good—the kind of person who helped little old ladies across lower Market Street and dug for change in the bottom of her faux-leather hobo bag when a bum on Haight stuck out a hand.

She tried to be kind. She would never, for example, tell her best friend, Michelle Garibaldi (who was brilliant, hysterically funny, and unfortunately built), that she looked like an armored personnel carrier in her new Marc Jacobs camouflage-print sheath. Instead, Annie found a darling Chloe jacket on super sale at a boutique on Fillmore Street and gave it to her friend as an "un-birthday" present. Michelle donned the jacket *over* the camouflage sheath. Instant streamlining.

Annie came from hardworking, intellectual stock. Her parents were math professors, and she definitely inherited the hardworking part, even if she sucked at math. Though her job as assistant art director at *HottieGirl* magazine was achingly dull—doing layout on "Back-to-School Fashion Musts" was not really her idea of a good use of a B.F.A. from Syracuse—she still tried to do it well. She'd held her position for four years and hoped that someday she'd be promoted. However, her boss was forever taking credit for her ideas, which Annie was sure contributed heavily to her lateral career nontrajectory. Though she often pictured herself marching into the editor in chief's office and sticking up for herself, she couldn't gather the nerve. Assertiveness was not her strong suit.

Annie tried to be respectful. For example, the thirtysomething muscular Greek guy at the Beanery on Ninth Avenue who sold her the occasional coffee-and-bagel-to-go? She didn't look down on him because he spent his life filling cardboard cups. She might, however, fantasize *going* down on him, after which he would ravish her on the counter, plastic coffee lids flying like miniature Frisbees.

That had to do with the asterisk. Her whole life, she'd had a fertile—Fertile-Crescent-level fertile—imagination. The things she imagined almost always had to do with sex. She never knew when it was going to happen, either; it was something she couldn't control. Annie Albright had the Tourette's syndrome of sexual imagination.

At age twenty-nine, she still looked like a college kid, thanks to cherubic cheeks inherited from her round-faced grandmother, Doris. Her dirty-blond hair was baby-fine and wispy. She tried to grow it, but every time it got an inch past her chin it seemed to recoil, as if allergic to her shoulders. She had a dimpled, Day-Glo smile and saucer-wide blue eyes, which she liked; thin lips and a bra size that matched her initials, which she didn't. Utterly lacking in curves and thin as she was—this really bit her inconsequential butt—she *still* had cellulite on her thighs.

How two math professors had given birth to such a girl was beyond her. Maybe her mother had been beamed up to another planet and impregnated by an alien with cellulite, which, Annie figured, would explain both her imagination and her thighs.

Her day started as usual, at the corner of Seventh Avenue and Irving Street, waiting for the N-Judah streetcar line to take her downtown to the *HottieGirl* offices. She wore a don't-notice-me navy skirt, white blouse, and navy cardigan ensemble (knowing she was so shocking on the inside made her want to blend in on the outside). She was with her boyfriend, Elliot Wenner, who'd spent the night at her apartment. Elliot, a wildly successful pharmaceuticals salesman, wore a tailored Ralph Lauren suit and Bruno Maglis with inner lifts that made him two inches taller than the five-eight he actually was. Even counting his being on the short side, Elliot was really good-looking. His blond hair was subtly gelled and spiked, his nails were buffed, and his skin glowed from weekly appointments at the Nob Hill Spa at the Huntington Hotel. Elliot considered being high-maintenance part of the good life.

They'd met six months earlier at the BridgePoint Assisted Living Facility on Nineteenth Avenue, where Annie volunteered once a week as an art instructor. Elliot was visiting his grandmother, a new resident, and Annie had been impressed with how solicitous he'd been of the elderly woman, as well as with his Daniel Craig–ish good looks. They'd ended up going for coffee, and Elliot went on and on about how much his grandmother meant to him, which touched Annie deeply. It wasn't until their third date that she found out that Elliot would be the sole beneficiary of his grandmother's sizable estate unless she forgave Elliot's older sister for marrying a Democrat, which didn't seem likely, since grandmother hadn't spoken to granddaughter since Bill Clinton's election. One of Elliot's less-than-sterling qualities was a strong what's-in-it-for-me streak.

Still, Annie believed that the good outweighed the bad. Elliot owned a two-thousand-square-foot loft in the Marina with floor-to-ceiling windows that overlooked the Golden Gate Bridge, an impressive wine collection, and every electric toy known to humankind. Nothing made him happier than buying things, and he was as generous with Annie as he was with himself. It was nice of him, but it still made Annie uncomfortable. Other than occasionally spending much more than she should on a rare but exquisite doll (she collected them—and not only because of the lurid fantasies they sometimes sparked), she didn't share his acquisitive nature.

Oddly, Annie never had sex fantasies about Elliot. Sex with him was okay, but he was the kind of guy who needed constant feedback on his prowess: Do you like this? How about this? Was it good for you? Was it the best ever? It was kind of exhausting, and it tended to interfere with whatever vision was running through her mind at the time.

They took the streetcar down Market Street. Elliot got off near City Hall to visit some accounts before he went to his home office. She found his good-bye kiss a little distracting because she had been imagining a torrid coupling between the tall black guy in front of her bopping to his iPod and an Asian girl in hospital scrubs.

At Market and Stockton, Annie hopped off. Instead of going right to work, she detoured to the San Francisco Marriott. She hurried inside and over to the concierge desk, where a uniformed young woman with two-tone hair and a kick-ass body greeted her with a friendly wave. Her Marriott name tag read ETHEREAL, LOS ANGELES, but her real name was Ethel, after some long-dead relative. They'd met via craigslist. Since then, Ethereal had turned into a prime source for Annie's hobby.

"Cool, you made it! It came by courier yesterday," Ethereal explained as Annie approached the desk. "Wait 'til you see." From a small box, she extracted a doll no more than five inches tall, with a head made of papier-mâché and a body of cloth. She wore a green silk ball gown and carried a tiny fan in her right hand.

"Talk about a nineteenth-century beauty," Ethereal breathed, handing the doll to Annie, who held it as carefully as she would a newborn. "She's certified. The certificate is in the box."

"Five hundred, right?"

"Yep. Worth every penny."

Annie handed Ethereal the check she'd already written, carefully placed the boxed doll inside her purse, and flew out the door. What a coup. This was her first nineteenth-century doll—they were very hard to find. A quick check of her watch caused her to pick up her pace, but she knew she'd still be at least ten minutes late. Her boss hated that. Every time it happened, she'd use two fingers to point to her own eyes and then to Annie's, as if to say, *I'm watching you.*

Annie flew through the lobby, tossed a hello to the security guard (in her mind, he was undressing his petite brunette assistant with his teeth), and rode the express elevator up to the seventeenth floor. She made a beeline for *HottieGirl*'s reception area and got through the heavy double doors before she stopped dead in her tracks. Employees were streaming out, arms laden with boxes of personal effects.

"What's going on?" she asked Billy, a paunchy guy from advertising who lived in short-sleeved drip-dry. He'd gotten drunk at the last Christmas party and tried to stick his tongue down Annie's throat.

"These fuckers just went out of business! May thirtieth is the end of their fiscal year. And what day is today, boys and girls?" He scooped up a *HottieGirl* notepad from the reception desk and dropped it into his box. "It's every man for himself— take whatever isn't nailed down."

Annie felt dazed and confused. "Wait—what do you mean?"

"Closed, folded, finished," Mary Fitzgerald, an underling in the fashion department, filled in. She grabbed a handful of pens. "Sales are way off, so corporate announced they're shutting down. Nice of 'em to give us some notice, huh?"

"You mean we . . . don't have jobs anymore?" Annie asked.

"Aren't you quick on the uptake," Mary observed. She spotted a couple of logo mugs and T-shirts and nabbed them too. "I can totally sell these on eBay." She made a move-along gesture to Annie. "Get going or get gone—they're padlocking the doors at nine thirty."

Dodging exiting employees all the way, Annie made her way back to the cubicle where she'd spent the last four years of her working life. As she took in the gray space, she realized she hadn't invested enough of herself in it to fill even the smallest of boxes. She picked up the pink corporate envelope that presumably contained her final paycheck, a pair of cheap earrings, some Burt's Bees lip gloss, and a framed photo of her with her grandmother. Everything fit in her oversized purse with her new doll. Then she joined the departing lemmings heading for the sea of unemployment.

So not good. This time, instead of fantasizing about it, she really *was* getting screwed. It was notoriously hard to find decent jobs in commercial art, and everyone from her department at *HottieGirl* would be out there pounding the pavement with her. That she had just dropped five hundred bucks on a nineteenth-century doll only made matters worse. It wasn't like she had massive amounts of money in her checking account, and her savings account didn't exist.

When she hit the sidewalk, she plucked out her phone and called Elliot to tell him the bad news, but got his voice mail. That was typical— he was with customers. Well, she'd just go to his loft. She needed a shoulder to cry on, even if it was two inches higher than where nature had placed it.

Elliot's building was on Marina Boulevard across the Marina Green, which was already crowded with dog walkers, Frisbee chuckers, kite fliers, and joggers from San Francisco's considerable population that considered nine-to-five employment a sign of mental illness. Annie had a key; she just let herself into the building and took the elevator up to the penthouse. She would soon be deposited in his thousand-square-foot living room with its spectacular view

As she stepped out of the elevator, she expected to see the bridge and the bay through the floor-to-ceiling windows in a space kept spotless by thrice-weekly maid service. Instead, she saw Elliot. She also saw Czuba, the Eurotrash performance artist who lived one floor down and who had a serious lip lock on Elliot. Both were stark naked.

The thought that flew into Annie's mind was that this had to be one of her fantasies, though it seemed odd that her very first fantasy about Elliot would also involve a performance artist well on his way to a serious case of rug-burned knees.

Elliot's eyes met Annie's. He paled. "Oh, shit."

Czuba whirled to see what Elliot's "oh, shit" was about, which caused an even greater "Oh, shit!" as he forgot to dislodge the appendage upon which he'd been lavishing his attention.

All Annie wanted to do was disappear. Instead, she stumbled back into the elevator, catching her heel on the uneven space between Elliot's living room and the elevator proper. Down she went, purse flying, her newly acquired five-hundred-dollar antique doll tumbling out and promptly decapitating itself.

In other words, Annie was having a really, really bad day.

two

Just one little tug.

Even as Annie carefully opened the packaging of the 1967 Chatty Cathy doll that she'd acquired two years before from an eBay seller in Regina, Saskatchewan, she knew she shouldn't. The box had never been opened; a mint-condition doll was worth much, much more. But Annie had been at home marinating in her own unemployed-with-no-boyfriend depression for a full week. Yanking Chatty Cathy's chain might just cheer her up a little.

When the first Chatty Cathy had been manufactured, it had been a technological miracle. You pulled a ring on the doll's back, a string extended, and Chatty Cathy uttered one of a dozen sayings at random. This 1967 model had sooty-lashed, limpid azure eyes that opened and closed, a sixties bouffant blond bubble of a hairdo, and a delicate white eyelet lace dress. Annie reckoned she was worth three hundred dollars now, which unfortunately was still two hundred bucks short of the headless nineteenth-century doll that even the Rosebud Doll Hospital probably couldn't restore.

A week earlier, when she'd returned from Elliot's loft, she'd set that doll on the shelf of the hallway case that housed her collection, directly on its own head. It struck her as an apt metaphor for just how far up Elliot's ass Annie thought his head was.

He'd called her endless times, leaving long messages on her voice mail. This had happened because their love life lacked imagination, he insisted, but that could change. The irony of this would have made Annie laugh if she hadn't been in such a funk. To think how careful she'd been not to let him know how truly overactive her imagination really was.

Instead of calling him back, she turned off the ringers on both her landline and her cell. She didn't even check her e-mail for fear that Elliot would try to woo her back with one of his patented persuasive missives. He did, after all, hold several corporate records for most transactions recorded in a single day and had an uncanny ability to sweet-talk his way past any medical office receptionist.

For a week, she'd ordered in pizza, watched soap operas and the Game Show Network, and basically eschewed both personal hygiene and contact with the outside world. When her landlord knocked on her door to ask why the *San Francisco Chronicle*s were piling up on her doorstep, she'd taken the newspapers with nary a word.

Chatty Cathy's box now open, Annie carefully extracted the doll. Maybe this moment would be the doll equivalent of the I Ching—a pithy and pertinent message about the mess she was in. She pulled the ring.

"May I have a kiss?"

Swell.

Annie kissed the doll on the cheek and replaced her among her two hundred sister and half dozen brother dolls. She briefly considered setting her atop G.I. Joe but couldn't summon the energy. Even Annie's imagination seemed to be in the dumps. She loved her doll collection in an utterly unreasonable way. What if she had to sell it?

Her stomach grumbled. Maybe there was a slice of anchovy pizza left from yesterday's delivery from Milano. She padded into the kitchen and peered into the nearly empty refrigerator. Ah. One lonely slice, hardening around the edges. She snagged it and leaned against the wall, chewing as she peered out her kitchen window, which overlooked the rear of a similar building on Sixth Avenue.

Annie lived in the Inner Sunset district, a neighborhood always not-quite-poised-to-become-cool, and notable mostly for some of the worst weather in the Bay Area. Every afternoon like clockwork, a blanket of fog would sweep in from the Pacific, dropping the temperature by twenty degrees in twenty minutes. The pea soup shroud seemed to reflect her mood.

Everyone kept their lights on because of the fog—she could see easily into her neighbors' apartments. In the flat directly across from hers, two gorgeous lesbians were doing what lesbians do with the aid of something long and double-ended. Meanwhile, from the apartment above her own, Annie anticipated the rhythmic *thump-thump-thump* she'd come to expect at three o'clock from the two University of San Francisco law students who'd just graduated and were now preparing for the bar exam. He was a moaner; she was a screamer.

You learned a lot about your neighbors when you were home during the day.

Annie licked tomato sauce off her pinky and eyed her cell on the kitchen table, tempted to call Elliot. In the past week, sex, sex, sex had been all around her in real life, but none of it belonged to her. If she called him, she could have sex too. If she didn't, then eventually she'd have to start dating. She hated dating. Why were guys so much more terrific in her imagination than they ever seemed to be in real life?

She heard the unmistakable sound of a key in her door. Oh, no. Elliot. She sprinted toward it, hoping to lock the dead bolt before he got in the—

Too late. It opened. Only it wasn't Elliot. It was her grandmother Doris, who frowned as she took in her disheveled granddaughter. Her grandmother still had a great body, due partly to genetics and partly to thrice-weekly Pilates at the Jewish Community Center. "You don't call, you don't e-mail, it's been a week. Who's throwing a PP?"

"It's a pity party for one," Annie explained, crossing her arms over her stained pajama top. "You are not invited."

"So I invited myself." Doris marched past Annie and dropped her chartreuse macramé purse, which matched one of the many colors of her handwoven poncho, on the coffee table in the living room. "Your place smells like fish."

"Anchovies," Annie said petulantly. "On my pizza."

"I can see, you're wearing half the sauce. What, are you saving it in case you get hungry later?" Doris headed for the kitchen, where she knotted an overflowing plastic trash bag. "I figured you had some tragedy that wasn't death. I'm right, right?"

"Right."

Doris nodded. "Of course, because if it *was* death I would have heard, so instead it has to be either work or love, but from the looks of you I would have to go for love—no one should look like that over their employment. So what happened?"

"It was work. I lost my job. *And* it was love. I caught Elliot cheating." She considered adding "with a guy," but it didn't seem like the kind of thing a person should share with her seventy-five-year-old grandmother.

"T.G., darling, though I didn't want to say it when you were shtupping him." Doris found a sponge and some 409 and went to work on the counter.

"What do you mean, 'Thank God'?" Annie demanded. "I thought you liked Elliot."

"*You* liked Elliot," Doris pointed out. "I kept my mouth shut. He was such a Republican, darling. Dollar signs for pupils. As for the job, it was all wrong for you anyway. You'll find something better. You have paper towels somewhere?"

"I guess. Under the sink. You don't have to clean for me, Gramma. I can do it."

"*Can* and *will* are not necessarily the same thing." She found the paper towels and took a much-needed second pass at the counter. "So how did you find out about Elliot?"

Annie's eyes flitted to her Betty Boop wall clock. Three fifteen. The USF students were overdue. "I walked in on him. The end," she said quickly. Her eyes flitted toward the ceiling. Was that a groan she heard? "You can go, Gramma. Really. I'll call you. I promise. And remember: your key is for emergencies only."

Doris shook the salt-and-pepper curls out of her soft gray eyes. "When was the last time you were out of this fishy apartment?"

"Um . . . a week."

"Put something on. You can shower later. We'll buy you some air freshener on the way. We're going somewhere so that I can give you patented G.M.A."

"Grandmotherly advice," Annie translated.

"Exactly."

Annie would have fought more, except that she could clearly hear the beginnings of a figurative oral argument from upstairs. And she couldn't pose an objection. "Fine. I'll be quick."

"Excellent," Doris said. "Because I know exactly what you need."

"Your neighbor Bella's house is what I need?" Annie asked, as Doris led her up the front walk of the white frame house in the far reaches of the Richmond district, over on the other side of Golden Gate Park.

"Trust me."

"We can't go to your place?" Annie glanced fondly at her grandmother's home next door, a clone of Bella's. It was located in the closest thing that San Francisco had to a Jewish neighborhood; Doris and Murray purchased it during the Korean War and had kept it ever since. While her husband was alive, Doris never worked. She was thoroughly devoted to him, her children, and grandchildren, to her volunteer work at her synagogue, and to staying in excellent physical shape. After Murray died, nine months ago, she substituted her friends for her husband. She was always willing to help one or more of them with their various ailments or psychological crises.

Annie adored her grandmother and she adored her house, though she realized that since Grandpa Murray had died, she'd rarely visited. Either Doris came to see her or they went to one of the many cultural events her grandmother loved. As they climbed Bella's front steps, Annie promised herself to come for Shabbat dinner at least once a month from now on.

"Bella adores you, and you haven't seen her in ages." Doris opened the front door and called inside, "Girls! We have a guest of honor!"

Girls? Annie was aghast. "I didn't even shower, Gramma. I can't meet anyone."

Doris made a dismissive gesture. "Your sense of smell goes after sixty-five. They'll never know the difference."

Bella's house was identical to Doris's on the inside, too. As Doris ushered her into the living room, Bella rushed forward for a hug. "Annie!"

Annie hugged the slender woman gingerly, certain that she smelled as funky as she looked. "Hi, Bella. I didn't know we were going to see anyone or I would have, um . . . cleaned up a little."

Well, at least she'd brushed her teeth.

There were six other women of Doris's generation settled

on various chintz-covered couches and chairs, with coffee cups and bowls of nuts or fruit in front of them.

"Girls," Doris announced, "some of you already know my granddaughter, Annie, Debbie's daughter. Annie, this is Irma, Ruth, Ettie, Roz, the other Irma, and Marge."

A chorus of "Hello," "Welcome," and "How's your mother?" greeted Annie as Bella steered her onto the bottle green love seat next to the taller of the two Irmas. A glass of iced tea materialized. Then her grandmother faced her friends, palms up in the air.

"So now let me tell you why Bella invited all of you here today," Doris began. "Let me ask you: when was the last time you felt fabulous all over?"

"Before Herbie died," said short Irma from the couch. She wore designer jeans and a Donna Karan warm-up jacket and looked to be in excellent shape. "God, I miss sex."

"Not me," Ettie declared. She was short and slender, with a long gray braid down her back. Annie vaguely recalled that she taught art at a junior college. "Well, at least not with Harry. A wonderful man, but in bed—a yawn."

Annie almost choked on her iced tea.

"Sorry, dear." Ettie nodded at Annie. "I didn't mean to shock you."

"No, no, that's . . . fine," Annie lied.

Tall Irma, who Annie was pretty sure was wearing one of those clip-on hairpieces, because the color of the hair at the back of her head didn't quite match the color of the hair at the front of her head, went wide-eyed. "You had a basis of comparison?"

"Certainly," Ettie affirmed. "I had a wild youth."

"I waited," Roz admitted. "Irving knew nothing and I knew less than nothing."

"You had three children, Roz," Doris pointed out, as she pulled a small trunk on wheels out from under the coffee table. "Evidently you both figured it out."

"Not really," Roz said. She wore a low-cut T-shirt that showed off an impressive cleavage, and lots of southwestern jewelry. "I'm just very fertile. I got pregnant every time we had sex." She lifted a hand to push a stray hair off her face, and her turquoise bangle bracelets slid up and down one graceful arm. "I bought him a book, once, from City Lights bookstore. It had pictures. I thought we could look at them together. He said, 'Who needs it?'"

"I was lucky," tall Irma said, setting her coffee cup on the table. "In that department, Herbie was gifted. But now that he's gone . . ." She spread her hands wide. "Nothing."

Doris raised a finger. "All of that is about to change. Ladies, we don't have our husbands around anymore. Which is why we need to take things I.O.O.H.—into our own hands. So to speak." With a flourish, she opened the trunk. It was filled with sex toys of every size and shape imaginable, and some sizes and shapes that even Annie had never imagined.

Annie looked from her grandmother to the trunk and back again. A thought struck her: Was it possible that her grandmother fantasized about sex as much as she did? Holy shit. Was it *genetic*?

"I have given every item in this trunk a personal trial run," Doris explained.

"Gramma!" Annie exclaimed.

"Don't Gramma me," Doris said. "You're a woman, I'm a woman." She looked around at her friends. "I started distributing for Funtime Industries a few weeks ago."

"But why?" Annie asked.

Doris arched one brow. "Fun."

Doris's friends chuckled.

"Oh, close your mouth, Annie," Bella said. "You look like you're catching flies." She went to the trunk and extracted a vibrator in the shape of a duck. "Do you think women over seventy suddenly aren't women anymore?"

Annie couldn't quite decide what to say. Because honestly, she'd never given it a moment's thought. She could hardly deal with the idea of turning thirty, much less seventy.

"Seventy-five is the new fifty," Bella declared, examining the duck's beak. "We're all widowed or divorced. And men our age want women who really *are* fifty."

Well, how unfair was *that*? Annie thought.

Doris gestured toward the open trunk. "Welcome to the wonderful world of B.O.B.—battery-operated boyfriends." She extracted a light blue vibrator with an extra prong extending from just above the base. "This one, girls, is called Ultimate Pleasure, and I can attest from personal experience that's exactly what it provides. The tip has no nubs, providing for insertion ease—although I can throw in free lubricant with every order, no problem—and there are rotating beads in the center, which provide an extra measure of satisfaction."

"What about the other prong?" asked tall Irma.

"Simultaneous inner and outer stimulation," Doris explained.

Ettie smirked. "Well, that would be a first. What about power?"

"It runs on double-A batteries." To illustrate, Doris flicked a series of switches at the base, and the various appendages started to hum. Annie scanned the faces in the room. Talk about playing to a rapt audience.

"It won't replace my Herbie," short Irma sighed.

"So name it Herbie," Bella suggested as she returned the duck to the trunk. "What else do you recommend, Doris?"

"I'll let you girls choose for yourselves. Funtime takes cash, checks, and all major credit cards."

"Anyone want more fruit?" Bella called out as she headed for the kitchen. "I have apples and bananas; you have to eat the bananas because in another day they'll go bad."

"Go and explore, Bella." Doris shooed her friend back into the living room. "Annie and I will bring the fruit, and more coffee."

As the women crowded around the trunk, Doris motioned for Annie to follow her to the kitchen, where she set the Ultimate Pleasure vibrator on the counter. "So, Annie darling. Do you have one of these?"

"I . . . um . . . no," Annie admitted, eyeing the vibrator, which looked very strange sitting next to a tasteful tiered-fruit arrangement.

"Murray bought me my first," Doris reminisced. "He never minded a little extra spice." She turned on Bella's coffeemaker. "When your mother and her sisters were little, time was of the essence. One of these can be very helpful in that department."

Annie was beyond shocked. "You and Grandpa . . . ?"

"Of course. Then, once the girls were out of the house, we had all the time in the world, but by then he wasn't what he used to be," Doris went on. "Then the Viagra came along, and it was S.S.S., day and night."

Sex, sex, sex. Dear God. It really *was* genetic.

"Anyway, this is for you." Doris took the vibrator from the counter and thrust it at her granddaughter. "Take it home, give it a test run, you'll sleep with a smile on your face."

Annie had no choice. She took it.

When she got home, she cleaned her apartment, took a long, hot bubble bath, and then spent the night with Ultimate Pleasure. It was nothing short of amazing. Just before she fell asleep, she had one final thought: Ultimate Pleasure might be a battery-operated boyfriend, but its designer *had* to have been a woman.

three

Charlie Silver rubbed his chin thoughtfully as he eyed the trio of cute blondes drinking at the far end of the bar. "Wisconsin," he pronounced.

"Minnesota, South Dakota, whatever," mused his friend Mark Wolfson. "Someplace with a lot of last names that start with Van. Van Dyken. Van der Root. I believe we are talking au naturel blonde top to bottom, and it's a thing of beauty."

"Yes on the no-need-for-color-touch-ups, no on the geography," Charlie insisted, draining his glass of Anchor Steam. He reached into his pocket, pulled out a ten-dollar bill, and slapped it on the bar. "Ten bucks says Wisconsin."

Mark raised the bushy eyebrows and one of the two chins that had made him a mainstay of character roles in theaters all over the Bay Area. "I will see that and raise you five. Even you aren't that good."

"Watch and learn, my friend." Charlie grinned as Mark extracted his wallet, then got the bartender's attention. "Hey,

Sal? Get a round of three Irish coffees going, with Jameson's, please. I'll signal you."

The bartender whisked away Charlie's empty glass. "What's the bet this time?"

"Wisconsin." Charlie caught the eye of the tallest blonde and offered a slight nod of hello, and then he turned back to the bartender. It was never good to come on too strong too fast; there'd be no more eye contact with the girls until the drinks were delivered. Still, via the mirror behind the bar, he saw the women sneaking peeks in his direction.

Sal shook his head as he started on the Irish coffees. "In my next life, Charlie, I want to come back as you."

"Hey, he's going down this time," Mark maintained.

Charlie very much doubted that. He and Mark had been coming to the Buena Vista Café here at Fisherman's Wharf for years; it felt as comfortable as his own living room. He'd met many a girl here, and each relationship—if you could call it that—was good, while it lasted. Most of them were extremely short-term, since this was one of the most famous tourist haunts in the city. Those were the easiest. No muss, no fuss, drop her at SFO for her flight home on Sunday night.

In the short term, Charlie was everything a girl could want—sweet, attentive, and very appreciative of whatever sexual favors were offered. This tended to make girls think long-term, and therein lay the problem. Charlie had no interest in the long term; on to the next was simply too much fun. Hence, the Buena Vista was the perfect hangout.

"So which one is tonight's lucky lady?" Mark asked. "I'm

guessing it's that tall drink of water. If she's double-jointed, I expect a play-by-play postmortem."

"Hey, you know I never kiss and tell."

"So don't kiss, and tell me the rest," Mark suggested.

Charlie shook his head. Whether or not he hooked up with the long-stemmed beauty, who was, at the moment, laughing over something her friend had said, he wouldn't breathe a word of it to Mark or to anyone else. Whether a relationship lasted a day, a week or a—well, they pretty much never lasted a month. But however long it did last, Charlie did not brag or boast. He might be a pickup artist, but dammit, he was a pickup artist with a *conscience*.

He and Mark had been friends since middle school; they lived only a block apart in the quirky Potrero Hill neighborhood of San Francisco, a locale known for the outstanding Goat Hill pizzeria and glorious sunny days when the rest of the city was fog-swathed. They were pretty different from each other. Charlie loved cities, and Mark was an outdoorsman who liked nothing better than to tackle the high Sierras with two matches, a pocketknife, and precious little else. But right from the start, they'd been an unbeatable team.

As a kid, Charlie hadn't thought about his looks much one way or the other. Then, during the summer before ninth grade, he shot up four inches over Mark and his voice dropped an octave to a sexy growl. His shaggy dark hair fell boyishly over his forehead, nicely complementing his deep-set hazel eyes. A job as a swimming-counselor-in-training at a day camp in Berkeley earned him a glowing tan, broad shoulders, and a well-defined six-pack.

When he showed up for day one of freshman year, girls were all over him like sugar junkies on Ghirardelli chocolate. And not just ninth-grade girls, either. Sophomores, juniors, and even one notable senior beauty took it upon themselves to teach Charlie the way around more than just his new school. Turned out he was a quick study.

In and of itself, that might have made Charlie reasonably popular. But the clincher was, he *saw* people—really saw them, noticing things that other guys couldn't or didn't bother to see. He couldn't fix his own car, couldn't do trigonometry worth shit, but when it came to picking up on the almost hidden clues about who a person was and what he or she was thinking, Charlie was a genius.

He remembered Rishan Sue Kennedy, a cute redhead in his American history class during junior year. She started coming to school with dark circles under her eyes, nibbling anxiously on her lower lip as she covertly counted out her money in the lunch line, then bought only a yogurt. Charlie took to buying extra food and insisting that he was full. Could Rishan Sue take some of it? Turned out Rishan Sue was the oldest of five kids, her mom was in the hospital, her dad had just lost his job, and Rishan Sue was working until midnight every day after school at a fast-food restaurant to help make ends meet.

Charlie never set out to become cool; it just happened. By senior year, all the girls wanted him and all the guys wanted to *be* him. When it became known that he was an amateur rock-and-roll historian who kept his several hundred concert ticket stubs in an old Superman lunch box, other guys started doing the same thing. Girls invited him to obscure concerts, hoping to impress him.

It only got better in college, and better still after he graduated from UC-Irvine with a double major in American studies and education. Instead of going right to work, Charlie took off for what was supposed to be three months in Europe. Those three months stretched into three years around the world, due to his uncanny ability to find women of all nationalities, sizes, and shapes willing to serve as his own personal international welcome wagon.

When he came back from his tour of the mattresses of Europe, the Middle East, and Asia, he found himself at a loss for what to do with his life. One college friend who had inherited a seat on the Pacific Stock Exchange urged Charlie to join his brokerage firm. That held no appeal. Other friends were in business or just finishing law school, but Charlie couldn't see himself doing those things, either. His world travels didn't just expose him to a few dozen exotic bedrooms— he'd seen how many people around the world were dying for a good education.

When Charlie decided to teach eighth grade at a charter school in the rough Hunter's Point section of San Francisco, his friends all tried to talk him out of it. Even Mark doubted that Charlie's charm would see him through gang wars and a salary that topped out in five figures no matter how long he taught.

Charlie had no idea if Mark was right or not, but he'd always gone with his gut. He did it again and signed a yearlong contract. If he hated it, he figured, he could always bail. Only he didn't hate it. In fact, tough as it was, he loved it. For maybe the first time in his life, instead of just feeling wanted, he felt needed. More than once he'd been able to avert a hallway fistfight (the only reason guns and knives weren't involved was because of the metal detectors at the front door) by observing the obvious telltale signs that weren't so obvious to others: the squinted eyes, the sidelong glance, an uneasy quiet when he stepped into the boys' room where the stall doors had been removed in a mostly futile effort to discourage drug dealing, or worse.

It was no shocker that he became the heartthrob of the Mays–McCovey Academy teachers' lounge, either.

Yet for all the female attention, he had no one that he would call his actual girlfriend. Most of the time, after a week or so, girls bored him. The ones who didn't bore him tended to run for the hills when they found out that he chose to work for the city and county of San Francisco and that his future earnings potential had been severely compromised by his career choice.

For his first few years at Mays–McCovey, it hadn't mattered. There was no lack of female companionship for himself—or for Mark, who was a bit like a remora on Charlie's shark. Now, as he'd approached and surpassed the big 3-0, he'd started to have occasional thoughts—which he quickly banished from his mind—about things like family, children, and bar or bat mitzvahs. It was disillusioning in the best possible way to see potential partners bolt for the hills once they figured out the spreadsheet for his future.

In the short term, it didn't matter. Meeting women for a

night, a couple of nights, or even a week or two of fun, was still no issue.

He glanced at the girls down the bar. This was the moment. "It's showtime," he told Mark as he headed for the fairer side of the bar. He'd been studying the girls. The tallest, who wore a red tank top, tight jeans, and had blond hair devoid of roots tied back with a green scrunchie, was obviously the ringleader. The two friends addressed their remarks to her. He knew he should, too.

"Excuse me, but can I offer you some native San Franciscan advice?"

The tall girl spun slowly on her barstool. "I don't know," she said with a flirty smile. "Can you?"

"I could try."

She regarded him from under lashes heavy with mascara. "My mom told me that I shouldn't talk to strangers."

"Then I'd better not be one," Charlie said with a disarming grin. "I'm Charlie Silver. Born and raised right here in San Francisco, although my parents retired to North Carolina five years ago. Don't know why anyone would leave the best city in the world, though. Don't tell them I said that." He held out his hand.

"I won't." The blonde shook his outstretched hand. "I'm Kristen. And these are my friends, Jeanne and Nella."

"From?" Charlie asked.

"Minneapolis," Nella replied. "But we all grew up in the same town in—"

"Wisconsin," Charlie declared.

Kristen's eyes went wide. "How did you know?"

"Some of it is your accent," Charlie admitted. "I heard you talking. That narrowed it to the Midwest. But the kicker is Jeanne's key chain."

He pointed to Jeanne's pocketbook, which rested on the bar to the right of a half-consumed Irish coffee. There was a key chain clipped to it—a small hunk of orange plastic cheese. "The cheese. Dead giveaway. Go Packers."

"Well, well, girls, it's *CSI San Francisco*," Jeanne quipped.

"So, what's your native San Franciscan advice, Charlie?" Kristen asked. "Never go to Fisherman's Wharf because it's full of tourists? Let me remind you of something, Charlie. *You're* here, too."

"Good point," Charlie agreed. "Mind if I taste your drink, Kristen?"

She handed it to him, and he sipped. "Yep, just as I suspected." He handed it back to her. "Next time, ask for a *Jameson's* Irish coffee. Of course, if you come and sit with me and my friend, you'll find that the bartender has already made you a round."

Kirsten turned to Sal, who was pouring three Jameson's Irish coffees at that very moment, per Charlie's instructions.

Five minutes later, they were all sitting around a table, laughing and drinking. Thirty minutes later, Charlie had Kristen's phone number. A half hour after that, Mark, Jeanne, and Nella were on their way to a blues club in North Beach. Charlie and Kristen were headed to the top of Mount Sutro to take in the view of the City.

After that, the night was still very, very young.

 four

"I have exactly twenty-seven minutes before I have to argue a demurrer in front of Judge Robertson LaRousse, and he hates women lawyers even though he used to be one before his sex change."

Annie's best friend, Michelle, grimaced as they settled onto a park bench and unwrapped the falafels that they'd purchased from a street vendor on the Market Street side of City Hall Park. "Remind me again why I went to law school?"

"Because you have a lot of hostility, you love to argue, and you love money," Annie replied, then licked some tahini off her pinky. She and Michelle had been best friends since they'd met at Syracuse as freshmen and Michelle had walked in on her then-roommate Paige, who was stoned on some lethal combination of E, alcohol, and what she thought were seratonin reuptake inhibitors but turned out to be high doses of prednisone. Said roommate had one foot out their sixth-floor window and was preparing to launch her first solo flight—Michelle moved to stop her.

Annie lived two doors down, heard the commotion, and came in just in time to yank Paige back from turning herself into a blood-and-guts Rorschach test on the plaza below. After the campus rent-a-cops and an ambulance had collected Paige, Annie and Michelle went for coffee and discovered they had absolutely nothing in common: not their looks, loves, life outlooks, or personalities. Yet they came to admire each other for exactly that reason. It wasn't only in love that opposites attracted. They shared an apartment for two years, and Annie was thrilled when Michelle came to law school at Hastings and then took an associate's job at McCutcheon Doyle. With the help of her parents and her signing bonus, she'd bought an enviably large flat in Noe Valley that had appreciated nicely in five years.

Annie chewed her falafel and held her face up to the noonday sun, though the fog spilling over Mount Sutro promised a gloomy afternoon. Ever since she'd experienced the Ultimate Pleasure two nights before—and repeatedly ever since—she'd been in a decidedly better mood. True, she had no job, no money, and a vibrator that was not exactly a great conversationalist, but somehow the funk she'd wallowed in for a week had been buzzed away.

Michelle had been Annie's first phone call the morning after the Ultimate Pleasure. She'd filled her friend in on both the negative—no job, no boyfriend—and the positive— her new B.O.B. Michelle's response had been something gentle and supportive like, "Are you fucking crazy?" She was working on the same motion she'd be arguing in twenty minutes, but demanded that Annie meet her for lunch the next day. Which was how dark-haired Michelle, in a size fourteen Ralph Lauren power suit, and Annie, in size four Lucky jeans and a 1940s-era red satin bed jacket, were dining both alfresco and on the clock.

A dark-skinned guy in a red and green dashiki strode by and gave Michelle a lascivious grin.

"Fuck," Michelle muttered. "Why is it that the only guys who are attracted to me are from countries where goats are part of a dowry?"

"What you need is an Ultimate Pleasure," Annie suggested. "All he wants to do is to make you happy."

Michelle fixed an evil eye on Annie. "You understand that you're deeply disturbed, right? You're talking about a *vibrator*." She did a quick check of her Chanel tank watch, polished off her falafel, and wadded up the wrapper. "His Wideness Judge Robertson awaits, so we need to cut to the chase." She opened her black Italian leather briefcase and pulled out a sheaf of papers. "Latex is not healthy. Neither is unemployment. You need to find a new job. And you need to start dating."

"Eventually," Annie murmured. A woman in a pink-and-white polka-dot dress was about to cross paths with a uniformed city cop directly in front of them. To her shock, the cop lifted the woman's dress with one hand and cuffed her to a tree with the other.

"Annie? You with me here?" Michelle barked.

Annie blinked. The cop and the woman passed each other.

Clearly the woman in the polka-dot dress wasn't really about to be a participant in a man-in-uniform fantasy.

"Sorry?"

"I signed you up for JDate."

"*What?* When?"

"When do you think? Yesterday, after you told me that Elliot was out and something that required double-A batteries was in. I printed out some of the best responses. Here." She thrust the stack of papers at Annie.

Annie cringed. The idea of signing up for a computer dating service was appalling. She was the kind of girl who had always let things come—or not.

"Come on," Michelle urged. "Look what your approach has gotten you. An ex who goes both ways and a pink slip. Take your lawyer's advice. *Read.*"

Annie sighed and read the first one aloud.

"You say you're a dark-haired powerful woman with deluxe curves and a mouth to match. I like dark-haired powerful women with deluxe curves and a mouth to match. I wonder if you'll use your mouth to—"

"Oh, sorry, that's mine." Michelle plucked the paper from Annie and slid it smoothly into her open briefcase.

"You signed up for JDate? But you're *Catholic.*"

Michelle shrugged. "Sue me, I like Jewish guys. Read on."

"I'm a forty-three-years-young computer consultant who has been fortunate enough to become very successful at a very young age. I own my own Gulfstream jet and dream about the kind of girl who would like to be wined, dined, and whisked off to some exotic locale for dinner as my copilot. I have all my own hair and teeth and would like a woman with same."

"No, no. I changed my mind. Throw that one out," Michelle decreed.

"Not that I'm remotely interested," Annie began, "but just out of curiosity, what's the problem with him?"

Michelle sucked in her cheeks. "Think, Anniekins. Would a guy who was really forty-three brag about having his own hair and teeth? This jerk is at least sixty-three. His teeth are probably implants and he has visible hair plugs." She shuddered. "Next."

"Sunrise, sunset, swiftly flow the days. I'm twenty-four, a successful actor-dancer-singer who wants to find that forever kind of love with the right creature. I'm not the run-around type and have grown weary of the dating scene. I would love to meet someone with a soft touch and a hard body who appreciates an artistic guy who makes a mean Mojito."

"What was I thinking?" Michelle lamented. "Definitely not him. 'Makes a mean Mojito' means he's working as a bartender like every other unemployed actor in this city. Also notice the reference to wanting to meet the right 'creature' and meet 'someone' who is 'hardbodied.' Definitely gay but had a ton of psychotherapy mandated by his parents and is trying to convince himself he's straight. Bottom line: he's passing and you don't want to get into that again. Take a big fat forget-it."

"I thought you only printed out the good ones!" Annie shuffled the gay/maybe-gay/maybe-not actor's sheet to the bottom of the pile.

"No, no. It's psychological warfare, though I spared you Arnie, who uploaded a pic of himself in a thong and high heels so that you'd really appreciate it when you got to *this*." She tapped an index finger on the next sheet of paper.

"I'm thirty-four and own my own boutique advertising agency in the City, but I'm still hoping to write the Great American Novel. I'm on the tall side, hazel eyes and brown hair if you care about those things, and stay in shape via competitive-level tennis. I own a house in Mill Valley and another in Squaw Valley, where I like to spend the summer fishing and the winter Black Diamond skiing. What do I look for in a woman? A female me."

"Gee, a female him," Annie mused. "I guess that means he can go fuck himself." She thrust the printouts toward Michelle. "We have absolutely nothing in common. I don't fish, I don't ski, I don't play tennis, and I don't do bachelors who live in Marin County."

"Oh, like you and Edible Elliot walked in lockstep," Michelle scoffed, taking the papers and shoving them into her briefcase. "Anyway, you already answered this guy. Via your attorney."

"You didn't. Michelle, I *already* don't like him."

"In fact, I did. In your witty and intriguing reply, you mentioned your background in commercial art, how *HottieGirl* had folded, and how you were looking for a job. Then he said there might be an opening at his ad agency, and maybe you could meet for coffee and he could tell you about it. You're meeting him in . . ." Michelle checked her watch again. "Two hours. At his office in the Marina. And I've got to get to court. Right now. Walk with me."

"Michelle—"

Michelle handed back the single printout from the ad exec, whose name was Eric Berry, then started up the sidewalk toward the courthouse so quickly that Annie had to trot to keep up. "Don't panic. You're meeting him to network. Maybe you'll find a job and maybe you'll meet his brother, who will turn out to be as strange as you are and the love of your life. My point is, you will be stuck with unemployment and the Ultimate Pleasure unless you get out there. You needed a nudge. I nudged."

Annie sighed. She knew Michelle was right. It was just so hard for her to "get out there." In her experience, life in her head was always more intriguing than life in the real world. Other girls wanted a guy who measured up to, say, their father. Annie wanted a guy who could measure up to her own imagination.

"Okay. As long as he doesn't expect me to play tennis with him."

Michelle stopped and took Annie by the arms. "Not to worry. You told him that you're just getting over a sprained ankle. Limp a little. And don't wear a bed jacket."

Eric Berry leaned across his desk toward Annie. "Thanks for coming to my office. I've been chained here for two weeks. We're doing a new thing for the California Avocado Growers. Stodgy bunch; they've hated everything we've come up with. So, Annie . . ." His as-advertised hazel eyes probed hers. As advertised, he was tall, good-looking, and in excellent shape. "Is your name short for something?"

"Um, no," Annie replied. She crossed her legs and rearranged her black portfolio where she'd set it on Eric's black desk. "It's, you know, long. For Anne."

"Ah." Eric clucked his tongue and sat back as if she'd just filled him in on a fascinating detail of her life. "I thought it might be Anne-Marie, something like that."

"Gee, are you allowed to be an Anne-Marie and Jewish at the same time?"

He didn't laugh. Not even a smile. Instead, he sipped from a bottle of Perrier as Annie took in his large and well-appointed office, with posters from various advertising campaigns for products ranging from California Organic Avocados to the Pacific Salmon Fisheries Association.

"So few people are completely Jewish anymore," Eric mused. "I'm half."

"Top or bottom?" Annie quipped. "Bottom is better, because then you don't have to deal with that pesky circumcision thing late in life."

Eric just stared at her. Annie flushed. Gee, she'd thought that was pretty funny, but evidently Eric didn't.

"I was joking," she added lamely.

He finally smiled. "So, Annie. What's your favorite area in Lake Tahoe to ski?"

"I don't actually ski. It is beautiful up there, though."

"You don't *ski*?"

He said this with the horror that might have resulted if Annie'd said, "I don't bathe."

"See, the thing about skiing," Annie began, "is that it's really cold outside."

The joke bombed like a turd after too much Passover matzo. Eric clucked his tongue again. "Let me take a guess. You don't fish, you don't play tennis—"

"I did once win a Ping-Pong tournament—"

"No offense, Annie, but I don't think this is going to work out personally. Let's take a look at your portfolio." He reached across his desk and opened it, looking at tear sheets from *HottieGirl*, flipping the pages, clucking his tongue again as he did.

Okay, the tongue-clucking thing was beyond annoying. What woman could put up with that? She had zero interest in him. On the other hand, she needed a job, and advertising agencies need art directors. The way he was examining her portfolio seemed to indicate that he was interested. Maybe there was hope.

Finally, Eric closed the portfolio. "A little young for us."

Annie was crushed. She wanted to say that *of course* the work seemed young; the intended age demographic of *Hottie-Girl* was somewhere between birth and fifteen and the intended age demographic of the California Avocado Growers was somewhere between forty and death. Didn't he have any imagination at all?

But she didn't say any of that. She never did.

"Well." She took her portfolio back and wound the elastic

band around it to keep it closed. She rose. "Thanks for look-ing at my work. Good look with your, uh, life." She started to get up, but Eric motioned her back into her chair with a smile.

"Annie, please, don't be so quick to throw away a new connection!"

Annie fiddled with the edge of her portfolio. "I'm sorry, but . . . what connection?"

"Excellent question!" He clucked his tongue again. "I like that about you!"

Huh? Annie felt as if she had just walked into a com-pletely different movie.

Eric walked over to a standing easel and turned around a thick piece of foam board that rested on it. While the back of the foam board had been white, the front was a blown-up graphic: APEX COMMUNICATIONS AND TELEPHONICS: A MUL-TILEVEL MARKETING PLAN FOR EXCELLENCE.

"Apex is, quite simply, changing the way America com-municates," Eric said. "It cuts your telephone and Internet bills in half. Who wants to save money, Annie? *America* wants to save money!"

"Uh-huh." Annie eyed the door longingly.

"And here's the beauty part," Eric went on. "If you sign up friends and family, you'll earn a percentage of their bills. And if they sign up any of *their* friends, you'll earn another percentage. Plus, Apex offers coverage equivalent to any of the other voice-over-Internet protocols. I'd be happy to give you a demonstration. Or show you the PowerPoint. Which would you prefer?" Eric looked at her expectantly.

"So . . . you're trying to sell me on a pyramid scheme?" Annie queried.

Eric put both hands over his heart. "Perish the thought, Annie! Apex is so much more than that!"

All righty, then. Annie rose again. "I'll just be leaving now, Eric." She edged toward the door.

"I can give you some literature to take with you!"

Annie fled. No more blind dating. *Ever.* At the moment, vibrating latex with no tongue to cluck was looking like the romance of a lifetime.

five

"These have been the most wonderful two days of my life," Kristen breathed. She ran a forefinger over his lips. "I just wish I had met you at the beginning of my trip, instead of at the end."

Charlie didn't necessarily share her sentiment, but he certainly had enjoyed the last forty-eight hours. Who would have figured that a girl raised on a dairy farm would be familiar with every position ever invented and a few that weren't yet? It's not like Holstein cows had creative sex.

The answer became clear when Kristen explained that she'd recently gotten a card game called Kama Sutra: 50 Ways to Love Your Lover in a goodie bag at a friend's bridal shower. Charlie was the lucky man upon whom she'd bestowed her new knowledge.

Charlie softly kissed the tender spot at the center of her elegant collarbone. "We'll always have Fisherman's Wharf," he joked sweetly, because she had mentioned how much she adored *Casablanca*.

"God." She sighed, then nuzzled her dainty nose against his cheek. "Why do you have to be so perfect and why do I have to live so far away?"

Charlie did a quick check of his bedside clock. He had an hour to shower, dress, and get Kristen in a cab to the downtown Airport bus stop, where she would meet her two friends for their flight back to Minneapolis. Then he'd make the short drive to school to see his eighth graders just before Kanye West came over the public address system. Principal Witherspoon was using rap with positive messages instead of bells to indicate the beginning and ending of class periods.

"I have something for you." He reached into his nightstand, took out a small box gift-wrapped in lavender paper, and handed it to Kristen. Her eyes went wide.

"For me?" As she sat up, the pale blue sheet slipped to her waist, baring a pair of achingly perfect pink-tipped breasts. She tore off the paper with a child's eagerness.

Charlie smiled, and not just at the breasts. The Parting Gift was a staple in his leave-'em-happy arsenal. He always tried to find something that truly fit the girl to whom it was given.

"Oh, Charlie!" Kristen held up a small, framed photo that Mark had taken of them with his cell phone. They were standing at the top of Lombard Street, looking down the "Crookedest Street in the World." Mark had e-mailed it to Charlie, Charlie had printed it and put it in a simple frame.

Now Kristen was gushing over it. Before he knew it, her arms were around him and her lips were heading south.

Before Charlie gave himself up to the moment, he decided that just this once he would go to school neither shaved nor showered, which would buy him fifteen extra minutes with Miss La Crosse Coulee Queen 2000.

There was nothing like going out with a bang.

"So, why did the Sharks and the Jets hate each other so much?" Charlie asked his students as he paced around his overcrowded classroom. There were thirty-two eighth graders in his first-period class, though when twenty-five showed up, as was the case today, Charlie considered it a good day. Many of his students came from homes where they'd learned to read gang signs before they'd ever opened a book. Ninety percent qualified for the state's free breakfast and lunch programs. Everyone knew someone who had been shot or stabbed; gunshot wounds were badges of honor.

When he'd started teaching eighth-grade humanities at Mays-McCovey four years ago, he'd asked the principal, Joe Witherspoon, who'd been at the job only two years himself at that time, if he could try his students on Shakespeare. Joe thought Charlie was crazy. Didn't Charlie realize that almost all of these kids read well below grade level? But Charlie persevered. Finally Joe gave him the go-ahead. Yes, Charlie could try it. But if it failed—and Witherspoon, as much as he liked Charlie, was sure it would—the Bard of Avon would have to go.

Honestly? Charlie hadn't been confident his plan would

work, either. His thinking, though, was that his students were perfectly smart but used to people assuming they were dumb. If he could find a way to make Shakespeare relevant to them, maybe, just maybe, he had a shot of opening them up to a whole new world.

He started by having them watch *West Side Story*. Afterward, they talked about it. There were always jokes about how dated the movie was, the cheesy clothes and hairstyles, the stupidity of fighting with nothing more than fists or a knife. But his students always got how the gang warfare in the movie wasn't very different from the gang warfare that permeated Hunter's Point.

After that, they would read scenes from *West Side Story* in class. Most of the kids would read, and most of the kids would read well, having just heard professionals do the lines in the movie. After *that*, Charlie would explain that *West Side Story* was based on *Romeo and Juliet*. Within weeks, he had everyone from truants to new immigrants putting their hearts into the Montagues and Capulets. They even performed scenes for family and friends, and they always got a standing ovation.

Charlie found that even the most hard-assed kids were affected by all of this. Their test scores improved significantly, as did their reading and comprehension levels. It was exciting to see. Charlie saw *Romeo and Juliet* as only the beginning. He knew his kids would respond to more of Shakespeare's work if it was just presented to them in the right way. *Macbeth*? He could start with the "Was the guy pussy-whipped?" angle. *Hamlet*? A tale of family revenge. If there was one thing you did not do in Hunter's Point, it was dis someone's family.

Recently, Charlie had applied for a Summit Grant, a monetary award given by a private foundation to be used for innovative educational ideas like his own Shakespeare program. The paperwork had been a pain in the ass, and he figured he didn't have much of a shot. But what the hell, it was worth a try. He could do a lot for his kids with ten thousand dollars.

"It was a racial thing," LaToya Jefferson offered, shaking the red yarn extensions that had been braided into an elaborate and very tall hairdo off her round face. "One group be honkies, one group be spics or whatever."

"One group *is* white and one *is* Puerto Rican, right," Charlie replied. In his class, you spoke proper English or you got corrected. That was Principal Witherspoon's mandate. "But that still doesn't explain why they hate each other."

"People don't like people who are different," Frederick Bickford offered.

Charlie thought that Frederick would know, as he took in his student's long frame slouched down in the much-too-small-for-him chair-desk combination. Frederick was the youngest of four kids; his single mom was a nurse's aide. He was also the smartest kid in Charlie's class, though he took pains not to show it off outside the classroom, lest he be accused of acting "white."

"Yo, we stick with our own, *Fa-red-er-ick*," Manuel Jesus explained, the taunt obvious in his voice. "You got a problem with that?"

"Excuse me? Mr. Silver?" LaToya waved a hand with inch-long nails painted a deep plum.

"Yes?"

"I'm *dying* in here, Mr. Silver." She fanned herself vigorously. "Seriously. I'm about to pass out."

There was mumbled agreement around the room. The Mays-McCovey charter school had formerly been a warehouse, and it was always ten degrees warmer than the outside temperature. Fortunately, San Francisco stayed reasonably cool. But on a sunny day like this in Hunter's Point, the school was baking, though the outer reaches of The City were still swathed in fog.

"Yeah, it's killer," Charlie agreed. "So here's the plan. Let's go get a drink from the fountain, and then we'll head out to the parking lot." He pulled a large bag of mini Snickers bars from his desk and saw their faces light up. "Every right answer, you get a Snickers bar. Two right answers? Share with your friends. You guys act up, you're right back in the hothouse. Deal?"

Kids were out the door in a flash, except for one boy in the back of the room who put his head down on the desk. Jamal Ashford. Charlie didn't know Jamal as well as he did his other students—it was the boy's first year at Mays-McCovey. He was skinny and small for his age, with an incongruously shaved head and a quiet manner. He did turn in halfway decent homework most of the time, which was more than Charlie could say for some of his students.

Huh. Odd. Jamal was wearing a long-sleeved shirt on what had to be the hottest day of the year. What would make a kid do that?

"Jamal?"

Nothing, except a snore. Wow, the kid was really out. Charlie stepped over to him and put a gentle hand on Jamal's narrow back. "Jam—"

The kid jumped out of his seat as if he'd been shot from a cannon, his eyes wild, one hand held up to his face. The open cuff of his sleeve slipped up his skinny arm to reveal a row of nasty purple bruises.

"Hey, buddy," Charlie said softly. "You fell asleep."

"So?" Jamal shook his sleeve back down.

"So the class just went outside 'cuz it's so hot in here."

Jamal stared at Charlie warily.

"Hey, things going okay for you, Jamal?"

The kid stuck his chin out belligerently. "Yeah."

Charlie shoved his hands deep into the pockets of his jeans. "Good, good. Just, you know, checking. Because if you want to talk—"

"No, I don't want to *talk*." Jamal picked up his books and held them in front of him like a shield. "Get the fuck out my face," he spat. Then he turned and fled.

"Come in, Charlie, come in. It's a bad time, but come in anyway."

Principal Joe Witherspoon's powerful and athletic body was still apparent under a decade of accumulated fat. He motioned Charlie into his diminutive office and wiped some sweat from his brow with a red bandanna. Witherspoon took pride in the fact that his own office was smaller than the guidance counselor's or the vice-principal's. He always said that if you were in education for the money or the glory, it showed you weren't as educated as you thought. "Too damn hot today."

Though their backgrounds could not be more different—Joe was a product of Hunter's Point himself, and a former Minor League Baseball utility infielder—Charlie admired him tremendously. He knew that Witherspoon could have become a baseball coach at any high school he wanted. Instead, he went back to graduate school, got a master's degree, and dove headlong into the public school system. When the opportunity came for him to open a charter school, free of the restrictions of the education establishment, he'd jumped. Witherspoon always said that he got as far as he did in baseball not because he was brilliant but because he was fundamentally sound both at the plate and in the field. That's what Mays-McCovey was all about—the basics of reading, writing, science, and math. In five years, its test scores had risen to the middle of the pack for the school district. Considering that Hunter's Point had never had a school before that was above the tenth percentile, this was a remarkable achievement.

"It won't take long," Charlie promised. The principal motioned him into a battered wooden seat. "We need to call Protective Services about one of my students. Jamal."

Witherspoon's face fell. "Jamal Ashford? The quiet kid. What do you know?"

Charlie laid out what had happened in class that morning—Jamal's sleeping, the bruises on his arm, Jamal cussing Charlie out, then running off. "He came back, but I hear from Dan that he cut science."

Witherspoon rubbed his chin. "Sounds like a mandatory

report to me." He reached into his desk for some forms and passed them to Charlie. "You know the drill. Complete confidentiality, don't talk about it with other school employees, respect the privacy of the student and family. Damn. I hate when this happens. When are these grown-ups gonna figure out that these damn children are *precious*?"

Charlie couldn't agree more.

Witherspoon sighed. "Couldn't have come at a worse time, either. I got some bad news this afternoon. School's gonna have to move, temporarily. State inspectors found asbestos down in the subbasement."

Charlie knew this was very bad. Many of the older buildings in San Francisco had problems with asbestos that were just now being realized. The building would have to be shut, immediately, and the asbestos encapsulated or removed. That would cost a small fortune, and a small fortune wasn't what this school had in its bank account.

"When?" he asked.

"They were here last week. I'm making the official announcement at this afternoon's faculty meeting." Witherspoon rubbed the space between his eyebrows. "Two steps forward and three steps backward."

"So, what's the game plan?" Charlie asked, knowing that Witherspoon would already have one.

"I've been on the phone for hours, begging, arm-twisting, whatever needed to be done. I told anyone that would listen that we're a year-round school and we simply cannot shut down, not even for a day, or we lose our kids."

"And?"

"And I found us temporary quarters at USF—I know the chancellor there from way back. It's gonna be a pain in the ass, running buses for our kids over there and all that. We can only stay until the fall semester. Then we have to find another home, or get this place up to standards."

"Damn." The kids at Mays-McCovey came from this neighborhood, and they walked to school. "If we reopen in some other area of the city—"

"Tell me about it." Witherspoon nodded. "It's all over."

Charlie folded his arms. "Okay, bottom line. How much will it cost to get this building to pass inspection?"

"Chump change." Witherspoon smiled thinly. "One point three million dollars. Give or take a few hundred thousand."

Charlie took out his checkbook. "Oh, why didn't you just say so?"

"If your last name is actually Hilton and you've been holding out on me, I will be a happy man," Witherspoon joked.

"I wish." Charlie put his checkbook back in his pocket. One point three million dollars was an impossible sum of money. Witherspoon might as well have said one hundred million. "If we don't raise the money . . . ?"

"It's *hasta la vista,* baby."

"Shit," Charlie muttered.

"Exactly." Witherspoon stood, a sure sign that the meeting was over. "Keep all this under your hat, okay, Charlie? Nothing worse than rumors. Faculty meeting at three fifteen. See you there."

"Will do."

When he thought about it later, Charlie didn't even re-member leaving Witherspoon's office, or wandering out into what passed for one of Mays-McCovey's hallways as classes changed. Yet there he now stood, as the youngest kids in the school—the first and second graders—practically danced by him. The first graders were going to math and science, the second graders to reading. There was real joy in their eyes, anticipation of another couple of hours in this safe, wonderful place called Mays-McCovey before they had to head back to the mean streets of Hunter's Point.

Then, just as quickly, the children were gone and the hallway was as empty as it would be tomorrow—as empty as it would be forever unless somehow the school came up with more than a million dollars. Charlie stood there a long time, feeling the emptiness, not just in the hallway but in his heart.

six

"This skirt looks like shit on me," Michelle moaned. "Why don't I just stick a huge sign on my ass that says: CAUTION, WIDE LOAD?" She checked out her rear view in her bedroom dresser mirror.

"Where'd you buy it?" Annie asked. She was sorting through the clothes in her friend's walk-in closet, because she knew that watching Michelle dress for a date—this time a sort-of-double-date with Annie—was always an adventure.

"Online. Nordstrom's. It's an Anne Klein fourteen-W, which is supposed to stand for Woman but please, everyone knows it stands for Wide, which does not do wonders for my ego, thank-you-very-much. What are you looking for?"

Annie didn't answer. She knew that Michelle loved to decompress after an insane day (and often night) at the firm by shopping online for clothes. Yet sixty percent of what she purchased had never been worn, because she tended to panic before a virgin garment's first public outing. As brilliant and confident as Michelle was in every other area of her life, all of her insecurities were located from the waist down. She didn't have an Achilles' heel; she had an Achilles' ass.

Ah, there it was! Annie remembered Michelle showing her the ocher and forest green paisley silk shirt from New Zealander designer Cherry Bishop. Now she snared it from its hanger, then stepped through the minefield of discarded clothes that littered the floor and handed Michelle the shirt.

"Try this," Annie suggested.

"I never wear that shirt," Michelle protested. "It's *paisley*."

"So?"

"So paisley is vintage. *You* do vintage. *I* do not. Plus why would I wear yellow and green—colors I fucking hate, by the way—with a black skirt? I don't even know why I bought it."

Fashion was not Michelle's long suit.

"Just try it," Annie urged. They didn't have much time before they met the guys at the Mark Hopkins hotel for Sunday brunch.

With a long-suffering sigh, Michelle took off the white cardigan that ended at the widest part of her hips—never a wise decision—and put on the low-cut Cherry Bishop. It showed off her considerable olive cleavage, was fitted under the bust where Michelle was small, and then fell in graceful folds past the hips to fingertip length, thereby emphasizing the positive and deemphasizing the negative.

"Oh. Wow." Michelle beamed.

"Exactly."

"How do you do it?"

"Proportions," Annie explained, looking around for the vintage Chanel ballet flats she'd kicked off during the what-should-Michelle-wear marathon. "I aced life drawing at Syracuse." She found her shoes under a green shift that Michelle had decided made her look like the Jolly Green Giant, sat on the edge of Michelle's bed, and slipped them on. "Hey, I have a great idea. Let's blow these guys off and go to the flea market. I can find you some really cute, flattering stuff and—"

"We are not standing them up," Michelle insisted, spraying a cloud of Passion perfume, then stepping into it, thereby keeping the scent subtle. This was a trick Annie had passed on from the "How Scents Make Sense" piece in last month's *HottieGirl*.

Michelle grabbed her purse and looped the strap over her shoulder. "Okay, my guy's name is Peter and your guy's name is Shamu. No, wait, that's a whale. Seamus. And yes, he's Jewish. His father married a woman from Dublin who converted. Why are you just standing there? We're already going to be late."

Annie trudged reluctantly past the mirror. She wore a summery floral skirt with a white tank top. Her lack of assets above the waist was more than apparent, but she couldn't muster up the energy to care. She could only hope the whale wasn't a boob man.

Sunday brunch buffet at the Top of the Mark, on the seventeenth floor of the storied Intercontinental Mark Hopkins in San Francisco's tony Nob Hill district, had been a city tradition for years. The restaurant occupied the entire top floor,

and had a three-hundred-and-sixty-degree view of the Bay
Area, from Mount Tamalpais in the north to San Mateo in the
south. If the day was clear, like this particular Sunday, diners
could watch sailboats racing various courses out on the bay.

The food and ambience were easily a match for the view.
The buffet featured fresh specialties, including a spectacular
table of seafood and another of desserts. In one corner, a
string quartet played Bach, serenading guests who ranged
from young to old, tourist to local, and gay to straight to (this
being San Francisco) those who defied sexual category at all.

Annie had been to the Top of the Mark many times with
Elliot, who loved expensive food and elegant surroundings
as much as he loved expensive things. She'd certainly never
been there with a blind date. It felt so awkward. Though she
fought the feeling with all her might, she found herself long-
ing for Elliot, even if he did come—literally and figuratively—
attached to Czuba, from time to time.

Because, really, was there *anything* more excruciating
than a blind date?

Michelle had set the whole thing up. She'd started chatting online with Peter Klein, a guy who had seen her photo
and profile on JDate. That had gone great, so they'd traded
cell numbers, and their first phone conversation had gone so
well that Peter invited Michelle to Sunday brunch at the Top
of the Mark. Michelle said the only way she'd meet him was
if he brought a friend along for her friend. Hence, Shamu.
No, wait—Seamus.

As Annie drank her first mimosa, she stole a sideways
look at her date. He was actually nice-looking, in a cuddly,

oversized teddy bear kind of way. He had jet-black hair, fair skin, and blue eyes. His somewhat Shamu-esque middle was partially disguised by the faultless cut of his beige cashmere sports jacket. He was, he had told her, a photographer for the *Chronicle*. That should have been interesting, but somehow it wasn't.

At least she didn't have to say much—Peter dominated the conversation, in a good way. Of medium height, with close-cropped chestnut brown hair, a rather large nose, and a fabulous smile, he'd spent years after college trying to make it as a stand-up comic. Though he had some minor success, he'd gotten tired of starving, and joined his dad's accounting firm in the Transamerica Building. He still kept his hand in performing, though, appearing at open-mike nights in North Beach every so often. At the moment, he was telling a long and funny story about how he got into a shouting match with a much older judge at the San Francisco Comedy Competition who didn't understand the pop culture references in his act.

The story went on and on. Annie found her attention wandering to a muscular busboy who'd just lifted a well-preserved middle-aged woman in a Pepto-Bismol pink suit onto the buffet, the woman's ass squishing a tasteful array of soft cheeses as he hoisted her legs over his shoulders.

"Annie? Wouldn't that be great?" Michelle was asking.

At the sound of her name, Annie shook her head and turned back to her tablemates. "Sorry?"

"I said, we'd love to go see Peter do his act sometime," Michelle repeated, obviously a bit miffed. "*Wouldn't* we?"

"Oh, sure," Annie agreed.

Peter leaned in to Michelle and launched into a part of his routine about a nephew who absolutely refused potty training. He spoke in an intimate voice clearly meant only for Michelle. Annie took it as a cue to go to the buffet. "I'm going to get some food," she told Seamus.

"I'll join you," he said.

They made their way to the long tables, where Annie concentrated on the salads and studiously avoided the soft cheeses. At the dessert display, a luscious piece of dark chocolate cake practically beckoned to her, but she could imagine the calorie count as it did. Someone really should do a study as to how it was that chocolate calories always went directly to the thighs.

"You're a chocolate girl, huh?" Seamus said, noticing the chocolate lust in her eyes.

"It looks really good, doesn't it?"

"Yeah," he said. "I feel sorry for women, I really do. Having to count every calorie sucks, huh?" He reached for the biggest slice of cake on the platter. Why was it a woman could so easily fall for a guy with a gut, but a guy with a gut still expected a woman to look like a *Maxim* babe?

Annie took a few slices of smoked salmon and then returned to the table. Seamus was there already. "You seem a little distracted," he observed.

Annie flushed. She'd just been imagining a foursome of Argentinian tourists in a variety of athletic positions on the floor. *Just stop*, she told herself. *Focus.*

"Sorry, I was . . . kind of . . . um . . . lost in thought, there."

"Are you a lawyer, like your friend?"

Annie shook her head. "Commercial artist."

"Oh, yeah? Where?"

"I'm sort of between jobs right now."

Seamus nodded and wolfed down a chilled jumbo prawn. Annie searched for something else to say. "So . . . photography. That must be interesting."

"Yeah, I like it, I get to do all the best crime scenes." Seamus nudged his chin toward Peter. "But if my friend here ever lands a Comedy Central gig, I'm his man. Hey, Pete, what color condoms do you want in your dressing room? Because it's going in the contract."

Michelle and Peter both guffawed. Seamus leaned over toward Michelle, who sat across from him, his eyes flicking to her cleavage. "Anyone ever tell you that you have a world-class laugh?"

"Do relatives count?" Michelle teased.

"Not unless it's a kissing cousin," Seamus teased back.

"My cousins are mostly under the age of fifteen and in various stages of orthodontia crisis," Michelle quipped.

"So were you born with that smile or are you just post-orthodontia?" Peter casually draped an arm around the back of Michelle's seat, and Seamus leaned so far forward in his chair that only a miracle of physics kept it from toppling over. How ironic. Both Michelle's date *and* her date were focused on Michelle. Annie could see that her friend was eating it up.

Well, that was fine. She felt not the slightest spark with Seamus, who seemed to be picturing Michelle's breasts in all their glory as he recounted some crime scene story about naked dead bodies found in compromising positions. Necrophilia was off-limits, even to Annie. So she gave herself over to the floor show of her imagination, where the very-much-alive string quartet had tossed aside their instruments to play each other.

They really were extremely talented.

The brunch ended mercifully early, and Annie decided to spend the rest of the afternoon at BridgePoint, helping the residents with their art projects. Sunday afternoon was always a good time to volunteer, because it was the day that residents with family most often got visitors. If any residents were alone, it usually meant there was no one to see them.

Fortunately, Elliot's grandmother was away for the weekend, so she didn't have to dodge either her questions or her scolding looks. Annie ended up working with a new arrival, an old Iranian man with a tenuous grasp on the English language and a wavering grip on reality. Annie spoke no Farsi and wasn't a trained geriatric psychologist, so he was a challenge. Still, she managed to help him construct an abstract cut-paper collage and then frame it. When, by a combination of babbling in Farsi and hand gestures, he indicated that she should hang it on the wall of his living room, Annie was thrilled. Even more thrilling was the heartfelt hug he gave her and the tears that welled up in his eyes. Though she couldn't make heads or tails of the collage—a random assortment of images and portraits—it clearly had meaning to him. That was all that mattered, finally.

She got back to her apartment around seven and changed

quickly into a pair of battered jeans and an old T-shirt, then on a whim pulled out her sketchbook and charcoal pencils, something she hadn't done since before she'd begun working at *HottieGirl*. First, she sketched the Iranian man's face. Then she did a close-up of his gnarled and veiny hands, somehow elegant and virile despite their age, holding a pair of scissors. She did a couple of versions of the hands—the second one was far better than the first—and then glanced at her clock, shocked to see that three and a half hours had passed. Not that there was any reason to go to sleep. It wasn't like she had a job to go to on Monday morning.

Next to her clock was the Ultimate Pleasure. Actually, maybe there *was* a good reason to go to sleep early.

She showered, dried off, and got into bed naked after closing the window shade and drapes and snapping off the light. She did some deep breathing as a plethora of erotic images from the day flew through her mind. Only when she found one that she liked—a cute, dark-haired guy she'd seen on the Muni bus to BridgePoint whose eyes had briefly met hers—did she turn on the Ultimate Pleasure to its slowest setting.

"Go ahead, darling, have a piece of chocolate cake. I love every inch of you," urged a deep, sexy male voice.

Annie almost jumped out of bed. Her heart was pounding. Who the hell had just said that?

She snapped on the light. Nothing. She was entirely and completely alone.

Okay, that was so weird. True, she'd been seeing sexual things in her mind's eye forever, but she'd never *heard* things in her mind's ear. Plus, it had sounded so *real*. Like some guy with the hottest voice she'd ever heard was lying next to her, murmuring in her ear. No. It was just a fantasy. There was reality, and there was fantasy. This was fantasy. She clicked the light off, lay down again, and tried more deep breathing. Just when she felt herself slipping into that utterly relaxed state . . .

"How about an aromatherapy massage?"

She bolted upright. Shit. God, it was such a great voice. It had the resonance of one of those TV announcers, but lacked all pretense. It was passionate, but honest, simple and unpracticed, and it held the intimacy of someone who *knew* her—really, truly, *knew* her.

"Wishful thinking," Annie told the darkened room, since, as she reminded herself, *no one was actually there*. She lay down again, determined this time to let the Ultimate Pleasure work its magic. So what if she had a vivid auditory imagination?

"You are so hot. Whatever you want, for as long as you want."

Annie sighed.

"God, I love your thighs."

"I don't."

"You're absolutely perfect, just the way you are."

Now, what girl wouldn't want to hear that?

Annie gave herself up to the moment. Repeatedly. Ultimate Pleasure seemed to know not only what to touch and how to touch it, but exactly what to say in that deep, sexy voice. If a guy could do that, give the absolute best physical pleasure while at the same time saying the absolute most perfect thing—

Holy shit. An idea began to form in her Fertile-Crescent imagination.

She reached for the phone and speed-dialed her grand-mother.

"Annie? It's so late. Are you okay?" Doris answered with concern in her voice.

"Never better," Annie declared. "I'm coming over to talk to you. Right now. And, Gramma?"

"What?"

"Whoever said that masturbation is not a productive activity was wrong."

seven

"Anniekins! Welcome to the Funtime family!"

Bernie Nadler didn't bother taking the smelly cigar out of his mouth before he enveloped Annie in a suffocating bear hug. She found her face smothered somewhere near the second scratchy button of his Polo knockoff, which stank of smoke.

From his protruding belly to his prominent comb-over, from his stogy to the scuffed shoes on his feet, right to the voice made raspy over too many years, Bernard Nadler looked like a pornographer from Central Casting. Only he wasn't a pornographer. He was the boss of West Coast operations for Funtime Industries, a public (NASDAQ, not NYSE) corporation with an enviable growth curve that just happened to specialize in adult toys and products.

"Nice to meet you, too."

Annie disentangled herself from Bernie's grasp and traded a look with her grandmother. She'd been warned that

Bernie left something to be desired in the couth department. However, Doris said, he was a genius at his job, responsible for countless innovations in the arenas of sex toys, novelties, lotions, and oils. Not only that, he'd recruited a growing sales force of housewives and retired women who had turned Funtime into the Avon of sex toys.

"I get a commission check every week," Doris had explained to Annie. "Also a sixty percent employee discount. I gave your mother's old clothes to Goodwill so that I could use her childhood dresser as a pleasure chest."

When Annie had rushed over to see Doris the night after Shamu, her grandmother had seen the possibilities right away. She termed Annie "my-granddaughter-the-genius-even-smarter-than-my-Murray-may-he-R.I.P.," then told her to sit tight. She'd talk to a lawyer, protect the idea, and then pitch it to Funtime.

Two weeks later, Doris had gotten the call from Bernie— come by the warehouse tomorrow and bring your granddaughter. Now, here they were.

"Ya got quite a little dolly there," Bernie told Doris, shoving his saliva-soaked cigar back into a corner of his mouth. "She takes after you."

Annie watched her grandmother smile at the compliment. It was true that Doris was still a great-looking woman for her age. But surely Doris and Bernie weren't . . .

No. Not possible. She definitely did *not* want to fantasize about that. To distract herself, Annie concocted some aerobic shenanigans between the African American receptionist and the Asian delivery guy at the shipping dock.

"Speaking of dolls, I'm sure you'll want to give your grand-daughter the grand tour, Doris." Bernie motioned to the interior of the warehouse and chortled. "Come and meet the silent partners!" He led the way through a huge open space that resembled an airplane hangar, except it was filled with boxes and products waiting to be boxed. Forklifts and laborers moved product from location to location. One entire corner was devoted to a UPS shipping station. "We ship seven thousand packages a day from this location," Bernie informed them.

"Forty thousand from the various Funtime warehouses around the country, ten thousand more from our new operation outside Berlin. Are we selling? You bet. Why? Because everyone loves a Funtime!" He cracked up at his own wit, ushering Doris in front of him with a meaty hand on the small of her back. "Ah, here we are. Dolly time."

Annie found herself looking at a cozy gingham couch and coffee table. Bernie used his cigar to gesture at the occupants. "Meet my dollies, Anniekins—Amber, Violet, and Nasty Natasha."

His vocal spin on "Nasty Natasha" made Annie want to take a shower; or at least it would have if she hadn't been both shocked and amazed by what she was seeing—three life-size dolls that looked so human she wondered if they had actual pulses. Amber was a leggy blonde in a very short schoolgirl's uniform, her knee-sock-clad legs demurely crossed at the ankle. Violet, a curvy redhead in a silver cocktail dress, had one ass cheek perched on the sofa's arm. Natasha was a raven-haired, leather-clad beauty with a sneer on her lip and a whip in her hand, draped over the back of the couch.

"You think supermodels are popular?" Bernie asked. "They got nothin' on my dollies." He crooked a stubby finger at Annie, beckoning her closer, and flipped Violet's cocktail dress up over her ass. "Anatomically correct in every way. There's a sucking sensation upon insertion, plus she's always lubricated. I invented that part—it has a five-year guarantee. As for the pubic hair, it's natural and attached by a special process that takes three days. That is, if you want pubic hair. You'd be amazed what a guy will spend for one of these."

Annie recoiled. A guy would buy one of these instead of meeting an actual girl? Why not save the money and get some psychotherapy? Then she thought more about it. Didn't she collect dolls herself? Didn't she have what could charitably be called a vivid imagination? She couldn't deny some particularly vivid fantasies about Barbie and Ken, who were so much kinkier than people might think. And hadn't she been spending an inordinate amount of time with Ultimate Pleasure? Was she really so different from a guy who would purchase an Amber?

Talk about your depressing inner monologue.

Bernie raised his eyebrows. "I know what you're thinking, Annie. There are a lot of lonely people in this world who deserve a companion. We make these dolls to order— eye color, bust size, facial expression. Men send pictures of how they want Amber's face to be, and we've got artists who execute it."

"Don't you think that's a little sad?"

Bernie shook his head. "I get fan mail. One guy tells me he was so lonely he was going to kill himself until Violet came into his life. A year later, he met a great woman and wrote to us asking if we knew anyone who wanted a used Violet. Not much market for that, I'm afraid, but we can recycle certain parts discreetly." He wagged his cigar at her. "Judge not, lest ye be judged."

"How about an older model?" Doris suggested. "For those who prefer a more mature woman?"

Bernie stabbed a finger in Doris's direction. "You're very direct, Doris, I like that. Maybe we should discuss it over dinner."

Annie was pretty sure she saw her grandmother blush.

"Thank you, Bernard," Doris said. "But I don't believe in mixing business with pleasure. Let's move along, shall we?"

Bernie led the way to the next area, which featured long metal shelves not unlike the ones Annie used for her doll collection. Instead of dolls, though, these displayed an enormous collection of sex toys and novelties. "I like to think of this as the Funtime museum of pleasure history," Bernie extolled. "One of everything we've ever sold." He pointed out heart-shaped chocolate thong panties he'd invented called "Eat Your Heart Out." There were pencils with penis-shaped erasers, windup animals having every type of barnyard sex, squirting latex cucumbers, and a computer mouse pad that allowed the wrist to nestle between a pair of voluptuous double Ds. Farther down was the vibrator area. Hundreds—thousands!—of them, an assortment so rich that it made Doris's trunk seem paltry in comparison. Annie perused them while Bernie engaged in a heated cell phone conversation about a production mishap in Taiwan.

"Tour's over," he announced, when the call ended. "I've got a fire to put out. Let's get back to my office, and I'll show you what we built. By the way, do you have a name for my newest toy?"

"I was thinking of calling him Mr. Vibrator," Annie replied.

"I like it," Doris said. "Every woman can give him the first name she wants. Mine will be Murray."

Bernie's office was a disheveled mess, nearly every surface covered with invoice slips, mail, and bills. There was another cigar buried in a breast-shaped ashtray and a dartboard featuring couples in various sexual positions—a blue-tipped dart was nailing a voluptuous woman's ass.

"Ever play that?" Bernie asked, as Annie and Doris squeezed together onto an ugly orange and brown tweed couch. "Can really spice up a Saturday night. Anyway, Anniekins, Doris— prepare to be wowed." He opened a drawer and brought out a phallic-shaped object that was, in Annie's experience, roughly the size of a reasonably well-endowed guy.

"Per your specifications," Bernie pointed out, then handed it to Annie. "Want us to leave so you can give Mr. Vibrator a trial run? The batteries are included."

"That won't be necessary," Annie demurred, turning the object over in her hand. It was just a simple, straight-ahead wand, save for a dozen small buttons at the bottom end.

"Turn it on," Doris urged.

Annie flipped the main switch and was pleased that the vibrator barely hummed. She'd given specific instructions to Bernie to reduce the noise factor, and he had, but it still wasn't silent. Her notion had been that the only noise Mr. Vibrator would make would be the things he had to say.

Bernie pointed to the bottom of the vibrator. "Try a button."

She did.

"Go ahead, darling, have a piece of chocolate cake. I love every inch of you."

Annie shrieked and dropped the vibrator, which bounced off her lap and then fell to her feet. Yes, a voice had come out of a microphone in its base, saying exactly what she'd instructed that it should say. Unfortunately, the voice had been Bernie's.

"You don't like?" Bernie relit his dormant cigar.

"It's . . . it's not what I expected," Annie admitted.

"Try the others."

All the phrases she wanted were there. *"May I give you an aromatherapy massage?"* *"Your thighs are perfect."* *"I can do this as long as you'd like."* *"You are so hot."* But they were all in Bernie's leering rasp.

She exchanged a quick glance with her grandmother, who shook her head disapprovingly. "At the risk of stating the obvious—Bernie, you used your own voice. It doesn't quite work."

Bernie took the cigar from his mouth as Annie eyed the vibrator on the floor. The magic was gone. "We can get another voice instead of mine, no problem. Funtime is committed to this project. Between you, me, and the lamppost, if I hadn't signed that damn confidentiality agreement, I'd steal it.

We're ready to start production, Annie-bo-bannie. You pick the new voice. Anything you want."

Annie picked up the prototype. A bit of indoor-outdoor rug lint stuck to the tip. She'd just put Bernie's voice out of her mind.

"Okay," she agreed. "I pick the voice."

"Fan-cosmo!" Bernie boomed. "We're in business. We'll give you ten percent of the net. Our attorneys will be in touch."

Doris recoiled. "Ten percent? Come on, Bernie, this is worth more—"

"*Net*, Doris," Bernie repeated, as his cell phone rang again. "That's my Taiwan factory, I have to take this. So you'll call me later. We're gonna have gorgeous sex together, dollies!"

eight

Charlie sat propped up by two oversized pillows and watched naked Sandra Bennington through the open door of his bathroom with great appreciation. She stood in front of the sink, brushing her teeth, her long, dark hair flowing down her creamy back, slants of morning light from the bathroom window highlighting her lush curves.

He'd met Sandra a week earlier at the Potrero Hill Cleaners. She'd been picking up her dry cleaning when he walked in to drop off his own. The Armani business suit she'd been wearing couldn't hide her lush Marilyn Monroe–esque curves; she was easily twenty pounds heavier than whatever arbitrary standard most of the girls he dated seemed to use as a guideline to acceptable. Yet Charlie had broad tastes when it came to women. Different shapes and sizes appealed to him. He definitely enjoyed the sensual feel of a round woman, and had enjoyed that feeling with quite a few. He loved the taut muscularity of athletic girls, and the sweet smallness of the slender ones. Honestly,

Charlie just loved women. He could find something delicious, to one degree or another, about most of them.

When he'd stepped into the cleaners', Sandra was at the counter. He took in her deep, dark doe eyes, high cheekbones, and full, sensuous lips, but also noticed something amiss. The hem of one section of her skirt had come undone. It was hanging unevenly against the back of her left calf. Rather than point it out, he stepped forward and asked the bubble-gum-chewing counter girl a benign question.

"Excuse me. Do you have some flash tape back there?"

"Yeah. We use it for alterations."

"Oh, that's great. Could you bring me some?"

"When I'm done with this customer." She indicated the curvy woman.

"It's kind of an emergency," Charlie insisted.

The girl rolled her eyes, but stepped over to a sewing machine, retrieved the roll of tape, and literally tossed it at Charlie.

"Here." He immediately offered it to the beauty in the suit.

"Sorry?" she'd asked him, eyebrows knit.

"Your skirt. It's coming apart in the back. This stuff is amazing. You tear off a small piece, peel the backing, press the adhesive side against your hem and then pull it off. When you press the material together, the adhesive will hold it in place. Instant fix. I'm Charlie Silver, by the way."

The woman flashed a winning, thankful smile. "Sandra Bennington. And thank you, Charlie Silver. I've got a huge presentation in an hour."

"That's always the time for a wardrobe malfunction," he said sympathetically. "What line of work are you in?"

"I'm a personal shopper," Sandra explained. "Tourists give me their list, I do the buying, and get a cut of what they've spent, sort of like an interior designer. But what I really want to do is to open my own boutique." She chuckled. "That's like an actor saying what he really wants to do is direct, isn't it?" She sat on one of the two folding chairs and went to work with the flash tape. "The presentation I'm going to? I applied for a business line of credit for my dream boutique and I'm on my way to meet with the bank."

"So the hem thing would have been kind of dicey," Charlie filled in.

"Exactly." She pressed the hem against the adhesive. It held perfectly. "I can't thank you enough."

"My pleasure."

"You must have a smart wife."

"No wife," Charlie told her. In fact, he'd learned the flash tape trick from one of his students. He'd popped a button on his shirt and she offered him a piece from home ec class—the shirt had stayed closed all day. The girl also explained that flash tape was a fashion must if you wanted to prevent thong ride-up. Coming from an eighth grader, that was far more than he needed to know.

By the time Charlie had gotten the ticket for his clothing, he and Sandra had made a date for a late bite that evening. By midnight, Charlie was having Sandra for dessert. They'd spent every night together since.

Then things had started to go wrong. Sandra invited him to her younger sister's wedding in Calistoga two weeks from Saturday—she was marrying a winemaker, and Sandra would be a bridesmaid. Charlie didn't want to go. In fact, weddings made him break out in hives. It was nothing personal—he liked Sandra very much.

He called toward the bathroom. "I got you a present!"

"I love presents!"

She rinsed her toothbrush and deposited it on the top shelf of his medicine cabinet—another thing that made Charlie break out in hives. Why did women think that just because two people were compatible in bed on more than three consecutive occasions that gave them medicine cabinet rights? First it would be a toothbrush. Then a lipstick would appear. Soon their stuff would start to breed and multiply, filling his bathroom with the flotsam and jetsam of all things female.

Not good. Really not good.

Utterly unself-conscious about her nudity—one of the many things Charlie really liked about her—Sandra padded back into the bedroom and gave him a sensuous kiss that included a spine-tingling nibble on his lower lip. For a moment, he considered postponing the gift giving. Then he remembered that he'd soon be getting ready for school and her toothbrush would be dripping on his top shelf.

"Let me get it for you," he whispered, then reached into the nightstand drawer and brought out an oblong wrapped package, about the size of a loaf of bread.

"Heavy," she remarked as she eagerly tore off the paper. It was a golden brick, with SANDRA B. etched into the surface. She'd told him that was what she planned to call her boutique.

"Your cornerstone."

"Omigod. You are the most perfect man," Sandra cooed,

then put the brick down on the end of the bed and snaked her arms around his neck. "I love it." She proceeded to show him just how much in a way that most of Charlie's girlfriends would never have shared at all, much less in the stark morning light.

Too bad. He really was going to miss her.

The middle-aged black woman peered at Charlie through a small glass window cut into the heavy metal door of the ramshackle house in the toughest section of Hunter's Point. "Who are you?"

"Charlie Silver. The teacher from Mays-McCovey. I called before?"

He could hear the sound of moving dead bolts, and then the door swung open. "I'm Mrs. Peabody. You got to be careful 'round here who you open up to. Come on in, Charlie, come on in." The moment Charlie was inside, the woman—a three-hundred-pound vision in a lime green polyester pantsuit—slammed the door shut and relocked it.

"We get some people who think I'm responsible for the court orders that put kids here. Truth is, I'm not, though sometimes I wish I was." She led Charlie into a large room just off the entryway. "Wait here. I'll call Jamal."

Mrs. Peabody gestured to an ancient couch covered in a beige Indian blanket and brown dog hair. Other than that, the living room was bare, save for several beanbag-style sacks on the floor—one leaking tiny white beads—and an old TV set on two blue milk crates.

"Jamal!" She cupped her hands and yelled weakly upstairs, then put a hand to her chest. "My asthma is acting up today and I can't get me no breath." She inhaled deeply and tried again. "*Jamal!* That ought to do it," she told Charlie. "He doesn't come down in one minute, there's no dessert. Amazing how well these children respond to no dessert. Much better than slapping them upside the head. Parents need to learn that. So you're his teacher? You make the report to Protective Services?"

"Sort of. To my school. They did it. It was mandatory."

Mrs. Peabody nodded. "Let's not get into the details. If you or I have to testify, it's better that you don't talk to the head of his group home. Some smart-ass lawyer could use it against us."

Charlie nodded, knowing she was right. Unfortunately, he'd been down this road before. "I agree. What I really wanted to talk to you about, Mrs. Peabody, was Jamal and school."

"Why you here, Mr. Silver?"

Charlie looked up. Jamal was at the bottom of the stairs. He wore long, baggy shorts and a 49ers jersey so oversized it hung nearly to his knees.

"Why *are* you here," Charlie corrected automatically, earning a small smile from Mrs. Peabody.

"I'm here 'cause they made me come here," Jamal replied, as if Charlie had been asking him a question. "Yo, some people lookin' for your ass, Mr. Silver," Jamal added. "Where you park your ride?"

"Just outside."

Jamal snorted. "Probably won't have no hubs when you get back there."

"Won't have any hubs," Charlie corrected. "It's a Saturn

and it's six years old; I doubt my hubcaps are worth much, but thanks for the heads-up."

Jamal shrugged diffidently.

Mrs. Peabody motioned Jamal into the room. "Mr. Silver wants to talk to you about school." Her head swung to Charlie. "Though I don't know why. It's June."

"Mays-McCovey is year-round," Jamal explained. He dropped onto the bleeding beanbag chair. "Right, Mr. Silver?"

"Right," Charlie agreed. "And there are some problems in the building, which is why we're meeting now at USF."

Mrs. Peabody frowned. "USF? That's on the other side of town. My boys go to the neighborhood schools. It's the only way I can keep track—"

"And the neighborhood schools are closed for the summer!" Jamal was triumphant. "So I'm on summer vacation."

"I'd like you to come back to Mays-McCovey, Jamal," Charlie said.

Stone-faced, Jamal folded his arms.

"You're a part of our school," Charlie added. "Everyone misses you."

"Like who?"

"Like me," Charlie admitted. "And LaToya—she asked about you. And Frederick. You guys were going to do your *Macbeth* project together, remember?"

"He smart," Jamal insisted. "He don't need me."

"He *is* smart. But so are you." Charlie turned to Mrs. Peabody. "What do you say? Can we get Jamal back at the school where he belongs?"

The housemother frowned. "Don't you think I have enough to worry about, Mr. Silver? I got eleven boys here. Youngest is seven, oldest is sixteen. Summer they all out on the street, but at least they're here in the neighborhood. During the school year they at three different schools. Now you want me to be thinking about a fourth?"

"It would be the best thing for Jamal educationally—"

"Let me tell you 'bout where you are, Mr. Silver. One out of five murders in this city happens in this here neighborhood. If you have a baby, it's three times more likely to die here. We got drugs, we got hookers, we got gangbangers, and it's my job to stand between those things and these boys who've been taken out of their homes because their mommies and daddies—whoever their daddies are—can't or won't do it. Or worse. It's a hard job, Mr Silver."

"I know that, but—"

"With all due respect, Mr. Silver, you do *not* know." She chucked her chin toward Jamal. "I let him go to school halfway across the city, who's gonna look out for him? He's a bitty thing. Who's gonna pay his Muni fare? Who's gonna fetch him if he gets sick? You don't have to think about these things, Mr. Silver, but I do. Jamal will go to Willie Brown Middle School like my other boys. In the fall."

Charlie snuck a glance at Jamal. The boy was grinning, but his blithe obliviousness to his own educational fate only redoubled Charlie's fervor. Willie Brown School was a disaster. Its teacher turnover averaged more than fifty percent a year, and more than fifty percent of the students never made it to high school. No principal had lasted more than two years.

"I've got that all worked out," Charlie told her. "Mr. Rodriguez, the Spanish teacher, will pick him up and take him home. If there's an emergency, Mr. Witherspoon says he'll be personally responsible."

Mrs. Peabody shook her head. "Jamal is a good kid, Mr. Silver. But I'm the one responsible for this boy."

"I don't want to go to your damn school anyways!" Jamal shouted at Charlie.

"Think about his future, Mrs. Peabody," Charlie insisted.

"Thank you for coming by, Mr. Silver," the housemother said. "I know your heart is in the right place."

Charlie took one last look at Jamal. He was wiggling a foot anxiously. Huh. Maybe he wasn't really so happy about giving up on Mays-McCovey at all. "Listen to me, Jamal. I think if you tell Mrs. Peabody you want to come back to Mays-McCovey, there's a chance she'll let you."

Mrs. Peabody snorted her disgust, but she didn't say anything. Charlie took it as a good sign.

He held Jamal's gaze and tried to will the kid to get his message. "You've got to decide you want it, Jamal. No one can do that for you. If you do decide, I'll be with you, all the way."

Mrs. Peabody snorted again. "Mr. Silver, I'll see you out now. Good luck with your hubcaps."

nine

Annie peeled off another label and stuck it to the manila exhibit envelope that was already marked *Merkin Corporation v. Nobley*. Since no one was supervising her or the other paralegal, she'd snuck a peek inside. It contained an authenticated copy of a handwritten letter from biotech pioneer Dr. Carl P. Nobley, who was threatening his former business partner and founder of Merkin Corporation, Bruce L. Merkin, with death by gunshot, strangulation, and/or poison . . . all in the same paragraph.

Michelle's law firm was representing Merkin, who had started the affair by suing the brilliant but erratic scientist for breach of contract. They'd paid him eight figures, he'd promised a breakthrough in the treatment of Alzheimer's. None had come. Nobley had countersued for intentional infliction of emotional distress. A jury in Palo Alto had acquitted Nobley on the criminal charges, but now the civil case was coming to trial in two weeks. Though Michelle had told Annie that a settlement was likely, the firm still had to go through the process of preparing for court. Since they were billing Merkin at four hundred and twenty-five dollars an hour, and since Annie was earning just eighteen of those dollars as a paralegal temp, they were happy to prepare as many exhibits as might be needed, and then a few more just for insurance.

It was a gig, though a monkey could probably do it more effectively. After five days of evidence labels, Annie was ready to tear her hair out, even though she was grateful to Michelle. Unemployment compensation insurance could take her only so far.

One of the exhibits had contained the newspaper clippings from the *Chronicle*. Merkin had been found dead in Nobley's bed, clad in Mrs. Nobley's thigh-high fishnets. Merkin Corporation claimed the body had been planted there after Merkin had been killed. Nobley claimed that Merkin had died during consensual sex. Normally, anything that involved beds and fishnet stockings would have been of at least passing note to Annie, but she simply couldn't work up even a smidgen of interest.

She'd certainly been making an effort to find a real job. She'd sent out résumés, made phone calls, and even had two interviews. Ethereal had recommended her to a friend in San Jose who was starting a magazine for doll collectors—how perfect would that be? Well worth the commute. But it turned out that the funding wouldn't be in for months. She'd also had an interview at a new advertising agency and had been excited about that one until she walked in with her portfolio and saw her former boss from *HottieGirl* on her way out with her own portfolio. It was no surprise to Annie when she didn't get the job.

There was a loud honking sound from across the small room. Annie winced. Her coworker, Richard—not Dick—Hertz, was pinching one nostril shut and blowing the other into one of an endless supply of tissues. He was a slight, balding man in his mid-thirties who claimed not to like people but who also treated anyone within earshot to the inner monologue he felt compelled to spew. On day one, Annie had heard about his childhood trauma brought about by his elementary school substitute teachers. Unfamiliar with their students' names yet conscious of the nicknames written on the seating chart, they would call out, "Who's Dick Hertz?"

Day two took Richard further back in time, to his birth trauma. He claimed to have minute recall of forceps being applied to his baby ass. Days three and four were about his sexual identity issues, since he'd decided he was gay when he was fourteen, changed his mind when he was seventeen, with a fair amount of experience in between that he was convinced had scarred him for life.

Annie did suggest at the end of day four that maybe professional psychotherapy was in order, but Richard claimed not to believe in it, explaining that he knew more than all the therapists put together and that he was sublimating his anxieties in his work. That made sense. Though he bordered on the intolerable, he was an extraordinarily efficient paralegal.

"Are you entering all those exhibit numbers on the master list? The partners check at the end of the day," Richard reminded her. The malodor of his garlicky lunch wafted across the table.

"Got it," Annie replied, switching to mouth breathing.

"Good. You know, I had an amazing dream last night." Richard reached behind him for a new stack of exhibits. "I was in a cigar-shaped boat, entering a yawning cavern."

"Sometimes a cigar is just a cigar," Annie quipped, labeling the next envelope in sequence and sending a mental plea to the Supreme Court in the Sky that Richard would not—dear God—share the minutiae of another dream.

Alas, her petition was denied.

"All my family members were there. I remember thinking about the word 'members.' Which you could take as, you know, a sense of belonging, as in a *member* of a club. Or you could take it as phallic, as in *my* member."

Suddenly Annie couldn't take another moment of him.

"Wow. Member! Speaking of, I need to call . . . my gym. Where I'm a member!" She sprang up and grabbed her purse.

"Just use the phone here," he suggested.

Too late. She was already on her way to the small kitchen at the far end the floor, wondering whether the benefits of eighteen dollars an hour outweighed the negatives of exposure to—

Her cell vibrated—there were strict rules at the firm about no ringing cell phones. She checked the number and flipped it open as she stepped into the kitchen. She was happy to see that someone had brewed a fresh pot of coffee. "Hi, Gramma."

"Hi, sweetheart. How's your day?"

"Terrible. I'm hiding out from Who's-Dick-Hertz."

Doris had heard about her coworker. She offered sympathy, then added that she had news that might cheer Annie up.

"You talked Bernie into raising the percentage?"

For the last several days, Doris had been engaged in heated negotiations with Funtime over the split on Mr. Vibrator. Bernie had come up from ten percent to twenty. Doris and Annie wanted fifty, but privately agreed to settle for thirty if they had to.

"Maybe better news than that. I got a call from my lawyer this morning. The probate judge is going to rule on Grandpa's estate today. At four. Any chance you can come to the main courthouse? Third floor, Judge Jenkins."

Annie knew she shouldn't—Who's-Dick-Hertz had a concentration-camp-level quota for the number of exhibit labels he wanted completed by a certain time. Still, if she worked triple-fast and hit her goal early, he'd surely let her take a personal hour at four, especially if she was willing to work late into the night as he did.

"Okay, see you then," Annie agreed.

She dropped her phone back into her purse, poured herself a paper cup of black coffee, and headed back to work. Fine. She'd have to endure—she checked her watch—three hours and twenty-seven more minutes of Who's-Dick-Hertz's dreams. At least he hadn't figured in any of her fantasies.

"All rise!"

A handsome African American man with a goatee

strode in, clad in judicial robes. He dropped said robes as well as trou on the way to his raised desk. As soon as his cute five-foot-nothing bailiff saw this, she stood and began undressing, too.

No, wait. Her clothes were intact. *Just stop it, Annie,* she told herself.

"Honorable Stephen Jenkins presiding, God save this honorable court," the bailiff called out.

Naked Judge Jenkins pounded his gavel. Oh, well. Annie was enjoying this part of her fantasy too much to rein herself in. He really was very hot.

"Be seated." His manner was no-nonsense. Annie wondered if that carried over to other venues.

Doris had gotten permission from the bailiff for Annie to join her at the petitioner's table with her lawyer. Doris was the executor of her late husband's estate, and though he had died nine months before, it had taken all this time for her to marshal the assets and find the latest copy of Murray's will, then more time for the court to investigate whether the will was actually valid.

"I apologize for my brevity this afternoon," the judge told them. "My son broke his ankle skateboarding in Golden Gate Park—he's being x-rayed as we speak. But I didn't want to delay this any longer." He opened a brown folder on his desk. "In the matter of the will of Murray A. Rosen, deceased October 17 of last year, case number 07-549942. It is the ruling of this court that the will presented for probate is valid and that Doris Rosen, appointed executor of the state of Murray Rosen by that same valid will, is indeed the executor."

"What does that mean?" Annie hissed at her grandmother. All Doris did was give her hand a little squeeze.

"Counsel?"

"Yes, Your Honor?" Doris's lawyer was a stolid-looking
woman that she knew from her synagogue.

"I'll trust you to go through the rigmarole with your cli-
ent about her rights and responsibilities. You can pick up my
order tomorrow morning at my chambers." Judge Jenkins
rapped the gavel. "We're adjourned."

"I hope your son is fine," the lawyer called.

"He will be, until he gets home to me," the judge joked.

The lawyer touched Doris's arm. "Okay, you're all set.
Call my office in the morning, and I'll messenger over a copy
of the order. Good luck."

"Thanks, Mavis," Doris told her. "I'll talk to you tomorrow."

A few minutes later, Doris and Annie were alone in the
courtroom. "I'm glad that's finally settled. I miss your grandfather," she told Annie. "Every single day. Every single minute. Every single breath."

Annie felt a knot in her throat. She reached for her
grandmother's hand.

"I'm all right." Doris raised her eyes and gave Annie a
smile. "He's taking good care of me. Even now."

"Is it . . . a lot of money?" Annie asked delicately. She'd
never discussed her grandfather's estate with her grandmother. It wasn't any of her business.

Doris shrugged. "Not enough to change my life. But why
would I change my life even if I could? I have my family, my

house, my health, my yoga, my friends, my shul, even my work. I'm happy enough. Who needs M.C.?"

"Marin County?" Annie guessed.

"Exactly." Doris shrugged. "It doesn't impress me." She gave Annie's hand a squeeze, then let go. "So, it's a nice estate. About four hundred thousand dollars. After fees and debts, let's say three hundred. I already have Social Security and our annuities. I'm fine. Like I said, it won't change my life."

"I know you'd trade it all for—"

"It won't change my life, sweetheart," Doris interrupted, "but it definitely can change yours."

Oh, no.

"I am not taking Grandpa Murray's money," Annie insisted, embarrassed that Doris felt her so incapable of earning her own living.

"What, you think I'm talking charity? Is that my style? You don't know me better than that?" Doris leaned toward Annie. "I'm talking *investment,* darling. In you. In us. In our project."

"Mr. Vibrator?" Annie ventured.

Doris nodded. "I told Bernie to go to hell today. He wouldn't come up over twenty percent, and your idea's worth more than that—plus the man gives new meaning to the words 'wandering Jew' with the hands on my ass—who needs it? Well, I do, maybe, but not from him." She took a breath. "Anyway, I called the factory in Taiwan and asked what it would cost to produce Mr. Vibrator. Nineteen bucks per, they can have the first order here in a week. And you hate that temp job. So, Y.Q."

"You quit," Annie translated. "Meaning, I quit?"

"Exactly," Doris agreed. "I'm backing you for a year. You'll get a draw against our profits. Will fifteen hundred a week do? I don't want you to worry about money."

Annie was floored. "Are you sure . . . ?"

Doris put a hand to Annie's cheek. "How could I not be sure? You're a brilliant girl. I'm simply investing in brilliance."

That her grandmother had this kind of faith in her touched Annie profoundly. She sent up a little prayer that she could live up to it.

The good-bye to Who's-Dick-Hertz was going to be sweet. She only wished that Doris could be there to see her say S.L.I.B.E.T.K.Y.

So long, it's been excruciating to know you.

 ten

"I started a joke," Annie sang along to the the Dirtbombs, blasting from her computer's speakers, as she tried to decide what to wear for her night out with Michelle. She was in a fabulous mood. She no longer had to temp; she didn't even have to look for a job. All she had to do was focus on making Mr. Vibrator a success, and she was working her ass off to do just that.

They started by setting up a company. Michelle was doing the legal work to incorporate and get them licensed, in return for a small cut of future profits, should there be any. Annie and Doris had decided to call their business Turn Me On, Inc., and money had already been wired to the factory in Taiwan that would manufacture the product. First would come a prototype for testing, and then mass production. Annie had decreed that it must be absolutely silent. No buzzing, at any speed. Internet research had led her to a NASA affiliate that promised to provide the parts to render Mr. Vibrator silent—except for the lovely and lascivious things that came from his "mouth." Once she received a satisfactory prototype, ten thousand Mr. Vibrators could roll off their assembly line in a week.

Annie was doing both packaging design and Web design herself. Their Web site, www.turnmeoninc.com, had been reserved and paid for.

She knew how crucial it was to get the right voice for Mr. Vibrator, so she'd booked a sound studio south of Market Street for two days of auditions and put a discreet casting notice in the West Coast version of *Back Stage*. She was careful not to mention in the advertisement the real purpose of the recordings that would be done, lest someone steal her brilliant idea. The advertisement called for auditions to do the voice-over on a "female affirmation CD." Close enough.

Her days were so full that she barely thought about Elliot. She'd go to bed at night so wound up from how fast all the pieces were coming together that she couldn't sleep. A romp with the Ultimate Pleasure took care of that. Ever since the first night when she'd heard that deep, sexy voice in her head saying all the things she wished a guy would say, she'd been able to conjure up his voice at will. While the Ultimate Pleasure engaged her body, the voice in her head engaged her mind. They had deep conversations and funny conversations, teasing and silly conversations, *every* kind of conversation. It was fantastic. Magical, even. Where that particular voice came from, she had no idea. But he always sounded the same. If only she could find *that* voice, she was certain that Mr. Vibrator would be a success.

She didn't exactly share this guy's voice-in-my-head thing

with either her grandmother or Michelle. Doris would think that she'd lost her mind. Besides, it was just too personal to admit to a grandmother, even one as liberated as hers. She would have told Michelle, who knew all about Annie's bizarre fantasies. But just as Annie had pulled out of her funk, Michelle tumbled into one.

Peter Klein—he of their double date at the Top of the Mark—decided to get back with an ex-girlfriend whom he'd never really gotten over. Seamus, Annie's date, had stopped by Michelle's place after a trip to the gym to offer her a well-padded shoulder to cry on. Eventually they'd started kissing on the couch, which was where Michelle discovered that the whale analogy didn't apply to all parts of his anatomy. When she turned down his offer to share, he'd whipped a hand into his gym shorts and taken the little worm for a notably brief ride before Michelle could stop him. She was having the couch fumigated and planned to send him the bill.

Unlike Annie, Michelle was a take-charge type, not one to wallow. Mere hours after she'd called the fumigator, she'd excitedly called Annie to tell her about the "greatest new dating thing" she'd read about in the San Francisco section of www.dailycandy.com: Dining in the Dark.

The concept for Dining in the Dark was that a group of singles met in total darkness in a private room at a restaurant. It was supposed to be a fantastic way for singles to get to know each other on a level other than the visual. The online story contained a testimonial from a fortyish woman who had met the new love of her life when he blindly popped a succulent morsel of sashimi into her open mouth.

Annie had zero interest in being fed raw seafood by strangers. However, Michelle wouldn't take no for an answer. She'd registered them for that coming Saturday night, which was why Annie was now standing in front of her closet, musing on what to wear. Finally she decided on her favorite faded jeans—at least she'd be comfortable—and a romantic white lace blouse with handkerchief-hem sleeves that fell in points to her knuckles.

Not that it mattered. No one would see her. Well, she'd just have to hum "I Feel Pretty" and go with the flow.

"What's the address again?" Michelle asked, as she motored her Lexus down Beach Street, not all that far from Elliot's loft. Annie no longer missed him. That was a good thing. On the other hand, if she'd still been with him, she'd have had an excuse not to go to this event. She peered at her MapQuest directions. "Three sixty-six Beach."

Michelle slowed down in front of a restaurant with a huge Hooters logo, then turned into a small parking lot. "I think this is it." It was half full, and she found an empty spot not far from the street.

"Hooters?" Annie asked dubiously. "We can't possibly be this desperate."

"Relax," Michelle assured her, as a black BMW pulled in opposite them. "The new owner just didn't take down the old sign. I read that online."

Annie watched a muscular guy in a leather vest with a bushy moustache hop out of the Beemer, calling his Great Dane after him. "Isn't he in the wrong neighborhood? I draw the line at animal husbandry."

"Yes on the jokes, no on the negativity," Michelle decreed. "Let's go." Like Annie, she'd worn jeans and a blouse, but also her usual makeup.

Just inside the front door, an effete man with a Mohawk and an ascot stood sentry with a clipboard. "Yes?" he asked pleasantly. "May I help you?"

"Dining in the Dark?" Michelle inquired.

"Breeder or non-breeder?" the man asked smoothly.

"I think you could call us pre-breeders," Michelle replied brightly.

"We're doing two events here tonight," the man explained. "I didn't want to steer you wrong, although it's always good to be open-minded about these things. Names?"

A moment later, their names crossed off the master list, they were pointed toward the "breeders" event. The main dining room was still being renovated. Chairs were piled up haphazardly, and the hardwood floor was only half finished. Across the main dining room, though, they spotted a black door with a white lettered sign:

DINING IN THE DARK
BREEDERS!
COME ON IN
LEAVE YOUR INHIBITIONS BEHIND!

Annie hesitated. "Um, I'm not really sure—"

Too late. Michelle was already opening the door.

The room was pitch-black. Annie literally could not see

a thing, except for a set of green glowing goggles that seemed to be floating in the air.

"Hello, and welcome!" A second pair of goggles materialized. The voice was male, and Annie felt her hand taken by a calloused palm. "I'm Chester. Next to me is Candi with an 'i.' We're from Sophisti-Katz Parties, and we're your hosts this evening. Just so you know, we're wearing night-vision equipment. You're in good hands."

Annie and Michelle introduced themselves; then Chester and Candi led them to what they described as a round table for twelve, explaining that four such tables were arranged around a large central area filled with luxurious pillows. They were seated with an empty chair between them because, as Candi explained, that was the best way to make new friends. Chester added that between drinks and the four courses of dinner, the waiters—who also wore night-vision goggles—would be moving the men from table to table. "Wouldn't want someone's hand in your sashimi unless you want it there!" Chester sang out.

Annie watched Candi's and Chester's goggles float away. This was a most bizarre situation, and very disorienting. She couldn't even see anyone to fantasize about.

"Now what?" she leaned toward where she thought Michelle would be. Before Michelle could reply, a pair of goggles appeared between them.

"What can I get you ladies?" Goggles asked. "I have Mojitos, Cosmos, or champagne cocktails."

"Maker's Mark, straight up," Michelle said.

"Make that two," Annie added. She rarely drank, but this situation called for alcoholic reinforcement.

"I'm sorry but we only have—"

"Do you have a bar?" Michelle interrupted.

"Yes. But if the drink isn't on my list I'll have to charge you extra."

"How the hell would you know who to charge?"

"*I* can see." The waiter sniffed. "*You* can't."

"Point well taken," Michelle said. *"Doubles."*

As the green goggles moved off, Annie leaned closer to Michelle. "Do we have to stay?"

"Of course. Think of this as a warm-up for choosing your voice for Mr. V."

Now, *that* actually made sense. Annie wouldn't be distracted here by looks. She could treat this as a business project. She wondered whether the cost of the evening might be deductible.

Goggles returned, and the drinks were pressed into their hands. Suddenly a deep gong sound silenced the room.

"Welcome, welcome, intrepid merrymakers! I'm Chester Westin from Sophisti-Katz Parties. Your appetizers are now being served. Gentlemen, we'll move you from table to table! And remember, you accompany a lady to the 'conversation area' with the pillows only if she invites you to do so."

Annie could hear the verbal air quotes around "conversation area," implying that a lot more went on there than verbiage. Swell.

"Your waiters can fetch you anything you might need to

make this evening truly special," Chester continued. *"Any-thing. Let the fun and games begin!"*

Anything you might need?

Dear God. Michelle had brought her to a blackout group grope. Not that she hadn't ever imagined one, but that was theory. This was practice.

"Shit!" Michelle exclaimed.

"What?"

"I just spilled my drink all over my pants. What am I, fucking Helen Keller here? Waiter? Waiter!"

Annie was tempted to point out that this outing had been her friend's idea, but it seemed mean to do so when Michelle was wearing a double shot of bourbon. Instead she groped for her napkin and handed it to Michelle, just before a guy with a helium-inflected voice settled into the seat between then.

"Wow, an empty seat. Man, this is so out there!" he chirped. "Hey, any girls around?"

"I'm Annie. To your left is Helen Keller."

He offered a high-pitched giggle. "I love a sense of humor on a chick. I'm in real estate, Annie. You?"

"She's a mentalist. She's seeing you leaving, *Alvin,*" Michelle quipped.

"Dyke." Alvin stood, bumping heavily against Annie as he moved into the darkness and called for a waiter.

Not exactly a promising beginning. Annie's stomach growled. Where were the appetizers?

She cautiously stretched out a hand to feel around for something—anything—edible. Her fingers hit something sticky. She put them to her nose. Duck sauce. What asshole had decided that a dish of duck sauce was a wise choice for those who could not see? What else? She hit something square and warm. Doughy on the outside. Promising. She put it to her lips and took a bite.

"Damn!" she yelped. It was spicier than the hottest jalapeño she'd ever tasted. She grabbed for her Maker's Mark and downed it in one long swallow. Now both her mouth and her stomach were burning.

"You okay?" The deep male voice was coming from her right. Whoever he was, he sounded legitimately concerned.

"Water!" Annie managed to gasp.

"Here, take mine." A large, warm hand found hers and curled her fingers around a glass. Annie lifted it to her lips and guzzled gratefully.

"Thank you," she said when she was capable of speech again. "I burned my mouth. In fact, I may have singed every internal organ."

He chuckled sexily. "Glad I could help. This is kind of crazy, huh? Gives a whole new meaning to 'blind date.' "

Wow. What a voice. Nice, empathetic, and not gay. Annie was about to introduce herself when she felt a large pair of hands kneading the back of her neck and then heading down the back of her lace shirt.

"Yum-yum," purred a male voice. "Don't *you* feel delicious."

Annie jerked forward. "Get your hands out of my shirt!"

Then she felt two more hands join his—someone was holding her hair up—and a tongue press against her neck.

Oh, no. I don't *think* so.

She slammed both elbows backward as hard as she could, making contact with soft body parts. With two deep and satisfying grunts, the groping stopped.

"Hello?" Annie called into the darkness. "The guy who gave me the water. Are you there?"

No answer.

"Water guy? You there?"

No answer.

"Michelle?"

No answer there, either. Annie reached over to where Michelle had been sitting, but hit only air. Then she heard her friend's distinctive laugh from the conversation pit. This probably meant that Michelle wasn't going to want to leave anytime soon.

"Excuse me," Annie called out to a passing set of goggles. "Where's the ladies' room?"

"To the right and down the hallway," Goggles replied.

"How am I supposed to find it?" Annie asked.

"By feel."

Funny. Goggles leaned over the table to deliver something or other. Annie didn't hesitate. Her hand flashed out, and she snatched the eye gear from his face.

"Sorry, but I really need these."

"Hey!"

"I'll be right back," Annie promised. She slipped the goggles on and everything glowed sickly green, as if it were radioactive. There was Michelle, making out with what turned out to be a good-looking guy in a black sports jacket and jeans. And he . . .

Oh, ick. Michelle had already been down this particular road. Annie stepped over sprawled bodies into the middle of the conversation pit.

"Michelle, it's me!" she hissed.

Michelle stopped in mid-kiss and looked up. "Annie? Is that you? How did you get the goggles?"

"I stole them." Annie leaned close to Michelle's ear. "Umm, I don't know how to tell you this, but the guy you're with has one hand on his joystick."

Not being shy, Michelle reached toward her partner's lap and caught him in midstroke.

"Jesus Christ! Shamu must have started a franchise! It's a fucking self-pleasure epidemic!" she yelped.

"Ready to go now?"

"I'm out of here," Michelle declared, and Annie helped her up.

"Hey, you can't leave!" whined her new friend. "What's up with that?"

"You, evidently. Enjoy flying Hans solo, asshole."

Once they were out the door, Michelle and Annie both cracked up.

"Hans solo?" Annie giggled.

"It just came to me," Michelle replied. "So, you didn't meet anyone?"

Annie thought about the guy with the soothing voice whose water she'd shared. But she'd heard only two sentences, and she had no idea who he was.

"Nope," she told Michelle. "No one at all."

 eleven

VOICE-OVER ARTIST NEEDED

SEEKING MALE VOICE-OVER FOR NEW FEMALE AFFIR-
MATION CD. BRING RÉSUMÉ. NO AUDITION TAPES
ACCEPTED. YOU WILL BE RECORDED WITH LINES PRO-
VIDED AT AUDITION. SELECTED ACTOR RECEIVES FLAT
FEE $2,000. FRIDAY AND SATURDAY, 9–5 ECHO
SOUND STUDIO. SIGN-UP SHEET POSTED 6 A.M.

"I am so nailing this," Mark confidently told Charlie as
they walked from the Muni stop on Market Street toward the
sound studio on Folsom Street. Though this was still a dicey
neighborhood after dark, Charlie knew it was gentrifying
like every other previously down-and-out part of the San
Francisco area, with the exception of Hunter's Point.

Charlie understood why Mark was so confident. He had
a deep and powerful leading-man's voice, even if he lacked

the requisite leading-man looks. That fact had finally paid off for him in a big way, since he had just been cast in the national touring company of *Hairspray*. He'd be cross-dressing as Edna Turnblad, the role for which Harvey Fierstein had won a Tony. Better yet, the show would actually start its tour in San Francisco, with a sit-down at the Geary Theater for fourteen weeks.

The only downside was that rehearsals wouldn't start for four more months. In the meantime, Mark still had to scrape together his rent money. Hence, this voice-over possibility, which was a lot better than his on-again-off-again gig waiting tables at a touristy restaurant on Pier 39, where tips of late had been somewhat south of shaky.

"We'll be in and out in like twenty minutes," Mark went on, as they stepped across Mission Street. On Saturday afternoon, traffic was light. "Everyone and their brother goes to these open-call things the first day. Poor fuckers get there at six in the morning to sign up. But four o'clock on the second day? It'll be empty," he predicted. "I'll be the last voice they hear, so I'll stand out in their minds—piece of cake. Then you can buy me that congratulatory beer. Or three."

The instant Charlie stepped into the reception area, he saw that Mark had been mistaken. Every seat and most of the floor space were taken up by guys waiting to audition. Some were filling out the release form, others were reading quietly aloud from a sheet of typed lines, trying out various cadences.

"Shit," Mark muttered. He went up to the girl behind the desk, who had blue hair extensions and a lethal-looking pierced lip. "Is there more than one audition taking place today?"

"Just the affirmation thingie," the girl replied, using a black nail-polished forefinger to push the sign-up sheet toward Mark. He signed it, picked up a copy of the same paper everyone else seemed to be reading, and wedged into a corner next to Charlie.

"I should have known." Mark sighed. "They don't care what physical type you are, so every asshole capable of speech thinks he's the right voice—easy two thou, the end. Sorry, man. This is gonna take a while."

"I'll survive." Charlie peered over Mark's shoulder, curious to see what would go on a female affirmation CD.

> *Your ass does not look fat. Have another piece of chocolate cake.*
>
> *What you need is an aromatherapy massage and a pedicure.*
>
> *You are so hot. Any man would be insane not to fall in love with you.*
>
> *You are the most fantastic, gorgeous, sexy woman in the world.*
>
> *I love your thighs.*
>
> *You're perfect exactly as you are.*
>
> *Tell me everything. I'll listen.*

Mark tried out one of the lines. *"You're perfect exactly as you are.* What a hoot. Who would listen to this?"

"Pretty much any woman I've ever met," Charlie opined.

"Get out of here."

"No, seriously. Women don't hear this kind of thing from guys, so I can see how it would help them feel better."

"Yeah, for both days of your deep and meaningful relationship," Mark joked.

"Okay, so I'm not in it for the long haul," Charlie acknowledged. "But who knows? Maybe if I met the right woman . . ."

"Bull," Mark snorted. "You are the king of the Parting Gift, man! I've seen you with women hotter than my fantasy women, okay? And they're all over you. But you *still* give 'em the kiss-off. Like that chick you met at Blockbuster a few weeks ago. Long red hair, killer ass?"

"Vivica," Charlie filled in. "Dental hygienist. She blushes all over," he recalled fondly.

"On a one-to-ten scale, that woman was an eleven," Mark insisted. "And what did you do after two weeks of playing hide the kosher kielbasa? You cut her loose."

Charlie wagged a finger at Mark. "See, now you misjudge me. *She* cut *me* loose. All I did was take her to a PTA meeting at my school. When we came outside, it was a crime scene for a triple homicide gang thing. She stopped returning my calls."

Mark stabbed a finger at Charlie. "You did that on purpose."

Charlie held up his hands. "You think I knew there'd be a homicide?"

"I think you knew something about your job was gonna turn her off," Mark guessed. "The shit pay, the neighborhood, *something*. If a chick makes it to two, three weeks with you, that's what you *do*, man."

Charlie couldn't really argue. He remembered how Vivica had asked for a movie rental recommendation. He'd suggested *The Producers*—the original Zero Mostel version—because it was the funniest movie he'd ever seen, and there was nothing sexier than seeing a woman laugh. Then she'd invited him to watch it with her. He'd noticed sadness flit across her face when Zero Mostel came on the screen. Later she admitted that he looked like her father, who had died the year before. He'd held her for hours while she talked about him. Yes, he'd known that one kind of intimacy could lead to another—and it had—but that wasn't why he'd done it. For however long he and Vivica were together, she was a real person to him, and that person needed to talk about her dad. It was as simple as that.

"*I love your thighs,*" Mark read aloud. "You think this is like a self-hypnosis kind of thing?"

"Could be," Charlie said. "I met this great woman in London named Layla. She was a hypnotherapist who helped people lose weight. In between sessions, they listened to her tapes. *You no longer have a desire to eat sugar.* She said it worked."

"Gee, let's cancel the gastric bypass thing," Mark cracked.

"I'm not saying it works for everyone," Charlie acknowledged. "But there's something to be said for the power of positive thinking."

"You didn't say that when I dragged your ass to Dining in the Dark last week. You stayed, what, ten minutes?"

Charlie clapped Mark on the back. "Face it, it fucking sucked. Be right back." He got up and crossed to the punk receptionist. "Where's the men's room?"

She mumbled something about going through the door, down the hall, turn, turn, turn, can't miss it, without once looking up from her copy of *Rolling Stone*. Charlie followed the directions until he got to the third turn, and realized he didn't know what to do next. There were unmarked doors to his right and his left. Well, he had a fifty-fifty shot.

He tried the door on the right. No bathroom—instead, it was the studio control room, where a cadaverous guy with a thin, graying ponytail sat under headphones on a stool scarfing down a Burger King burger. On his lap was a red book titled *Russian for Beginners*.

Well, wrong doorway. He was backing out of the room when the guy said, in a truly atrocious accent, "девочка, можно купить вас напиток?" Charlie realized he had to be listening to a Russian-language program.

"Купить вам, не вас," Charlie corrected in a loud voice. His time in Tver had been put to good use. "It's actually девушка можно купить вам напиток."

The guy opened his eyes and took off his headphones. "Say something?"

"Sorry. I didn't mean to interrupt. Carry on."

"Wait—hold up, man. You actually speak Russian?"

"Some," Charlie acknowledged. "Great country. Fascinating. Beautiful."

Equally beautiful had been the three weeks he'd spent with Galina, an acrobat with the Tver city circus. It was amazing what an enthusiastic triple-jointed girl could do.

The bearded guy grinned and patted an empty stool next to him. "Cop a squat, man. This fucking language is insane!" He held out a hand. "Name's Rocket."

"Charlie Silver." Charlie sat, calculating that his bladder could hold out for a few more minutes. Quirky people always interested him. He studied Rocket as he wolfed down another piece of burger. The nail on his right pinky finger was long, which meant he either snorted coke or used it as a guitar pick. Or both.

"I'm a sound engineer," Rocket explained, throwing the paper wrapping from his burger into a trash barrel. "I'm getting married in three months. Fifty-two fucking years old and I'm getting hitched for the first time. Ain't that a bitch? To a Russian girl I met on the Internet. Can you fucking deal?" He reached for a can of Red Bull on his console. "You married?"

Charlie shook his head.

Rocket pointed a forefinger at him. "Now, see, that's the attitude I used to have. Then I got my ass pussy-whipped. Valentina Kuriakova. What a gal. Never thought it would happen to me. My old lady's parents are coming from Smolensk for the wedding; she wants me to be able to talk to 'em. Why couldn't I fall for someone from Honduras, man? I fucking *know* Spanish." He showed Charlie his open textbook and pointed. "Can you read that?"

Charlie read the phrase aloud to him, and suggested an

easier way to say the same thing: "I'm honored to be your son-in-law."

"Hey, thanks, man, that helps. If I can just remember. One too many Pink Floyd concerts, if you get my drift. You here for the voice-over gig?"

"My friend is. I just tagged along."

"I'm the engineer—hey, I guess the studio was a big fucking clue." Rocket barked a laugh at his own joke. "On my break. There still a lot of guys out there waiting?"

"Oh, yeah. You're gonna be here for a while."

"Shit, I cannot do this in a non-altered state." Rocket reached into a small drawer under the mixing board. "How do you say 'Do you want to torch one?' in Russian?"

Charlie chuckled, because he actually knew the answer to that. His acrobatic friend and all her circus friends were very big on recreational drugs, though the laws in Russia against their consumption were very strict. He'd met a contortionist who could blow smoke rings with three different orifices. Quite a talent.

"А не хочешь закурить марихуану?"

"You coulda just said my dog is humping your knee, for all I know," Rocket snorted. He struck a match and lit the end of a blimp-size blunt. "I do this shit much better with THC in my bloodstream." He sucked hard on the joint, held his breath, and passed it to Charlie.

What the hell, Charlie thought. He'd be here for a while. He took a hit and passed it back to Rocket.

"Fucking female affirmation tapes," Rocket scoffed in a

strangled voice, then exhaled a long stream of smoke. " 'Your ass does not look fat.' I've heard that five hundred times in the past two days. What asshole with a hard-on would tell a chick her ass looks like a Hummer? Hey, you wanna take a shot? I've got the lines here, somewhere."

"I'm no actor," Charlie demurred.

"Neither are most of the assholes out there." The engineer handed Charlie the lines on a file card that he unearthed from under a pile of papers, then flipped some switches on his board. He pointed to the microphone hanging over Charlie's head. "What the fuck, man—it pays two grand."

What the fuck was right, Charlie thought. Plus it was a damn good reefer. He passed the joint back to Rocket. Why the hell not take a shot at the recording? Rocket snubbed out the joint and stuck the roach in a drawer, then sprayed the air with an air freshener, as Charlie studied the lines.

"Ready?"

Charlie nodded.

"When I point to you."

Rocket pressed a button on his console and held up three fingers, then two, then one. Then, he pointed a skinny forefinger at Charlie.

"Your ass does not look fat," Charlie read, in a normal tone of voice. The same voice, in fact, that he would use were he really alone with a woman he liked. It was easy, especially in his stoned state, to picture one of the many beauties he'd known in the biblical sense right there next to him. He never lied to any of them, ever. He just found what was wonderful and beautiful about them and concentrated on that.

He did the same thing now. Galina. Sandra. Vivica. And a cast of dozens.

"Have another piece of chocolate cake."

Rocket gave him a big thumbs-up, so he went on to the next affirmation.

"What you need is an aromatherapy massage and a pedicure. You're perfect exactly as you are. I love your thighs. You are so hot. Any man would be crazy not to fall in love with you."

When he got through them all, Rocket nodded emphatically and switched off the microphone. "Hey, you need to sign a release. I have 'em here somewhere. If they pick your recording, they'll send you two grand. I should record the fucking thing myself, take my bride on a kick-ass honeymoon to Mendocino. Ah, here they are." He dug out a clipboard, wrote the number 514 on the top paper. "Fill out the top page and sign it at the bottom."

Charlie did, while Rocket entered some information into his laptop. Fact was, Charlie didn't need the money all that badly. He had grown accustomed to living on what he made. In fact, he could think of at least two better places for it to go. First was to his school, but two thousand dollars would be a mere drop in the bucket of the $1.3 million they needed to raise; which was why a major fund-raising effort would need to gather steam. Second was his friend Mark, whose needs were more immediate—to pay his rent until *Hairspray* went into rehearsal. Two thousand would do it.

It was a no-brainer. Charlie scrawled Mark's name and address on the form and then filled out a W-4, too. He didn't know Mark's Social Security number, so he left that off. Let them call Mark for it, he thought as he headed back to the reception area, mellowed by Rocket's reefer. What the hell. It was his good deed for the day. He'd given his best bud a second shot at winning the voice-over lottery.

twelve

Michelle popped open her briefcase, took out a loose-leaf binder, and handed it to Annie. "Congratulations. Turn Me On is officially a California corporation. You're the president. Doris, you're vice president, and I'm—God help me, my Catholic grandmother in Chicago who goes to Mass every day would kill me if she knew—secretary and treasurer."

"Amen," Doris said, then hugged Annie. "Mazel tov, darling. You're in business." She sat down in one of the two over-stuffed maroon chairs she'd given Annie eighteen months before, when Murray had gotten so sick.

"You mean *we're* in business." Annie put the binder on her coffee table. Strewn about the floor were various sketches that she'd done and discarded for Mr. Vibrator's packaging. In fact, she'd transformed her living room into an office, purchasing secondhand furniture—desk, chair, filing cabinets, and drafting table—at a place on Mission Street, moving in her iBook, and buying herself a top-grade printer. Of course, it didn't matter much if her living room looked like an office when she had zero idea of how to run a business. What if she failed?

She hadn't even told her parents back in Michigan. Neither had her grandmother. There was no doubt that her mother—Doris's eldest daughter—would be appalled at the gamble Doris had taken with Murray's estate. As for the product itself—well, if her mother knew what the gamble was being taken on, she'd *plotz*.

"Call my friend Christina tomorrow," Michelle instructed Annie, who saw a Wells Fargo business card clipped to the paperwork. "She'll help you with the corporate bank accounts and your checks."

"Thanks," Annie said gratefully. She looked from Doris to Michelle. "You understand that I don't know what I'm doing."

"So you'll learn as you go," her grandmother said amiably. She was creating a needlepoint of the Book of Life that she hoped to have done by the High Holy Days in late September.

"Did you get the voice-over CD yet?" Michelle swung her legs sideways over the chair and kicked off the Manolos she'd worn to work. She'd been in court all day and had complained that the shoes hurt her feet.

Annie shook her head. The auditions had been the previous weekend, and she was still awaiting delivery of the CD. She'd had a brief phone conversation with the engineer—Rocket, he said his name was—who'd done the actual work. He claimed he was having a bit of trouble keeping all the recordings organized, but Annie could expect a

CD messengered to her within the next day or two. That was four days ago, and she was starting to get concerned.

"Call me if it doesn't come in tomorrow's mail," Michelle instructed. She absentmindedly massaged her calves. "I'll send a lawyer's letter on the big letterhead. That tends to scare the shit out of people. What's the rest of your progress report?"

"Oh, you know," Annie said lamely. "Packaging design, kind of."

"'Kind of'?" Doris echoed. "C.B.C., Annie, darling."

C.B.C.?

"Confidence begets confidence," Doris explained. "You have to believe in you before anyone else is going to. When I'm done with this, I'll make you a nice wall hanging. Can we see?"

The idea of displaying her packaging concept for Mr. Vibrator made her feel sick to her stomach. Doris had lent her the Funtime catalog, extolling the virtues of their vibrator's very discreet brown paper packaging. If you mail-ordered, the return address said simply "F.T. Industries." Inserts referred to the item as a "personal massage unit." Words like "sex," "vibrator," "insert," and "orgasm" were scrupulously missing from the enclosed instructions.

Funtime was the industry leader, Doris had pointed out. Why reinvent the wheel?

Only Annie knew she *had* reinvented the wheel, but she wasn't sure it would even roll. Well, hell. Her grandmother and Michelle would have to see it sooner or later.

"Okay." She went to the largest drawer in her file cabinet

to retrieve her prototype package and held it out for Doris and Michelle with both hands

"Oh, my God, Annie." Michelle's mouth dropped open.

That had to be bad, Annie realized, wincing.

"It's . . . it's . . . " Doris stammered.

Really bad, Annie concluded.

"I'll do it over. Really," she assured them.

Michelle shook her head. "Are you insane? Why would you do that? It's fabulous! Don't you think, Doris?"

"I adore it," her grandmother agreed. "Another mazel tov."

Wow. Annie had not been prepared for that reaction. Instead of plain brown packaging, she'd gone with bright colors. Instead of a solid box, she'd chosen a narrow clear cellophane top through which the shaft could be seen. For the moment, she was using one of Funtime's run-of-the-mill models just to give an idea of what the battery-operated boyfriend would look like in the box. She'd decorated the box with a cartoon drawing of a handsome guy of indeterminate age. Circling his head were various cartoon balloons of a few choice things the purchaser could expect.

> *You're perfect exactly as you are.*
> *Have another piece of chocolate cake.*
> *Any man would be insane not to fall in love with*
> *you.*

"You really like it?" Annie asked shyly. She had to be sure they weren't just being kind.

"It's fabulous," Doris decreed. "My grandmother, my mother's mother, may she rest in peace, was also an artist. You're a credit to the family name even though you're an Albright and not a Katzenellenbogen like her or a Rosen like me."

Michelle looked aghast. "Katzen *what*?"

"It means 'cat's elbow,'" Doris translated, as if this explained anything at all.

Michelle got up and paced. "Okay, the box rocks. We're all in agreement about that. Now we need to talk about a marketing plan. I don't think we sell Mr. V like Funtime sells their stuff, with distributors at parties."

"Because?" Annie asked.

"Because within a month some company in China will do a knockoff and you'll be completely fucked," Michelle replied.

Huh. The night before in bed, after a session with Mr. V and still unable to sleep, Annie had come to the exact same conclusion. Mr. Vibrator was high concept. High concept could easily be ripped off.

"You're right," she told her friend. "That's why I'm thinking we need to hit the market with something really big and really hard."

Doris and Michelle just stared at her.

"Really big and really hard?" Michelle repeated.

"Okay, poor choice of words," Annie allowed. "But you get the idea. What I mean is, I think we need to be Web-based. Come to my iBook. I'll show you what I've got."

For the next half hour, Annie took her grandmother and Michelle through the preliminary design she'd done for the www.turnmeoninc.com Web site. She'd stayed up late several nights studying the sites of companies like Funtime. Most were cheesy-looking, done on the quick and the cheap. A few were incredibly salacious, sites meant to titillate instead of sell. A few more were supposedly pro-women, but absolutely humor-free. Still others treated vibrators like lawn furniture, complete with lists of features and a mind-numbing array of specs. That no one cared about.

After hours on those sites, one question had been on Annie's mind: Where's the fun? If the meeting she'd had with Doris's friends had taught her anything, it was that girls and women—of every and any age—really *did* want to have fun.

With this in mind Annie had designed a fun Web site that featured special pages depending on the age of the woman doing the buying. There was a click if you grew up with Kelly Clarkson, another if you grew up with Mariah, another for Pat Benatar, another for Blondie, and another for Grace Slick. This went all the way back to Patti Page and Doris Day. Each of those clicks took you to marketing information specially tailored for that buyer's demographic, including what Annie thought would be the pièce de résistance: a funny www.homestarrunner.com-type animated cartoon that humorously showed a typical male foible for the age group.

The twentysomething cartoon guy, for example, left his girlfriend high and, while not dry, less than satisfied, to go play ball with his high school buddies who still hadn't figured out that they weren't in high school anymore. The thirty-something cartoon guy was work-obsessed. The fortysome-thing cartoon guy was too busy looking in the mirror at his thinning hair, and the fiftysomething guy bought a Harley and joined a middle-aged motorcycle gang. After each humorous cartoon guy left his girl wanting more, the perfection of Mr. Vibrator was introduced.

Each cartoon ended with an order form.

"Holy shit, this is genius!" Michelle exclaimed.

"More than genius," Doris agreed. "It reminds me how back in my day, adult movies were this hush-hush thing. Nice girls never admitted to watching them, and nice boys would never even ask. Then along came this film called *Deep Throat*, which had an actual sense of humor. Everyone was talking about it, and everyone went to see it, including all the ladies in my Hadassah group. It changed everything." She took Annie's face in her hands. "Plus I want to tell you how proud I am you put in a cartoon for the Rosemary Clooney generation, darling." She kissed the top of Annie's head.

This was fantastic. Michelle and her grandmother really, truly liked—

The doorbell rang, interrupting Annie's thoughts.

"It's the Chinese I ordered," she announced. "Let's eat."

She hustled to the front door. When she opened it, though, instead of the Asian deliveryman from Little Buddha, she found herself looking at a very tall, very skinny guy with a scraggly ponytail.

"Hey, I'm Rocket. From Echo Studio."

The sound engineer, Annie realized.

"Hi."

"Hey, sorry I didn't call first." Rocket held out an envelope. "It's got your CD. We were going to send it by messenger tomorrow, but I was heading home and thought you might want it sooner. I, like, told you you'd have it yesterday or something, I think. Yeah, I'm pretty sure."

Actually, he was three days late, but Annie was too happy to finally have the CD to point that out.

"Thanks," she told him.

"Invoice is in there." He tipped an invisible hat. "Hey, good luck with that female affirmation thing. *Dosvidanya!*"

Michelle paused Annie's portable CD player and yawned hugely. "No more," she pleaded. "I can't stand it. We've heard everything male with a functional voice box in San Francisco."

"Also Berkeley and Oakland," Doris added. "They're all starting to sound the same to me. What time is it?"

Annie rubbed her bleary eyes, stretched out a kink in her neck, and craned around so that she could see the clock on her iBook. "Almost one."

"Great. I have to be back in court at nine," Michelle moaned.

They'd been at it for three and a half solid hours. Empty cartons of Chinese food littered the carpet; dozens of tiny silver foil balls from a jumbo bag of Hershey's Kisses adorned the coffee table. They'd listened to literally hundreds of voice-overs. Some of them were quite good. Some of them made Annie wonder about the relative sanity of the male half of the population. None of them was perfect.

There had been a lisping Truman Capote soundalike: *Your ath duth not look fat.* A dozen guys from foreign countries with heavy accents—Indian, German, French. One inventive guy did each line as a different cartoon character's voice, though hearing Eric Cartman say, "You are the most fantastic, gorgeous, sexy woman in the world" was not exactly an aphrodisiac.

There was the guy with the nervous giggle that made him sound like a serial killer, and quite a few imitations of various presidents of the United States. One threw in "Oh, baby" before each sentence, like Barry White. One guy changed the lines completely. That wouldn't have been too bad, except he'd substituted "I want to do you like an animal in the barnyard" for "Would you like an aromatherapy massage?"

They'd worked their way through nearly five hundred voices, and only two dozen or so names had been circled as *maybes*. All had nice voices. All had read convincingly enough. But none was *the voice* that Annie was looking for.

"Come on, just a few more," she pleaded. Tired as she was, she didn't want to quit. She displayed the master list of names that had come with the CD. "He's in here. I just know it."

"And soon he'll be in women all across America," Michelle cracked. "We hope, anyway. If you can forge on, so can I. Doris?"

"I'm in," Doris agreed tiredly. Her needlepoint had long since been put away.

Annie checked the list. "Let's see . . . we're up to number four hundred and seventy-one. There are five hundred and sixty-four in all."

"Great," Michelle muttered, and started the CD again.

"I'm Fred Tannin," the next voice insisted, sounding incredibly annoyed. "Your ass does *not* look fat! Have *another* piece of chocolate cake! What you *need* is an aromatherapy massage *and* a pedicure!"

Next. A mouth-breather.

Next. A prospective cast member of *Sesame Street*.

Next. Channeling Liberace.

Next.

"My name is Bryce Buffalo," said a deep voice.

Not bad. Not bad at all.

"I'm number four hundred and seventy-five. Your thighs are perfect. Have another piece of chocolate cake."

"Bryce Buffalo . . ." Michelle mused. "Wait. We heard him before!"

Annie frowned. "We have?"

"Who can remember?" Doris asked wearily.

"Because he's got that stupid name." Michelle took the master list from Annie and flipped to the first page. "Yep. Here he is. Number eighty-seven—Bryce Buffalo. The sneak. He auditioned twice."

"Maybe he was just being smart," Annie mused. The more she thought about it, the more sense it made to her. "It's kind of ingenious. He probably did it differently each time to double his chances."

Michelle and Doris allowed it, though Michelle groused as she excused herself to the bathroom that the stoner engineer shouldn't have let anyone audition more than once, but then he probably didn't even know his own name, much less the name of the auditioners. Doris took the impromptu break to call out the reserves—a pint of Ben and Jerry's Chubby Hubby and three spoons.

Meanwhile, Annie lay with her legs dangling over the top of her couch. What was she being so obsessive about? There were plenty of good voices. All she had to do was choose one and let her friend and grandmother go home to—

Hang in there. If it had been easy for us to find each other, maybe we wouldn't appreciate how amazing it is that we actually did.

Annie sat up so quickly that she wrenched her neck.

"Are you okay?" Doris asked, a spoonful of ice cream halfway to her mouth.

It had been the voice—*his* voice. But it hadn't been on the audition CD; it had come from inside her head.

"Yep!" Annie chirped. "Everything is fine! Great!" She knew her voice was a shade too bright. "Let's get back to work. Only . . . let's see . . . five dozen more."

She started the CD even without Michelle in the room. Voice after droning voice. Michelle came back. The auditions didn't get any better. And then—

"Your thighs are perfect. Have another piece of chocolate cake."

When Annie was in middle school, she and her cousins used to have fun by hyperventilating together. They'd breathe in, out, in, out, as fast as they could, and then stick their thumbs in their mouths and blow. The room would spin, their knees would weaken, and the world would turn upside down for split seconds that felt like eternity.

That was how Annie felt when she heard the voice inside her head on the CD.

"Him. That's him," she whispered, every inch of her concentrating on his voice.

"Tell me everything. I'll listen."

"What you need is an aromatherapy massage."

"It's deep, honest, natural, masculine—I like it," Doris commented.

"Me, too," Michelle agreed. "Would I have sex with this voice? Definitely. Put him in the maybe—"

"No." Annie turned off the CD player. "This is him. The one. The only one."

"You're so sure?" Doris asked.

"Positive." Annie flipped through her master list to the right page. "His name is . . . Mark Wolfson."

"Hold on," Michelle said through a mouthful of ice cream. She swallowed and spoke again. "We heard a Mark Wolfson seventy guys ago. He's in our maybe pile. Come on, check. I have a memory for these things."

Annie checked the list. Michelle was right. They'd heard Mark Wolfson. They'd put him in the *maybe* pile.

"He auditioned twice, too," Annie decided.

"Great. Smart guy. I'm going home." Michelle pulled on her shoes and got to her feet. "We found Cinderella Man, and the vibrator fits. Call Mark What's-his-face in the morning and tell him he's two grand richer. I have to be in court in seven hours. Come on, Doris, I'll drop you."

Annie thanked them profusely, walked them to the door, and said good night. There was still so much she wanted to do—copy Mark's voice onto her computer, upload the file to Taiwan, and tell them to make a half dozen prototypes. She'd probably have them in about a week.

After she did it, she found Mark's first audition and listened to it again, over and over, and she cleaned up the wreckage of the evening. One part of her was elated. She'd found her guy. But another part of her—the silly, ridiculously romantic part—was a little disappointed. Which voice was Mark's own, and which was nothing more than a professional variation of tone and inflection?

Her head said she had no way of knowing. But her heart told her that the last version she'd heard was authentic.

Mark Wolfson. He was her man.

thirteen

"Mark Wolfson? Hi, this is Annie Albright calling again about the female affirmation voice-over you did for us? I, um, don't know if you got my last message, but I'm calling again just to make sure you got the check that we sent. I'm glad you put down your Social Security number on your first form so that we could send you your money. So, I just wanted to tell you again what a great job you did. And . . . maybe you could call me back, just so that I can confirm you got the money."

Annie hesitated a moment, picturing Mark's broad face, friendly smile, and dark, thinning hair. Not classically handsome, true. But he had a nice face, an inviting face. She'd Googled him and downloaded a file folder's worth of material, including half a dozen photographs from various theatrical productions in which he'd appeared. She learned that he'd graduated from the theater program at Carnegie Mellon. That was nice—it meant he was at least literate. He'd appeared at Equity theaters all over the country, and especially here in the

Bay Area, where his reviews were uniformly good. She was surprised to realize that she and Doris had actually seen him in a production of *Uncle Vanya* at A.C.T., where he'd played Professor Serebryakov.

For a moment, that stumped her. Why was his voice doing things to her now that it hadn't done to her before? Then she remembered this was a guy of many voices.

It was so weird to be calling him, considering the things he'd done to and with her in her imagination over the past week or so. And it was maddening that he never returned her calls. She wanted to meet him so much. She longed to hear him say something else. Anything else. But he had a standard greeting on his voice mail, so she didn't even get that satisfaction.

"Anyway," Annie went on, "I'd love to meet the man behind the voice. Did I already say that?" She giggled nervously, then winced, because she sounded not unlike the "tittering" auditioner whom they'd nicknamed the Serial Killer. She cleared her throat. "If you're out of town, Mark, you can call on my toll-free number at 888-555-4532."

She hung up and slumped in the kitchen chair. It was nearly three o'clock, which meant that the lesbians across the way would be getting set to go at it. Ditto the law students, who seemed to have gotten into role playing—she occasionally heard something about letting the nice nurse take the bad boy's temperature.

Of course, since she'd selected Mark's voice for Mr. Vibrator, she was in her own threesome—Mark's voice, the Ultimate Pleasure, and her own imagination. Yet something was lacking. She wanted more than his voice. She wanted him. According to her research, he often spent his summers doing stock at Flat Rock Playhouse in North Carolina. Maybe that was where he was now, Annie reasoned, brightening considerably. She could look up their summer schedule and see if he was appearing.

Just as she got up to go to her computer, her doorbell rang. It was Rhonda, the muscular, perpetually cheerful FedEx delivery lady who competed as a bodybuilder in her spare time. Since the business had gotten under way, she and Rhonda had become casual friends. Rhonda had even invited Annie to a competition she was about to do in Oakland.

"Hey, Rhonda, whatcha got for me?"

"Big package. From overseas."

Annie's heart skipped a beat. "From Taiwan?"

"You bet. Sign here."

Annie scrawled her name on the paper on Rhonda's clipboard and took her package. She'd thought about this moment so many times over the last couple of weeks. Now, it was finally here!

She carried the box into the bedroom. One quick rip and it was opened. Out spilled six prototype editions of Mr. Vibrator. All were Caucasian—they'd talked briefly about Asian, Latino, and African models, but they decided to keep things simple at first. If this model worked, they'd branch out. She took one of them in her hand. It was smoother than the Funtime version; the texture felt nearly like skin. With one finger, she flipped the main power switch.

Nothing.

It took Annie a moment to figure out that the factory hadn't inserted any batteries. Well, that wasn't a problem. She had plenty of them in her nightstand. It was ironic to think about tax-deductible orgasms, but Michelle had assured her that double-A batteries were a legitimate business expense.

Five minutes later, the batteries were loaded, the lights were out and the window shades drawn. Annie had even turned the ringer off her phone. The nurse and her bad-boy patient didn't appear to be home; all was quiet. It would be just her, and Mark. She pressed his button.

I love your thighs.
You're perfect exactly the way you are.
You are so hot.
I won't stop. I won't stop.

And he didn't.

Three hours of bliss later, there was only one thing on Annie's mind, besides the fact that she was running low on Emotion Lotion.

She wanted to talk to Mark Wolfson.

Actually, she wanted to do more than just talk to him; she wanted to put her money where his mouth had been, so to speak. If Mr. Vibrator turned into a commercial success, clearly Mark should share in it. In addition to the check for the flat fee she'd already sent him, he would deserve a bonus. Surely that was a legitimate reason to call him again.

Her cell was on the nightstand; she had Mark on speed

dial. As his phone rang, she put together a message in her mind, since she fully expected to hit his voice mail again, just like she had every other time she'd called. Evidently her messages hadn't been enticing enough to get him to call her back. But this time, when she told him about the bonus she wanted to offer, surely that would get him to—

"Hello?"

It took Annie a moment to realize that there was a real live human being at the other end of the phone.

"Hello?" the voice said again. "Someone there?" The voice was male, with a strong Brooklyn accent that didn't sound anything like the voice she'd come to know. In the biblical sense.

Well, Mark's an actor, Annie reminded herself. He probably had a million voices. Maybe he was in character for a role he was about to play, or—

"Yo, this isn't funny. Who the fuck is it?" the voice yelled.

"Hi!" she said quickly. Her palms were sweating; she wiped one on the leg of her jeans. "This is Annie Albright. Is this Mark Wolfson?"

"Nah, babe, sorry. This is Andrew. I'm sublettin' his apartment 'til he gets back." Annie could hear a dog barking through the phone. "Down, Beastie!"

Annie sagged with disappointment. After all this time, Mark was away? For long enough to sublet his apartment?

"I'll take you out in a minute!" Andrew yelled.

"Oh, I wasn't calling for a date, exactly," Annie explained.

"I was talking to my dog."

Annie winced. "Right. Of course!" She gave a little laugh,

pretending she'd been joking around, too. "So, is there some-place Mark can be reached?"

"I don't think so. He went back east to hike the Appala-chian Trail."

The Appalachian Trail? She had been leaving message after message for her fantasy man and all that time he'd been on *the Appalachian Trail?* Geography had never been Annie's long suit, but she did vaguely recall that the Appalachian Trail went all the way from Georgia to Maine. Which was a hell of a hike.

She curled her feet under her. "Well, he must have a cell phone with him," she reasoned. "I'd really like to speak with him."

"Hey, me too. The goddamn stove is on the fritz and the landlord isn't supposed to know I'm here." The dog barked again. "Hey, I really have to go. The Beast is ready to gnaw off my leg—it won't be pretty."

"Wait, don't hang up!" she cried, because she just couldn't bring herself to give up. "What if there was . . . I don't know . . . an emergency or something? There has to be a way to reach him!"

"He said if there was an emergency to write to him at General Delivery in Damascus, Virginia. He'll be there in a couple of months. That's the best I can do you for, babe."

"Thanks, anyway."

"No worries. Hey, do you know anything about stoves?" Andrew asked.

Annie sagged back on the couch one more time. "No. If by some weird chance Mark calls you, ask him to check his messages. Okay?"

"You got it. And if you want to hear my band—we're kinda in that retro punk groove—we're playing DNA Lounge on Saturday. Brooklyn Bumz. That's us. That's why I'm in Frisco. So, what do you look like?"

Oh, jeez. Annie had no interest in flirting with the guy. For one thing, he had a terrible voice. For another thing, even though she knew it was stupid and ridiculous and juvenile, she felt as if she'd be cheating on Mark. She didn't even want to stay on the phone long enough to explain that no one said "Frisco," that Frisco was a town in Colorado.

"I'm . . . old," she said, because it was the first thing that came into her mind, and she didn't want to hurt his feelings. "So, good luck with your band."

After she hung up, she just lay there, staring up at the ceiling. She was hung up on a hiker who could do voices. But he didn't know, or care, that she existed. He'd come home to her check, and that would be that.

Just one more stupid fantasy.

 fourteen

"Annie, sweetie, hand me the kugel," Doris said, holding out her hand. "Y.A.L.A.B. Do you feel okay?"

"You ate like a bird," Annie translated for Michelle. They'd just cleared the dishes from Shabbat dinner and were helping Doris clean up in the kitchen. Back in the dining room, five of Doris's friends were telling stories about their grandchildren, their bridge game, how they were not too keen on the new associate rabbi, and their physical ailments, though not necessarily in that order. They were waiting for Doris to bring in her famous homemade apple strudel. Doris had made two; one regular, one with Splenda, for short Irma, who was diabetic.

"I'm fine," Annie assured her, and handed the chafing dish to her grandmother.

"She's just nervous," Michelle explained. "She can't eat when she's nervous. Unfortunately, when I'm nervous I eat everything." As if to illustrate the point, she two-fingered the last potato pancake from the serving dish and popped it into her mouth.

"What's to be nervous about?" Doris demanded, smoothing plastic wrap over the leftover kugel and sticking it in the fridge. "Everyone here loves you."

"Thanks, Gramma, but you're used to selling sex toys. I'm not."

In the past nine days, Annie had done her best not to think about Mark Wolfson, who, while in action every night in the privacy of her bedroom, was also missing in action in real life. She'd tried to concentrate on her business plan for Mr. Vibrator, and had even semi-succeeded. First she'd dropped a prototype off for Michelle at her office (swathed in bubble wrap, with the envelope marked PERSONAL, just in case someone else was tempted to open it) and delivered another to Doris, so they could conduct their own . . . assessments. Both had called late the same night. Michelle had rated the device a fifteen on a scale of ten. Doris had said that she hadn't had this much fun since October 19, 1987, when Murray had seen their stock portfolio take a pounding. This had caused him to wax philosophical about what was really important in life, and it certainly wasn't money, after which he'd spent the evening pounding the love of his life, namely her.

Annie was thrilled, of course, and thrilled further when she brought a fourth prototype to Ethereal at the Marriott and Ethereal had called an hour later from work—Annie hadn't asked how her friend had managed to test it out at the hotel—to claim that it was almost enough to make her give up men forever.

So, Mr. V had gotten glowing reviews from women of all ages. For a moment, she was tempted to leave one on the doorstep of the lesbians across the backyard and then sit up in her kitchen at three o'clock to see if any action developed—could Mark be inspiring even to them? But she decided that a truer test would be Doris's friends, the ones who had come to Bella's house for the Funtime party. Some of them had purchased things from the Funtime collection that afternoon, but others claimed they found it embarrassing. *Feh*—who needed it, and who could afford it on Social Security, anyway?

It had been Doris's idea to invite the ladies over for a Shabbat dairy potluck dinner, after which Annie would demonstrate—so to speak—Mr. Vibrator. It being Shabbat, Doris wouldn't take any money if her friends wanted a model of their own, but she assured Annie that her friends were completely trustworthy.

"I'm not very good in front of a crowd, Gramma," Annie admitted. She turned her attention to the dishwasher.

"This isn't a crowd, it's my friends, many of whom have known you since you were in diapers," Doris pointed out. "Bella even changed a few of them." She gestured wide, and the dozen slender, brightly colored bangle bracelets slid up her arm. "Think of yourself as an Avon lady, only with a more fulfilling product."

"That you created, marketed, and own," Michelle added, as she cut Doris's strudel into thick pieces and arranged them artfully on a bone china platter. "Who made the brownies over there, Doris?"

"Roz. She was never much of a cook. So eat A.Y.O.R."

"At your own risk?" Michelle ventured as she arranged the sugar-free strudel.

"Exactly." Doris reached into a cupboard and brought out a box of sugar-free cookies, adding a few to the sugar-free-strudel platter. "Roz is always on a diet. And the doctors don't want Ettie eating sugar, so I want to be sure there's enough."

Annie put teabags and a carafe of hot water onto a tray. "How's she doing?"

"She's here, isn't she?" Doris shrugged. "Wonderful, considering it's just been two weeks. Her son only hired the aide because she's so weak on her right side. But with physical therapy, she could come all the way back." She clapped her hands together. "Okay, ladies, are we ready for dessert and the unveiling?"

"It's not a headstone, Gramma."

Doris looked thoughtful as she poured coffee from her coffeemaker into another carafe. "You could think of a headstone as a reminder of happier times, when your loved one was still with you. Your invention does the same thing—in a more . . . tangible way. Come on."

They carried the trays into the living room. It was the same cast of characters as Doris's Funtime presentation—Roz, the two Irmas, Bella, Marge, Ruth, and Ettie. Only now Ettie had a sweet-faced Jamaican girl named Tarshea to assist her with anything she needed.

"I was going to come in and see if you needed help," short Irma said, "but Roz was telling a hysterical story about staying at the Hermitage last week when she went to visit her grandson in Nashville. Tell them," Irma urged.

"I had that machine with me, you know, the one I put over my face for my sleep apnea," Roz explained. "It looks like something out of a science fiction movie. Anyway, it was a very warm night, and I hate the air-conditioning in hotels, so I decided I would leave it off and just sleep in the nude."

Annie nodded and set the tea tray on the table.

"Well, I was very tired," Roz explained, "so I slept right through my wake-up call. When I didn't show up at my grandson's for breakfast—you all know how punctual I am—he got worried. So he called the hotel and asked security to check on me." She reached for a sugar-free cookie. "I wake up with this outer-space mask over my face, completely naked, and a huge security guard is standing over my bed. To tell you the truth, I thought I was dreaming, and I didn't want to wake up!"

The women convulsed with laughter, as did Michelle. Annie blushed. Okay, she knew it was ridiculous to blush. One of her personal favorite fantasies had to do with a security guard and handcuffs, where—

Well, that didn't matter.

Once everyone had dessert and coffee or tea, Doris took the floor. "Girls, my Annie has a presentation she would like to make." She beckoned to her granddaughter.

All eyes swung to Annie. She was seated by her grandmother's dining room hutch. Before the guests had arrived, she'd stashed one of her Mr. Vibrator boxes on the bottom shelf. Now, being careful not to knock over the still-burning Shabbat candles, she retrieved it and got to her feet.

Oh, God. Everyone was looking at her. Her mouth was so dry. She had to pee.

"Well . . ." Annie cleared her throat. Inhaled deeply. Exhaled. Gulped. Inhaled again.

"Come on, Annie," Bella chided. "We're not getting any younger here."

"Jeez, say it before I take a third piece of strudel," Michelle demanded. "Annie invented a new sex toy."

Annie winced. That wasn't exactly the way she'd planned to begin. "It's not exactly . . . I mean, it's more than a sex toy," she told them. This was it. The moment of truth. If she didn't believe in her product, it wouldn't matter if it was the best invention since cell phones, no one else would believe in it, either.

I can do this, Annie told herself. *I can.*

Slowly she gazed around the room, making eye contact with each and every woman there. "Let me ask you. What is the sexiest kind of man?"

"One who's breathing?" tall Irma quipped, then forked another bite of strudel into her mouth.

"Without the aid of a respirator," Roz added.

"His own teeth!" Marge hooted.

"And a lifetime supply of Viagra!" short Irma said.

Everyone laughed heartily, including Annie. And just like that, the fear left her. "Let me ask you, what do your women friends give you that men don't?"

Everyone seemed to contemplate this for a moment. "Honestly?" Ettie finally said, with a bit of a slur from the right side of her mouth. "When I was younger I used to think it would be better to be a lesbian. Because I had such wonderful women friends. I still do. With men?" She shrugged. "I could never be myself."

"You're always too something—loud, pushy, fat," Michelle snorted, reaching for the third piece of strudel she'd been trying to resist.

"Or not enough something," Bella put in. "Like in the boob department."

There were chuckles of agreement.

"Murray wasn't like that," Doris insisted. "Do you want to know the very best thing about him? He made me feel beautiful."

There were sighs around the room. Bella patted Doris's arm.

"You were so lucky, Gramma," Annie told her. "Every woman deserves that."

"Well, of course," tall Irma agreed, crossing one designer-jeans-clad leg over the other. "But that's like peace in the Middle East. Impossible."

"Maybe not," Annie said. "Some of you bought the Ultimate Pleasure from my grandmother. It made you feel good—*momentarily*. But it didn't make you feel beautiful. It didn't make you laugh. Well, now meet a man who does all that, and more. This is Mr. Vibrator." She extracted the prototype from the box and held it up.

"What?" Marge asked. "It's just another vibrator."

"Not hardly," Michelle insisted. "Turn him on, Annie."

Annie did. The room was utterly silent.

"No buzzing," short Irma marveled.

"I hate buzzing," Bella agreed.

"You turn him on—no buzzing—and he turns you on," Annie said, pleased with her own off-the-cuff wit. "Now, let's say you just experienced twenty minutes of bliss with a man who knew exactly how to please you. What is the very, very best thing that could happen next?"

"Twenty more minutes?" Roz wondered aloud.

"If you want," Annie agreed. "Or maybe, this." Annie pushed one of the discreet buttons at the base of her invention. Out came Mark Wolfson's sublime voice.

"Your thighs are perfect. Have another piece of chocolate cake."

For a moment, there was dead silence.

Oh, God, Annie thought. *They hate it.*

She tried again.

"Your thighs are perfect. Have another piece of chocolate cake."

Bella's eyes went huge. "That's . . . that's what I dream of a man saying to me after sex!"

Annie pushed the button twice this time.

"Tell me everything. I'll listen."

Roz cracked up. "That's hysterical! Morty never said that to me in his life!"

"Any man would be insane not to fall in love with you."

"I adore it!" short Irma exclaimed. "He's even circumcised. Let me try!"

Suddenly everyone in the room was clamoring to press Mr. Vibrator's buttons. Doris and Annie had discussed how this presentation might go. This cacophony was Doris's prearranged cue.

"Girls, I tried it out." Her voice silenced her friends. "And my granddaughter deserves a testimonial dinner. I'm getting two, in case one of them breaks down."

"They won't break down, Gramma," Annie assured her.

"I even give a money-back guarantee. It wasn't easy to create a superior product. Safe. Waterproof. And completely silent, unless you push his button, in which case he will say one of twenty-five different wonderful things, and you never know which wonderful thing he'll say next. That's why Mr. Vibrator will sell for $89.99."

Annie scanned the room to see what reaction this price would bring. She'd done her market research; there was just one model in her price range. Sold only in England, it was called GoldMember, was plated with fourteen-karat gold, and didn't say a thing in any language.

"You could add a one in front of that $89.99 as far as I'm concerned," short Irma opined. "I love it!"

"He's just *adorable!*" Marge added.

"Cute, funny, satisfying—what's not to love?" Bella asked.

Annie traded looks of excitement with Michelle. This was going even better than either of them had dared to hope.

"Girls," Doris began, "how many of you would part with ninety dollars of your Social Security to go home with your very own Mr. Vibrator tonight, if you could?"

Annie held her breath. Then, one by one by one, all of Doris's friends raised their hand. Except for Ettie. She turned to Tarshea. "Tarshea, darling." Ettie nudged her chin toward her right hand, which lay heavily on the armrest of her chair. "Please."

Tarshea lifted Ettie's hand.

Then she lifted her own, too.

 fifteen

One of the advantages of year-round school was that Charlie got monthlong vacations. In October, which everyone said was the nicest month of the year to be in San Francisco. And in January—January was great. He'd go to Lake Tahoe—with Mark when Mark wasn't in a show. They'd gamble a little and snowboard at Alpine Meadows or Squaw Valley. Now April—that was great. It was the start of baseball season. Twice in the last four years, he'd followed the Giants on road trips to Los Angeles and Arizona, enjoying the spring sunshine as much as the baseball itself. As it turned out, some really lovely women also followed the Giants around the country. One memorable girl from the Haight had a tattoo of the Giants' mascot on an intimate body part Charlie hadn't even known it was possible to tattoo.

Truth was, he needed the time off. Teaching at Mays-McCovey was a challenge on its best days and physically exhausting on its worst. Summers were particularly tough.

Friends of his students who went to different schools were all on vacation, which meant his kids were tempted even more than usual to blow off school. It was common to have ten, fifteen kids absent on a hot summer day.

After a tough week, this particular Saturday found Charlie utterly wiped out. There had been a tendentious faculty meeting the afternoon before to discuss the state of the fund-raising campaign. Joe Witherspoon announced that a quarter of a million dollars had been raised for the asbestos-removal effort. Which would have been encouraging, except that he'd gone on to explain that he'd hit up each and every possible donor with deep pockets—groveling, bullying, or guilt-jerking them into giving as much as they could give—and it still fell far short of what they needed. The meeting had turned ugly when three teachers announced that they'd already sent in applications to other schools; they had families to support and couldn't risk a shutdown of the academy without having other work lined up. Charlie couldn't fault them. If he'd been a family guy, maybe he'd have done the same. However, since he was probably the least likely male to become a family guy anytime soon, he felt he could hang in there with Joe and fight the good fight.

Small wonder then that he'd spent Friday night alone at the Buena Vista, drinking Irish coffees and chatting up two French girls visiting from Lyons. They were staying at the "Fairmount," one explained with a delicious accent. Perhaps Charlie would like to come to the Fairmont and see if he could illustrate just why the hotel had that name? Both girls were beautiful: slender Françoise had a sleek cap of dark hair and Danielle was a voluptuous blonde. But Charlie's heart wasn't in it, and he never, ever went through with an assignation unless his heart was one hundred percent involved for however long the assignation lasted. So he kissed both girls on both cheeks, bid them adieu, and went home alone.

Saturday dawned not much better. There were so many things he could do—ride his bike to Golden Gate Park, watch the Giants play the Mets, or even settle down on his back porch and read the biography of the Marquis de Sade that he'd purchased but never gotten around to. And of course, he could always pick up women. None of it appealed, though. He puttered restlessly around his small house, intermittently watching *Sex and the City* reruns on TV and attempting to retile a bathroom that had needed retiling since the day he'd moved in. He was glad when he heard the mail drop through the slot of his front door, just because it would give him some direction for a minute or two.

There were a few bills. The new *Harper's*. A couple of advertising circulars. And a thin white envelope with an address label on the front and a return address of the Summit Foundation in Washington, D.C.

His heart sank to somewhere near the San Andreas Fault, because it was a thin envelope. Damn. Anyone who ever applied for anything knew what a thin envelope meant. Thick meant good, thin meant bad. How many women had ever considered that irony?

Well, no use postponing the inevitable. He tore open the envelope.

Dear Mr. Silver,

It is a pleasure to inform you that your application for a Summit Grant has been approved by the committee. The funds that you requested will be disbursed to your educational institution within ninety days, pending the completion of final documentation. You can expect that documentation to arrive at your school this week.

In addition, we are also pleased to inform you that on the basis of subsequent investigation by the Foundation, you have been selected as one of twenty-five national finalists for the High Summit Award, a special honor we are instituting this year to honor five outstanding North American educators. We base our decision on a variety of factors, including your work in the classroom, your track record of success, and recommendations by educators. A personal interview with the Foundation will assess such arenas as intelligence, leadership, moral fiber, communication skills, capability as a role model for your students, and potential for future professional development.

The High Summit Award is personal to the teacher, and not to the institution. It is designed to free the teacher to concentrate on her or his teaching environment without the constant worry of how to make ends meet on a teacher's salary.

The award is in the amount of one million dollars as a lump sum. It is the intent of the Foundation to have that award be an after-tax amount.

Please accept our congratulations on your nomination,

*and contact our office at your earliest convenience to confirm
receipt of this letter and arrange for your personal interview
here at our offices in Washington, D.C.*

Holy shit.
Holy shit!
Charlie read the letter twice more before he began to believe that it could possibly be real. As a rule, he didn't drink
during the day. But he opened the cupboard where he kept
the Flagman, got out a shot glass, and poured himself a stiff
one. He downed it in one swallow like they did in Russia, followed by a big bite of a kosher pickle to take the sting out of
his throat. Then he reread the letter again. And again.

Jeez, what should he do now? There were so many people
he wanted to tell. Witherspoon, of course. His other friends
and colleagues at the school. His parents at their new home
in North Carolina, and his sister, Carol, and her husband in
Cleveland. If only Mark were here, instead of tromping
around somewhere in the mountains. Mark would be so
psyched for him.

But wait—he knew he shouldn't get ahead of himself. If
they didn't raise enough money to save the school, the funding for his Shakespeare program wasn't going to mean squat.
On the other hand, if he got one of the five High Summit
Awards . . .

A million bucks. Jesus. He imagined getting the money
and turning it over to Joe to save the school. How cool would
that be?

Who were the other finalists? He was suddenly dying to know. His chances were one in five. Basically, those odds sucked ass. On the other hand—

His doorbell rang. Jehovah's Witnesses? Someone handing out literature for the upcoming mayoral election that wasn't 'til November?

He opened the door and found himself looking down at the small, dark, angry face of Jamal Ashford.

"You ought to live somewhere a person can *find*, dawg," Jamal spat. "I been walking all over the damn place."

Charlie hadn't seen Jamal since the trip he'd made to the group home a few weeks earlier. When he'd left, he'd thought there was a shot that Mrs. Peabody would let Jamal continue at Mays-McCovey, even after the temporary move to the USF campus. But he'd received a terse phone message from the woman the following week—Jamal would be attending the neighborhood school in the fall.

Now, here the boy was on Charlie's doorstep, all five foot one of him. Jamal wore baggy blue shorts, a long-sleeved brown FUBU T-shirt, and basketball shoes without laces. He had a ratty backpack slung over one shoulder.

This was actually the first time that a student—former student—had showed up on Charlie's doorstep. "Jamal. How are you?"

Jamal scowled and shrugged.

"What brought you to Potrero Hill on a Saturday?"

"My feet, fool."

In other words, he had walked. That had to be three and a half miles. "From Hunter's Point? Up the hill?"

"Yeah, up the hill, you know another way?" Jamal gave an eye roll at Charlie's stupidity. "Damn, ask me inside, fool."

Charlie knew the prudent thing to do would be to keep Jamal out on the porch. Who knew what a troubled kid might claim if he was in your house with you alone? On the other hand, if he kept Jamal out on the porch after he'd asked to come in, Jamal would likely turn right around and walk away and Charlie would never find out what was bothering the kid enough to make him walk all the way to Charlie's house in the first place.

"Happy to hang out with you, Jamal," Charlie said, "but how about cutting down on the cussing and the name-calling." Charlie stepped back to let the kid pass. "You must be tired. Have a seat. You want a Coke or something?"

"'Kay."

Charlie came back with two Cokes and a box of Cracker Jacks left behind by a former girlfriend who adored them, so for the two weeks of their relationship he'd kept them stocked for her. Jamal was sitting on the edge of Charlie's brown leather couch, backpack leaning against one skinny knee, nervously jiggling one leg crossed over the other.

"Here ya go." He handed the kid the Coke and the Cracker Jacks, then sat on the easy chair kitty-corner to the couch. Whatever was up with Jamal, it wouldn't do any good to come right out and ask; that much Charlie knew. "So how's your summer going?"

"Okay." Jamal tore off the top of the Cracker Jacks, upended the box and poured some into his mouth.

"Whatcha been doing?"

"Stuff."

"How's it living at Mrs. Peabody's place?"

"Okay." Jamal cracked open the Coke and took a long, thirsty swallow.

"Does she know you're here?" Charlie asked, in the same offhand tone as his other queries.

Jamal shook his head.

"She'll be worried, don't you think?"

Another shrug.

"Tell you what. Let me call her, tell her you're here, just so she won't worry."

Jamal shrugged again. Charlie took this as a good sign. If there had been a problem at the group home, like if one of the other boys was bullying him, Jamal would have told Charlie not to call.

He took out his cell, but didn't place the call. "So, what else is up, Jamal?"

"I thought you were gonna call her."

Ah, so Jamal *wanted* him to call Mrs. Peabody. Interesting. "I'm thinking maybe there's something that you want me to tell her. That's why you walked over here."

Jamal took his time chewing another mouthful of Cracker Jacks. "Maybe," he finally mumbled. "It ain't gonna do jack, though."

"I can't try to help if I don't know what it is," Charlie said.

Jamal scuffed his sneakers into the beige carpeting, eyes downcast. Finally he blurted it out. "I-wanna-come-back-to-school."

"Yeah?" Charlie asked. "Well, we'd like to have you back."

"But like I said . . ." He finally raised his gaze to meet Charlie's. "You can't make it happen."

Charlie saw the hope in Jamal's eyes, the real kid behind the bravado.

"I can give it my best shot. What's Mrs. Peabody's number?"

Charlie pressed it into the phone. The housemother answered on the first ring.

"Hello?"

"Mrs. Peabody? This is Charlie Silver. Jamal Ashford's teacher at Mays–McCovey?"

"Yes, I remember you. Jamal isn't here. He's playing ball in the park."

Charlie grinned at Jamal "Actually, I had an unexpected visitor here in Potrero Hill, Mrs. Peabody. Jamal is here with me."

"That a fact."

Clearly Mrs. Peabody was not thrown by this news. Charlie realized that she was used to dealing with far more difficult matters than a resident who goes for a really long walk to talk with a former teacher.

"Is that boy bothering you?" Mrs. Peabody asked.

"No, ma'am, not at all," Charlie assured her. "And I'll give him a ride home. But before I do, I want him to tell you why he walked three and a half miles to talk to me. Go ahead, Jamal." Charlie held out the phone.

Jamal took it reluctantly. "I wanna go back to Mr. Silver's school," he told Mrs. Peabody. "A lot."

Charlie waited as the housemother talked to Jamal. He watched the boy's face fall.

"She say I ain't got no transportation," Jamal reported, thrusting the phone back at Charlie. "I *knew* you couldn't help," the boy added, his face going dark.

"Don't give up on me so fast." Charlie spoke with Mrs. Peabody again. "What if I pick Jamal up on my way to USF and drop him off on my way home?"

"He'll spend all that time sittin' around!" Mrs. Peabody exclaimed. "Before school, after-school meetings and such."

"If he has to wait for me after school, he'll use the time to study." Charlie's eye caught Jamal's. "Won't he?"

"Yes, sir," Jamal reluctantly agreed.

"Well, then, bring the boy home and we can discuss it," Mrs. Peabody allowed. "And Mr. Silver?"

"Yes?"

"If there were more teachers like you, we wouldn't be in this mess we in now. Thank you. Thank you so much."

Charlie said good-bye and hung up. He grinned at Jamal. "Done. I'll drive you back and we'll iron out the details."

Jamal stuffed the now half-empty box of Cracker Jacks in his backpack. "Why you being so nice to me?"

Charlie looped an arm around the boy's skinny shoulders. "Because I like you, Jamal."

All of Jamal's posing fell away. He was just a kid whose parents had done him wrong, reaching out. He gave Charlie a big grin. "You okay, too, Mr. Silver."

And that, Charlie thought as he ushered the boy out, was almost worth a million dollars all by itself. But another thought followed on its heels: if he didn't get the High Summit Award, a thousand Jamals would lose the very thing that now held those kids together—their school.

# sixteen

"Product?" Michelle asked.

"Check. We've got ten thousand packaged in the warehouse in Valencia, and Taiwan is ready to go at a moment's notice to produce another ten thousand a day." Annie crossed the word "product" off her final checklist.

"Accounts receivable?"

"Check. We take Visa, MasterCard, Discover, American Express, but prefer PayPal. All those accounts are operative as of nine o'clock this morning." "Accounts receivable" got a line through it on Annie's list.

"Shipping?"

"Ready, via UPS ground, included in the price. People hate to be gouged on shipping and handling, so the charge for overnight delivery—if it's requested—will be our actual cost. Everything will be fulfilled via Your Shipping Source, also in Valencia. We get a sliding discount depending on how many a day they're doing."

"Sounds good," Michelle acknowledged.

"I think that covers it," Annie agreed, and looked at her checklist—everything that could be crossed off was crossed off. Marketing, Web services, licenses, accounting— Who would have thought that starting up a business would be so complicated? Yet here she was with her best friend, standing in front of the computer monitor in her living room on yet another foggy San Francisco morning. The night before, Doris's friends had not only declared they'd part with their Social Security money for their own Mr. Vibrator, but had insisted on an auction to decide which one of them would go home with the demonstration model. Tall Irma won, and had already called Annie to express her satisfaction. She would, she promised, make a donation to her synagogue in Annie's name.

Michelle twisted a pencil into her thick, dark hair to hold it up in a messy bun. "There's one thing left to do, then."

Annie got butterflies in her stomach just thinking about it. "Go live, you mean." She knew everything was ready, that there was no more preparation that could be done, but the idea of actually getting on the Internet and taking orders was a little nerve-racking. Of course, she didn't expect more than a few orders the first day. But what if she didn't get any orders at all? What if no one wanted her product? What if Doris had gambled Grandpa Murray's money on Annie's big idea and that big idea was a big fat flop? What if—

"You're thinking so hard you're giving *me* a headache," Michelle complained.

"It's just . . . what if I'm a flop?"

Michelle shrugged. "I'll still love you, loser. Come on. Take it live."

"Okay. Here goes."

Annie moused the cursor over to the little purple valentine heart on the home page that read TURN ME ON and clicked twice. A moment later, a scrolling banner across the bottom of the screen announced, "We're live!" Next to the valentine was a counter, which Annie had designed so that if she clicked on it, it could show orders by the hour, by the day, by the week, or overall. She clicked on it. 00000. Oh, God. One order. Please? Just one order. Just so she didn't have to look at all those zeros.

Michelle reached across and turned off the monitor. "As your secretary-treasurer and unofficial counsel, I recommend you spend the day away from your apartment so you don't get incredibly anxious and/or depressed."

Annie nodded, though her eyes traveled longingly back to the now dark screen. One order. Just one order. "Want to go out and get breakfast?"

"Can't. Told you, gotta go to the office to prep a witness." Michelle slipped into her Ralph Lauren jacket. "I'm looking at a boring-ass, seriously long night."

Annie walked her to the door. "Thanks, Michelle. For everything."

"It was fun." Michelle reached up to the doll shelf and rearranged Malibu Barbie and Ken into a very compromising position. "At least *she'll* have fun tonight." She frowned at Annie. "Wait, don't you have a date?"

Annie made a face. She did, but she wasn't looking forward to it. The date was courtesy of her grandmother, and how could she possibly say no to Doris? The guy was a thirtysomething podiatrist from Los Angeles named Alan, who'd just moved to San Francisco and joined Doris's synagogue after an ugly divorce. Doris had met him at an oneg and told him about her granddaughter. Reportedly, Alan had begged her for Annie's number.

Annie had reluctantly given her grandmother the okay. At least the phone conversation earlier in the week hadn't been too painful. Alan said he kept a catamaran at the yacht club across the bay in Tiburon. Would Annie be interested in an afternoon sail?

Not really. Frankly, she'd been looking forward to spending Saturday afternoon with Mark Wolfson's voice and a really great fantasy. Besides, wasn't sailing something that was done by windswept WASPs with excellent muscle tone? And she was neither WASPy, windswept, or particularly toned.

Still, she said yes. "I'll call you with a progress report," she promised Michelle.

Her friend kissed her cheek. "Tomorrow. I'll be with a senior partner today who makes us check our cell phones at the door. Hope you have as much fun as Barbie."

"Ready about?" Alan called.

"Ready!" Annie managed.

That meant push the tiller forward as far as it could go and then duck her head. The first time, she'd nearly been knocked overboard. It wasn't that Annie didn't like sailing—well, okay, she didn't like sailing. Sailing had turned out to be the equivalent of a gym class from hell at sea, with an

instructor—Alan—barking out commands in a strange sailing language.

And that wasn't the worst part of it. What Alan had described as an afternoon sail had turned out to be a full-fledged
yacht club race on the turbulent waters of San Francisco Bay.
With the wind blowing at twenty-five knots and the tide
rushing outward to the ocean, the catamaran kept slamming
into whitecaps the size of the Transamerica Pyramid. Despite
her borrowed yellow slicker, she'd been drenched within five
minutes, and felt her fine hair plastered to her head—drowned
rat was not her best look. Yet Alan seemed too absorbed in his
love of the race to notice her much at all.

"Hard to lee!"

She pushed the tiller forward, and they scrambled to the
other side of the cat.

"You doing okay, Annie?" Alan shouted over the howling
wind. He was slender, athletic, and obviously very competi-
tive, with clear blue eyes, a thin nose, and a short brown beard
that shined with ocean spray. "You're looking a little pale!"

"Oh, I'm fine!"

That was bullshit. Every time they hit a whitecap, she felt
a little queasier. The wind blew a clump of wet hair into her
mouth. She spat it out.

Liar. Tell him to take the damned tiller.

Omigod. Mark's voice. On the wind.

"It's not his fault," Annie mentally replied.

*Who takes a girl who's never sailed on a sailboat race for a first
date? He doesn't really want to get to know you. He wants to impress
you. Big difference.*

"Why don't you come tell me that in person? Don't hide behind eight inches of plastic that warms to the touch!" was her mental plea.

Nine.

"Nine?"

"Nine what?" Alan asked. He tightened the sheet that controlled the single sail, and the catamaran heeled up so far out of the water that only one pontoon maintained contact.

Oh, crap, had she said it out loud? She *had.*

"Nein," Annie repeated, though her stomach lurched.

"Oh, nein! 'No' in German. I didn't know you were bilingual."

"Yeah."

"Hey, do you want to take the mainsheet for this final leg?" Alan motioned to the line in his hand. "I think we've pretty much blown our chance of winning."

What an asshole. You should hurl on those brown Top-Siders. This is not the guy for you, Annie.

She shook her head. "Sorry if I wrecked it for you!" she called to Alan. "I'm not feeling all that great."

Alan nodded sympathetically. "It's a little rough out here, I know. There's only about ten minutes left. I'd like to try to finish; I could use the points for the racing ladder. Can you make it?"

"Sure."

Bullshit.

Mark was right. Within five minutes, Annie was adding organic matter to the bay. Then she sat with her head between her knees while Alan piloted the catamaran across the finish line, and then back to the relative calm of the yacht club cove.

"You can open your eyes, we're back," he announced as he made a mooring.

Ten minutes later, they were on terra firma, and Annie felt a bit better as he escorted her into the clubhouse. It was quite lovely, all burnished wood and nautical fixtures. She showered and changed into jeans and a sweater in the women's locker room, and then came out to the restaurant bar to meet Alan. She found him immaculately dressed in white pants, a pale blue button-down shirt, and a blue blazer with some kind of crest on it, though he'd been wearing jeans and a tennis shirt when he'd picked her up at noon.

God, she hoped they didn't have a dress code. On the other hand, maybe that wouldn't be a bad thing. They'd kick her out, she could go home, and—

"Margarita?" he offered.

She shook her head. Alcohol was the last thing she wanted. Alan seemed miffed when she asked for hot tea. Yet he got over it when the mâitre d' showed them to a table with a wondrous view of the club, the cove, the bay, and the Marina district of the City in the distance. She wasn't feeling at all talkative, but Alan made up for it with a meal-long monologue that segued from his background to his medical practice to his politics to the "Grade-A bitch" also known as his former wife. He referred to her as The Debbie. In fact, the monologue stayed on The Debbie from the middle of the main course right through dessert.

Annie just kept nodding, sipping her tea, and picking at her food, while she fantasized about five or six couples doing all sorts of interesting things to each other at the other tables. It was amazing, really, the creative things you could do with Long Island duck and the chef's special glaze.

Alan pulled his 1975 Jensen Interceptor in front of Annie's building. He didn't turn off the engine, or even offer to walk her to the door.

"So, this was fun. Can I see you again?"

Before Annie could even formulate a polite alternative to no-fucking-way, he answered his own question.

"I'll call you."

There is only one guy for you. Don't give up on me.

Annie smiled. Mark. If only.

Alan moved in for a kiss. Annie stretched out her right arm in a blocking maneuver that could be mistaken only by a narcissist for an offered handshake.

He took her hand. "Great, Annie. We'll talk soon."

She fled, bolting up the stairs in record time and heading straight for the shower, to wash both the lingering salt out of her hair and the memory of the last wasted ten hours out of her consciousness. No more Alans. No more sailing. No more divorced assholes who hated their ex-wives. Annie felt like sending The Debbie a sympathy card.

She towel-dried her hair and put on her oldest, most comfortable sweats. A glass of red wine later, she started to feel better.

Annie. Come to bed.

Oh, yeah. Much, much better.

"I'm going to check my Web site," she said aloud, because

what the hell. She might very well be insane, but at least she was being insane in the privacy of her own apartment. "I want to make sure it's working."

Go on, then. But hurry. I want to show you how much I want you.

She padded into her dark living room and noticed through the window that the lesbians across the way were having a party. Well, she'd have her own party soon enough.

With one finger, she reactivated the monitor—the first thing she saw when the screen illuminated was the Turn Me On! scroll rolling across the bottom.

Don't be upset if there are only a few hits, she told herself. *An empire isn't built in a day.*

She moused over to the purple valentine and clicked it.

No.

It couldn't be. That was impossible.

The counter at the upper left displayed the digits 45236. Then, before her eyes, it rolled to 45237.

And then to 45238.

No goddamn way.

Heart pounding, she snapped on the lights and searched for her landline—it took her a full minute to find it buried under a stack of files on the floor.

What was PayPal's number? Or Visa? Or MasterCard? She tore through files in her cabinet. There! Written on the cover of Accounts Receivable.

Ten seconds later, she was talking to a business representative at Visa.

"Hallo?"

"This is Annie Albright of Turn Me On, Incorporated, in San Francisco. Can you give me an account status report as of eleven o'clock this evening?"

"Yes, Ms. Albrecht, Iwouldbehappytohelpyou," said a female voice with a heavy singsongy accent. Indian? Bangladesh-ian?

"Sorry?"

"Ifyouwouldjustbesokindastogivemeyouraccountinformation."

"Did you say something about account information?"

"Exactly. Ifyouwouldjustbesokindastogivemeyouraccountinformation."

"What?"

"Pardonme?"

"What about account information?"

"Exactly."

Annie was starting to feel desperate. "What account information?"

"YourpasswordpleaseMissAmyAlbrecht."

Annie didn't bother to correct her name. "Could you please, please, please speak more slowly?"

"Certainly, Miss Albrecht," the woman replied. Her accent was just as thick but thankfully at half the speed. "If you would just be so kind as to give me your account information and then your password."

"Is there a way I can key it into the phone?" Annie asked. "That might be . . . easier."

"No, miss. I assure you that I will get it properly."

Annie gave her the requested information. Twice.

"Very well, Miss Albrecht. As of eleven o'clock this evening Pacific Daylight Time, your active Visa business accounts receivable balance for Turn Me On, Incorporated contains a positive balance of nine hundred and seventy-seven thousand dollars and fifty-four cents."

Oh, my God.

"Could you repeat that?" Annie said weakly.

"I cannot speak any slower, ma'am. Nine hundred and seventy-seven thousand dollars and fifty-four cents. As of eleven o'clock. If you should like to stay on the line, I will be able to provide you with the balance as of midnight in a very few minutes."

Annie had a choice between letting the glass of wine fall from her shaking hand or downing it. She downed it. Then she hung up and called Visa right back, on the reasonable possibility that the woman in Bangalore or Delhi or wherever had mangled the information, or that she herself had been unable to penetrate her barely penetrable accent.

Nope. Everything was accurate. Mostly. In fact, the callback lady—who spoke better English than Annie—was able to give her the midnight balance: one million, twenty-five thousand, six hundred and eleven dollars, and eighty-five cents.

Annie couldn't believe it. She now had another asterisk to put next to her name.

Rich.

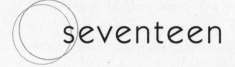# seventeen

"Watch your step down," Annie cautioned Doris, as the older woman stepped carefully into the communal hot bath at the Kabuki Springs and Spa in San Francisco's Japantown district. Doris was nude, as were Annie and Michelle. In the spa's traditional Japanese communal tub room, swimsuits were barred.

They were in an open space with both hot and cold tubs large enough for dozens of women, plus sauna, steam room and showers, and the spa-goers were of all ages, shapes, and sizes. At the moment, three elderly Japanese ladies at the far end of the pool patio were ladling ice water over each other. Not far from them, two middle-aged Caucasian women were sitting on chaises, deep in conversation. No one seemed to care that anyone else was naked, or that the bodies on display were less than perfect.

When Doris had suggested coming here, Annie had found the notion unnerving. She had no desire to get naked

in front of a bunch of women she didn't know, and even less
desire to bathe with them. The reality of all the naked female
flesh—gray pubes, flaccid breasts, hanging stomachs—cut seriously into her geisha orgy fantasy. Worst of all, the notion
of seeing her grandmother's well-preserved lush curves in all
their glory was more than a little disconcerting in theory. Yet
now that she was here, Annie was finding the experience
quite freeing.

"Now that you're rich, we should insure your feet for a
million each," Michelle quipped. She'd been in the pool for
a few minutes, and her cheeks were red from the water's
104-degree temperature.

"I've always been worth a million," Doris remarked, "even
when Murray and I didn't have any money." She lowered herself into the steaming water. "Speaking of—would you two
like to know the secret to getting any man you want?"

"I don't think we follow your mental dot-to-dot." Michelle lolled against the edge of the tub.

Doris let out a small sigh of satisfaction as the water covered her to her neck. "To get any man you want, you have to
believe that he would be willing to pay you a million dollars
for the privilege of having sex with you."

Annie thought about that for a moment. "But . . . why?"

"There's a second part," Doris added. "You have to believe you're worth it."

Annie smiled. "I love that."

"Good," her grandmother said. "Now go from loving it
to doing it."

Easier said than done. It had been ten days since the

Mr. Vibrator Web site had gone live. Her life had changed completely, and yet she didn't *feel* any different. She lived in the same apartment, had the same clothes and the same friends, and apparently had the same life. Yet everything had changed, because that first day's flood of orders for Mr. Vibrator had been no fluke. In fact, it was just the beginning of a sales firestorm. During Annie's prep for the launch, she'd considered the theoretical possibility of viral Internet marketing, where buzz could generate instantly and your message could multiply exponentially. She'd never imagined, however, that it would happen to her. But it could, it had, and it still was. She'd followed the postings about Mr. Vibrator on listservs and bulletin boards. Friend was telling friend who was telling friend, and the orders kept rolling in. The kicker had come when Annie got an e-mail herself from a former colleague at *HottieGirl,* linking Annie to www.turnmeoninc.com. She had to laugh at that one.

When Annie had departed for the baths this morning, something like 150,000 Mr. Vibrators had already been sold and paid for. Roughly half of those had shipped, and the rest would be in the fulfillment pipeline by the end of the week. The factory in Taiwan was getting close to its production capacity, but had made arrangements with another facility to take the overflow. There was no possibility of running short. In fact, they were now giving Annie a high-volume production discount.

Most gratifying of all had been the incredible testimonials that were being posted to the Mr. Vibrator Web site. Annie had been wise enough to allow for buyers to post their comments in text, podcast audio, and even YouTube-style videos. Though she'd had to screen out a number of these testimonials due to overly explicit content—quite a few users had uploaded their interpretations of Mr. Vibrator as an action toy—there were hundreds of others that she could post. Annie was convinced that the testimonials were one of her best sales tools.

The previous afternoon, Annie, Doris, and Michelle had met with their corporate accountant, who'd delivered the startling news that the company had already grossed close to $15 million in sales and was showing a profit of more than $11 million. Under the articles of incorporation, Michelle was entitled to ten percent of that profit, Doris to thirty-nine percent, and Annie to the rest. The accountant had presented them with three checks, holding a liberal amount back for taxes and other liabilities. Annie's check amounted to $4 million.

Annie only wished she had been there when Michelle marched back into McCutcheon Doyle and tendered her resignation. Michelle had gleefully reported what the managing partner had said to her: "You'll be making half a million dollars a year within the next three years, Michelle. You're crazy to turn your back on that." Michelle had gone into a laughing fit and offered to stay on through her current trial. She was told to pack her things immediately.

Annie was the last one into the water. She slid down until it covered her head completely, then popped up to find her grandmother smiling at her. "You know, I always wanted to come here," Doris confided. "But I could never afford it."

The spa was, Annie knew, ridiculously expensive. Somehow it had caught on with local and visiting celebrities. But for the first time in her life, she didn't have to think about what something cost.

"You can afford anything you want now, Doris," Michelle reminded.

Doris's shrug made little waves ripple across the steaming pool. "What I want, money can't buy."

"You want Grandpa back," Annie guessed.

Doris smiled sadly. "It's a funny thing about having had a Big Love," she mused. "It's a joy most people never know. But like everything else in life, it ends. And having had that joy—well, it's very difficult to lose it."

Annie felt an ache in the back of her throat. Would she ever get to experience the kind of Big Love that her grandparents had had?

Doris reached for Annie's hand. "But also, Annele, I wanted for you to find yourself. And that, my darling, has happened. I'm very proud of you."

Annie beamed. "Annele" had been Doris's pet name for her since she'd been a toddler. She loved her parents, but honestly she felt closer to her grandmother, whose approval meant the world to her. She knew that without Doris, there would be no Mr. Vibrator. In fact, she'd probably still be in her apartment bumming about Elliot.

"Ms. Albright? Ms. Garibaldi?" Two spa attendants dressed in white cotton drawstring pants and loose black tunics approached the pool.

Annie raised a hand. "That's us."

The taller of the two smiled at her. She was Asian, with a long salt-and-pepper braid. "Your spa treatments are ready.

You both will have the Javanese Lulur body treatment with the extended massage?"

"If that's what Annie signed us up for," Michelle said. "Whatever that is."

The attendant looked at her closely. "Your first time here?"

"Yes," Annie confessed. "For all three of us."

She nodded. "You will be back, I am sure. We will bring all of you to the main lobby in two hours. Mrs. Rosen?"

Doris opened her eyes. "Yes?"

"We'll return for you in a moment. You have the classic Shiatsu."

"Are you okay alone in here, Gramma?" Annie asked, as she moved toward the steps out of the pool.

"Of course," Doris said. "There's only one thing I want to know."

"Yes?"

"Shiatsu, I get. But what the hell are they going to be doing to you two?"

The tall Asian explained as Annie and Michelle were escorted to a meditation room in anticipation of their treatments: the Javanese Lulur body treatment was an Indonesian-based set of protocols that involved the application of scented oils to the skin, followed by a rubdown with a turmeric-and-rice exfoliant, followed by a yogurt-based cream, and then finally an exotic flower bath.

"Just hearing that is making me hungry," Michelle cracked.

"Perhaps you'd like a light refreshment?" the attendant asked. "Our vegan soy mini muffins are wonderful. We have bran or carrot-honey. You'll find them in the meditation room. Please help yourself."

The meditation room was small, lit only by dozens of aromatic candles, with jewel-toned velvet-cushioned couches, bamboo walls, and a waterfall that slipped over hundreds of smooth stones. Michelle picked up a mini muffin from a tray table and popped it into her mouth. "I know you're not going to believe this, but it tastes good." She reached for two more and handed one to Annie. "I'm ready to move in here."

"It's fabulous," Annie agreed, but she couldn't help sighing when she said it. She put the muffin back.

"The weariness of the suddenly rich?" Michelle queried.

Was that it? Annie couldn't put her finger on why she was feeling inexplicably sad. "It's all just so . . . strange. All I had was an idea."

Michelle examined the muffin plate and picked up a different flavor; something orange with nuts on top. "That is like saying that string theory is just an idea. What you had was a conceptual breakthrough for three and a half billion people." She popped it into her mouth. "Mmm. Carrot. Yummy." She chewed, then washed it down with a glass of herbal tea. "So what's bugging you, really?"

Suddenly Annie knew. Or maybe she'd known all along but just didn't want to say it aloud because it sounded so desperate and stupid. Still, if you couldn't sound desperate and stupid to your best friend . . .

"It's the voice," Annie admitted.

"Mr. Vibrator's voice? What's wrong with it?"

"Nothing," Annie assured her. "It's great. More than great, don't you think?"

"Hundreds of thousands of women agree with you. Including me," Michelle said. "What's that guy's name again—Mark something?"

"Wolfson. Mark Wolfson." Annie loved just saying his name aloud.

"Right," Michelle agreed. "I'd like to personally thank him for the fact that I no longer check JDate three times a day and I now go to sleep with a smile on my face."

"The truth is . . ." Annie took a deep breath. "I'm kind of obsessing about him. I really want to meet him."

Michelle shrugged. "So call. Ask him to meet you—I don't know—at the Wishing Well." This was a neighborhood bar at Seventh Avenue and Irving that Annie loved.

"It's not that simple," she cautioned Michelle.

"Bullshit." Michelle used her hand to mime a cell phone. "'Hello, Mark? This is Annie Albright. You don't know me, but you just made me a fortune and I'd like to buy you a drink. If you come, I'll give you a hundred grand tip.'" She closed her hand. "Who wants to bet he'll say yes?"

"Me," Annie said. "I tried. He's out of town—I spoke to his apartment sitter. He's out trekking the Appalachian Trail."

Michelle looked askance. "People really do that? Voluntarily?"

"Evidently."

"So let's see . . ." Michelle mused. "What are your options?"

Before Annie could reply, yet another attendant, this one short and African American, appeared in the doorway. "Excuse me, ladies. I'm Cassandra. Annie? Are you ready for your treatment?"

"Good luck," Michelle called as Annie followed Cassandra out of the meditation room and down a wood-paneled corridor. Cassandra opened a door, and Annie found herself in a small sandalwood-scented treatment room barely big enough for a massage table and the attendant.

"Sit on the table," Cassandra instructed, as she took a small stool out from under it. "I will begin by massaging your feet with aromatic oils that clear the chakras."

Within thirty seconds of Cassandra's ministrations, Annie felt herself drifting into a state of relaxed bliss.

Come find me, Come find me. Mark's voice whispered.

Ah. There it was. It instantly made her feel better. What good was being filthy rich if you didn't use it to bring you happiness? Crazy as it might seem, Annie felt certain that her happiness—maybe even her Big Love—lay in the man behind the voice of Mr. Vibrator. Mark Wolfson. She would figure out how to find him. But it was going to have to wait until after her chakras were balanced.

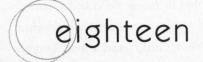eighteen

"Mr. Silver?"

An African American woman in her late twenties clad in a tweedy blue suit opened the door to the waiting room at the Summit Foundation, where Charlie had been nervously waiting for his first interview. Under his navy sports jacket and new white dress shirt he could feel a line of sweat trickle down his spine. It was disconcerting, because usually he was cool under pressure. But then, he'd never before felt a million dollars' worth of pressure.

He put down a copy of the foundation's annual report, which he'd been leafing through. In actuality, he'd downloaded it as a PDF a week ago, part of his self-imposed homework for this interview. He knew everything there was to know about the Summit Foundation and could recite chapter and verse about its various projects both here and overseas.

Charlie stood. "Please, call me Charlie."

"Charlie. I'm Linda Fannin, a project associate here."

Linda offered him her thin, perfectly manicured hand. He took it, noticing a small ring on her pinky with the tiniest of daisies etched into it. She was very attractive, tall and elegant, with skin the color of creamed coffee and almond-shaped eyes above a nose just a tad too long for classic beauty. Her hair was coiled into a glossy bun at the back of her head. "Welcome to Washington." She held his hand a beat longer than necessary.

Charlie recognized that special light in her eye, but he was careful to keep his gaze neutral. He hadn't come to Washington to flirt. Not this time. "Thank you," he said, smiling. "Actually, I've been here before. With my eighth-grade class."

"You accompanied your students?" she asked.

Interesting. There was the slightest British lilt to the word "accompanied." Plus, an American would have just said, "You brought your students?" So either Linda Fannin was the child of British expatriates who'd moved here when she was a kid, had gone to boarding school in England, or was simply unbelievably pretentious.

"I didn't mean I came with my students," Charlie confessed, hoping he sounded charming as opposed to pathetic. "I meant I came when I was in the eighth grade. As a student."

Linda laughed, an excellent sign. "When did you get in?"

"Last night."

The foundation had flown him first class from SFO to Dulles so he'd be fresh for his initial interview, and booked him into a junior suite at the Omni Shoreham not far from Dupont Circle. He was grateful for that, just as he was grateful that the names of the nominees had not been made public. Charlie thought how awful it would be to have your family, friends, colleagues, and students get their hopes up, only to have them dashed. He himself was playing it very low-key. No one knew that he'd been nominated, and no one was going to know.

"I thought perhaps we'd go for a walk on the Mall and chat a bit," Linda suggested. "Then I'll bring you back here to meet the committee."

"Sounds great," Charlie agreed, wondering if every finalist got the walk-on-the-Mall portion of the proceedings.

The foundation's offices were in the Watergate complex, so it only took a few minutes for Linda to lead the way to the Mall. His instincts were right; she was the youngest daughter of British parents who'd come to work at the National Institutes of Health when she was just a girl, and then decided to seek American citizenship.

"Have you been to the UK?" Linda asked.

In fact, Charlie had been to the UK He'd spent considerable time with a lovely student named Gemma in London, and then with an even lovelier teacher named Catriona in Edinburgh, Scotland.

"I have. It was . . . memorable."

"Ah, a girl," Linda guessed. She gave him a knowing sidelong look. "You can relax, Charlie. I don't report to the committee. This is quite refreshing for me. The average age of our finalists is somewhere north of fifty and south of death."

Well, that answered his question about whether or not everyone got the Mall tour.

They cut through a small wooded area that led to the Mall—it was filled with tourists picnicking or just taking advantage of the shade to rest. "So, tell me about your school," Linda urged. "Mays-McCovey—have I got that right?"

Charlie gave her a quick rundown on his school. She listened intently, asking probing questions about the academic program, how many of the children were in the free breakfast and free lunch programs, and more. "You're sure you aren't part of my interview?"

"Definitely not. But I am very proud of the grants we award, and extremely interested in the candidates to whom we award them."

A few hundred yards' walk took them to the Vietnam Memorial, the long black wall that he'd seen in photographs but never in person. It seemed to shimmer in the afternoon sunshine. Though there were a thousand people or more gazing at it, he could hear tufted titmice screeching in the overhanging trees. It was that *quiet*.

When he saw an elderly woman with a walker running two fingers over a name on the wall—it had to be her child that she was remembering—he realized that his mother's eldest brother, Franklin Auerbach, had to be here somewhere. He'd been killed during the siege at Khe Sanh. Maybe he could even make a rubbing of Uncle Franklin's name and send it to his mother in North Carolina. She'd appreciate that. He'd have to make up some excuse about why he was in Washington, but that wouldn't be too difficult.

Ten minutes later, he'd excused himself from Linda, saying that this was something he wanted to do alone. She understood completely. Using the guidebooks designed exactly for this purpose, and cadging a sheet of white paper and a stubby pencil from the Park Service employee in a booth at one end of the wall, he carefully searched for the section of the wall containing his uncle's name. Since Khe Sanh was an early battle, it was on the left side of the wall as he faced it.

And there he was: Lance Corporal Franklin Auerbach, USMC. A man he'd only heard about, dead at the age of twenty, who never got to experience computers, or DVDs, or the Super Bowl, or even the considerable advantages of the women's liberation movement that had brought so much joy to Charlie's life. Charlie took the sheet of paper, held it against the black stone, and made the rubbing. Then he folded it carefully and put it in the back pocket of his trousers. Whatever else came of this trip, he would have this.

He looked for Linda, and found her waiting patiently on a bench to the south of the memorial. "Meaningful?" she asked, as she got to her feet.

"Very."

"So, Charlie, I was thinking. Your first round of interviews will take you to about five this afternoon. If you don't have plans for dinner, I was wondering if you'd like to join me. I know a fabulous Ethiopian place in Adams Morgan."

Damn. He loved Ethiopian food. And Linda would look great sitting across a table from him, her slim fingers wrapped around a piece of *injera* bread, which would in turn be enveloping a tasty bite of *kitfo* or delicately spiced soft green lentils. But he had a feeling that that could easily lead to something significant after dinner, which seemed like a really bad idea.

"I wish I could," he told her, "but my kids just turned in five-page book reports. I promised they'd have them back after the holiday. So it'll be me, a red pencil, and room service."

For a moment, he saw disappointment flit through her eyes. Then she brightened. "Well, if things work out, this won't be your last trip to Washington this summer. Our final eight contenders will be returning in late August. How about a rain check, then?"

"Sounds great," he agreed.

Charlie noticed a small Asian man nearby who was selling flowers from an old-fashioned pushcart. "Hold on a sec," he said impetuously, and bounded over to the old man. He bought all the daisies the elderly man was selling, just under three dozen, and carried the simple flowers back to Linda.

"My favorite!" she exclaimed, when he pressed them into her hands. "How did you know?"

It had been the daisy etched into her pinky ring, but Charlie never told his secrets. "Just had a feeling."

Linda's eyes shone as they turned and headed back toward the Watergate. "I have a feeling, too. That the committee is going to love you."

"When I think about what that money could do for my kids . . ." Charlie hesitated. "Anyway, I hope you're right."

She gazed happily at her flowers, then back at Charlie. "I've been in this position for five years, Charlie. I haven't been wrong yet."

Charlie considered himself a reasonably experienced interviewee. He'd been interviewed for college, interviewed before he got his graduate teaching degree, and he'd interviewed for various jobs. Principal Witherspoon had famously kept him captive in his office for more than two hours, though the principal had done as much talking as Charlie had, if not more. He'd even been interviewed by the *International Herald Tribune* at a Paris café for a story about what Americans did in Paris on Thanksgiving. (In his case, what he'd been doing was a tall, lithe actress with the Comédie-Française named Françoise, but he diplomatically focused on his visit to the Louvre instead).

But he'd never had a more peculiar interview than the one that afternoon with the committee of five that would choose the High Summit Award winners.

First, there'd been the committee itself. Dudley Donovan, an octogenarian name partner at a prestigious Washington, D.C. law firm, who walked with two canes but whose mind had lost none of its snap. Reginald Martinez, the Republican former secretary of education. Lenny Leonard, storied former NFL star turned head coach of the Oakland Raiders right across the bay, who'd forsaken a third eight-figure coaching contract to attend divinity school and establish a church in Houston. Lin Mei, the diminutive but combative Washington bureau correspondent for CNN. And last, an actual Nobel laureate, the left-leaning economist Pablo Goldstein.

Second had been the location. Not a conference room at the Watergate, but a private room at a restaurant-bar in Georgetown, where there had been plenty of food, a reasonable amount of beer and wine, and a conversation that had ranged from politics to literature to educational philosophy and back again. At one point, Goldstein and Leonard had gotten into a heated argument about discipline in school that everyone else seemed content to simply observe. Then, as if by prearrangement, Lin asked Charlie his opinion on the question: whether parents needed to be informed whenever a child was taken out of the classroom for disciplinary reasons.

Charlie answered honestly and directly, realizing that he couldn't satisfy both Goldstein and Leonard with what he had to say, and hoping that reasonableness of his position would at least gain their dual respect.

"It depends on the school, and it depends on the kid." He saw Donovan nod, so he thought he had a good beginning. "Some of my parents want to know everything—that kind of involved parent is a gem. But some of my kids couldn't tell you where—or even who—their daddy is. Many are being raised by a single mother, and many more by a grandmother. Often these women work two, sometimes three jobs to try to make ends meet. Oftentimes I can't even get hold of them. And then there are the parents with substance abuse problems who either aren't tracking their kid at all or use a call from a teacher as an excuse to administer corporal punishment. This is one of the many reasons why it's so important to know each individual kid and his or her circumstances."

"But you aren't a social worker, Mr. Silver," Mei pointed out.

"I would say that knowing a kid's circumstances is part of being a good teacher." He thought for a moment. "I don't have to tell you that there's a lot of bluster in a junior high school classroom, and more at my school than most. But what kids really want, I think, is to feel known. To feel like they matter."

"I think I understand you, Charlie," said Martinez. "I grew up in Calexico, California. I was one of those kids who could have easily slipped through the cracks. I had a teacher in fifth grade, Mrs. Wolfenbarger, God rest her soul, and for some reason that woman really *saw* me."

Charlie didn't know much about Martinez, other than that he was a Republican. But he realized immediately that though they might differ in politics, they probably had more in common than any other two people in the room.

"Perhaps I could come out and visit your school," suggested the former Cabinet official.

"My kids would love that," Charlie said. "They're having a tough time right now, worried that we might not ever get back into our school building. It makes them anxious."

"We're up to speed," Donovan assured Charlie in his croaky voice. "Damn shame."

"A school is not a building. It's where the teachers are," Mei pointed out.

"Not if kids can't walk to the damn building," Martinez said quietly.

"Amen to that," said Leonard with a big grin. A former

defensive lineman, he took up his whole chair and then some. He looked at his watch. "We've kept Charlie for four hours. How about we let Linda take him back to his hotel? I think we're all agreed we'll be seeing him later in the summer. Right?"

One by one, the committee members nodded emphatically.

"Congratulations, Charlie," Martinez said. "You just made the first cut."

nineteen

"Omigod. Get these things away from me!"

Annie, who had just plopped down to rest on the bank of the swift-running mountain stream, swatted with both hands at a swarm of midges that were doing everything they could to fly into every open orifice on her body. She was fortunate to be wearing long pants tucked into her hiking boots, and quickly rolled down the mosquito netting that was part of her bush hat, though not quickly enough to bar several hundred midges from invading her nasal cavities. She instinctively squeezed her nostrils together. Too late. She fished a tissue out of her backpack and blew dead insect parts from her nose. "People do this for fun? *Mark* does this for fun? I'm dying here!"

Michelle, whose mosquito netting had already been deployed, screwed the top back onto the water-filtering squeeze bottle she'd refilled in the stream, then drank thirstily. "Stop complaining," she ordered. "I'm the one hauling around thirty extra pounds."

"If you want the *delicious trail food* we're eating—"

"Not eating," Michelle interjected.

"Exactly my point," Annie said. "I'd say twenty-five."

"Gorp without M&Ms? Raw peanuts and raisins that taste like rabbit turds. Freeze-dried scrambled eggs and whatever they put in it that passes for bacon? I'd kill for a Snickers."

Annie yawned. Exhausted, she lay back against her over-stuffed backpack.

"I take it you want to rest for a while?" asked their trail guide, whom they'd found back in Damascus, Virginia. Nancy was thirty, with knotty muscles and the short, style-free brown hair of a woman who cared more about function than form. Her voice was deep and booming. Annie immediately had suspected some hormonal confusion, confirmed the day before when she'd awakened to pee and had found Nancy shaving her chin.

"We *are* resting, Nancy," Michelle confirmed.

"You know your own limits," Nancy declared in a tone that made clear her disdain for their slothlike limitations.

Still, Annie was extremely grateful for the woman. Nancy's backpack carried twice as many supplies as hers and Michelle's put together, and she never complained about anything. She'd even hiked ahead to pitch their tent and cook their dinner before Annie and Michelle came straggling into camp. When they separated on the trail, they were always in touch, since she had insisted that they buy high-quality walkie-talkies before they left Damascus.

After three days of hiking, Annie knew she'd never been

so sore in her life. Muscle groups she hadn't known existed were aching, and she had blisters on her blisters.

"There's another two hours of daylight," Nancy reported. "The campground is about four miles up the trail. It's a pretty nice clearing. If you really can't hack it, I can signal for a chopper to drop in and bring you girls out."

"Yes!" Michelle exclaimed in a voice that Annie guessed approximated her response to a particularly fulfilling experience with Mr. Vibrator. "We want the chopper!"

For an instant, Annie was tempted. She hated everything about hiking through the wilderness, including the cute, furry woodland creatures that Nancy warned should not be approached lest they be rabid. The idea of being transported back to civilization by means other than her hiking boot–encased aching feet was extremely appealing. But were she to do that, it would negate the entire reason she was in the wilderness.

Mark Wolfson was out here, too, somewhere to the south, heading in their direction. Whether "somewhere to the south" was a mile or a hundred miles, Annie did not know.

"No chopper," Annie decreed. "Go ahead, Nancy. We'll catch up."

"I'll have dinner waiting," Nancy promised. "Freeze-dried tuna wiggle and Tang. See you up the trail." With a quick wave and five quick leaps over some protruding rocks, Nancy crossed the stream and bounded off into the woods.

Michelle dug a bag of M&M-free Gorp out of her backpack and offered it to Annie.

Annie shook her head. "Just five minutes. Then we're walking again."

"Ten," Michelle decreed, as she closed her eyes. "Or I feed you to the first rabid squirrel I see."

Annie lay on her back and studied the fleecy clouds as they floated by. They'd taken a flight from San Francisco to Charlotte, North Carolina, and then a death-defying puddle jumper to Bristol, Tennessee. From there, they rented a car—a convertible Mustang, at the insistence of Michelle—and drove to Damascus, Virginia.

Damascus was—there was no other way to put it—deeply bizarre. As the unofficial southern headquarters for Appalachian Trail through-hikers, the casual on-the-sidewalk traffic was roughly ten males to every female. Michelle had perked up considerably at the ratio, until it became apparent that the passing male parade was uniformly bearded, ill-washed and ill-dressed, with a habit of referring to each other by strange trail nicknames like Roper, Wolfdog, and Captain Bizarro. Most carried the same ski-pole-style walking sticks that they'd used along the trail. Annie couldn't even work up any good fantasies about them.

Their first stop in Damascus had been a bed-and-breakfast, where they checked in for the night. The next was the town post office, where Annie had the bright idea to give the postmaster a stamped letter addressed to Mark Wolfson; she watched as it got rubber-banded to a thick stack in the "W" slot of General Delivery. Despite the odor emanating from the long-bearded, long-nailed, trail-hiker dude in line behind her, Annie was elated.

Those rubber-banded letters meant that Mark hadn't yet stopped by the post office to get his mail, which meant that he was still out there someplace on the trail south of Damascus.

Well, then. There was only one thing to do. Get outfitted at one of the numerous outdoors stores that dotted the town like marshmallows on a pumpkin pie and start walking south on the trail. Logic dictated that if they kept walking in one direction and Mark kept coming in the other, eventually their paths would cross. She'd brought one of the photos she'd downloaded; she was sure she could identify him.

Twenty-four hours on the trail nearly nixed that idea. She and Michelle had no idea how to hike, what to do in a thunderstorm, how to purify their water, how to pitch a tent, light a cookstove, or what to use as toilet paper in the woods when you've forgotten to bring the real thing—situations they encountered during their first day out. They felt lucky to stagger back to Damascus the next day with their dignity and limbs intact.

Fortunately, Annie had determination on her side. Some conversation with a female hiker they encountered had led them to Nancy, who they were told could always be found at the Baja Café. With a combination of cash and gratitude, they convinced her to be their guide before they finished their unlikely breakfast of eggs and frijoles.

Annie sighed and adjusted her backpack under her head. Maybe what she was doing was insane. What non-athletic city girl and her even-less-athletic best friend hiked the Appalachian Trail to find a *voice*, for God's sake? In the past three days they'd crossed paths with dozens of northbound hiking males.

Ninety-eight percent clearly looked nothing like Mark—Annie had the photo she'd printed from the Internet in her backpack. The two percent who were possible matches turned out to be someone else. She knew because she asked.

Off in the distance, Annie heard the now-telltale crack of twigs under hiking shoes. She sat up to see who was coming—was it Mark? No. It was a boisterous pack of Cub Scouts led by a Dick Cheney look-alike in ill-advised regulation khaki Cub Scout shorts.

"Do you girls need help?" The Cubmaster scratched one sweaty armpit. He had noticeable man-boobs under his shirt.

"We're fine," Annie assured him. "Just resting."

"You kids keep going!" the man told his troops, then smiled confidentially at the girls. "Well, if you two are heading to Damascus and want some company, we're staying at the Best Western for a couple of days. Just ask at the front desk for Bubba Dickens. I've got me a single."

"Oh, yeah, we're all over that, Bubba," Michelle told him. "Hey, give the Scouts you're so ably leading a few six-packs—that oughta knock 'em out. Then we'll come over and play with your chest. What size bra do you wear?"

Bubba glowered, then stomped off after his kids.

"Did I offend?" Michelle asked, batting her eyelashes.

"I'm remembering his name so that I can report him," Annie said. "How can he be allowed to lead children?" She slung her backpack on. "Ready to go?"

"You realize you will owe me for this for many years to come," Michelle warned.

"Yep." Annie started across the wide mountain stream, trying to get her feet on the same rocks she'd seen Nancy use, plunging her walking sticks into the water for extra balance. It wasn't easy—the stream was quite deep and very cold. Nor was Annie a Nancy. Halfway across, she lost her balance and landed heavily in the frigid water.

"Shit!" she shrieked. "It's fucking freezing!"

"Your pack!" Michelle shouted.

Annie watched helplessly as her pack floated downstream. Michelle scrambled after it on her side of the stream. As Annie struggled to regain her footing, she heard a shout from the other side of the stream, and then the sounds of heavy crashing through the underbrush.

A male voice shouted: "I'm on it!"

Annie certainly hoped so. All she could do was slosh through water up to her waist and struggle up onto the opposite bank, squishing and dripping with every step on dry land. She pulled her walkie-talkie from her pocket to call Nancy for help, but the device was waterlogged and useless. "Shit," Annie spat.

"Hey. Bad break. I've got your pack, though!"

She looked up. It couldn't be. But it was.

It was him. Mark Wolfson, looking much like he did in the Dr. Faustus photograph, only with a longer beard. Annie stood there dripping and shivering. She'd waited so long, longed so much, for this moment. It would have been right out of a fairy tale, him saving her backpack like this, if not for the fact that she looked like a drowned rat.

But wait. She'd just heard him speak. He didn't sound

anything like the voice of Mr. Vibrator. Still, she reminded herself that he was an actor with a lot of voices.

"Hey, you don't want to get hypothermia," Mark said. "Have you got a towel and dry clothes in your pack?"

Annie nodded. Something about this just didn't feel right.

"Dry off and get changed," Mark suggested, "Are you with someone?"

She still didn't look at him. "My friend Michelle. She went after my backpack on the other side."

"You get changed, I'll get Michelle," Mark said. "Oh, wait, let me do this first." It took him less than thirty seconds to set up a small butane cookstove and get some water heating. "For tea. When I get back. What's your name?"

"Annie."

"Annie," he repeated, then nodded. "Change."

He left his own backpack, picked up his walking stick, and bounded across the river as easily as Nancy had. Annie dug out her towel, dry pants, shirt, and socks, and changed as quickly as she could. The only thing uglier than her dripping wet was her dripping wet in ugly white cotton trail underwear. Fortunately, by the time Mark crossed the creek back to her, helping Michelle from stone to stone, she was fully dressed.

"Hi, Annie!" Michelle shouted. "This is *Mark*!" Michelle stabbed a finger in his direction. Clearly she'd already figured out that this was *the* Mark.

"Yeah, we exchanged names already," Mark said easily. The water was boiling, so he dropped in a teabag and some sweetener. "I nearly bit it on a stream like this a few miles back. It happens to everyone."

"So . . . drink that tea, Annie," Michelle said. "I'm going to go . . . hunt for blueberries! Right. I love blueberries!" Before either Annie or Mark could say anything, she headed down the dirt path that paralleled the stream.

Mark glanced at Annie. "She might have a problem with those blueberries, seeing as she didn't take a container with her."

"Maybe she's going to eat them all," Annie replied, since it was the best she could come up with.

"How are you feeling?" he asked.

"Like I just walked into a theater after stepping in a big pile of dog shit." She sipped her tea.

"That's quite a metaphor. I'm a stage actor—when I'm not doing this."

"I know," Annie mumbled.

Mark was silent for a moment. He looked at her more closely. "Did you just say, 'I know'?"

Annie nodded. "I think I did."

He rubbed his bearded chin. "So . . . either you're clairvoyant or you're the world's biggest theater buff and you've seen me in something. I live in—"

"San Francisco," Annie filled in. "I live there, too. Actually, you auditioned for me recently, and um . . ."

This was ridiculous. She put down the tea and forced herself to meet his eyes.

"It was a voice-over thing. We chose you."

It took a moment, then Mark snapped his fingers. "That

female affirmation tape thing. All right!" He pumped his fist a few times. "Mailbox money. There's nothing an actor likes more than to make money when he's not working. Did you send it yet?"

"Yeah."

"Wow, great, thanks! What a coincidence, huh? Us running into each other out here."

"Umm . . ."

Wrong guy.

The voice. In her head. Of Mr. Vibrator. This was all wrong, and Annie knew it. The voice was right. She should feel a magical connection with Mark. He should feel a magical connection with her. He was nice enough, he'd made tea for her and rescued her backpack, but what he was most concerned with now was whether the check had already been in the mail.

Wrong guy, Annie.

"Annie? You okay? Did you hit your head when you fell?" Mark asked.

"No, sorry, I . . ."

Damn. She'd come all the way out here for nothing. It didn't matter that Mark Wolfson's name had been on the voice recording, or that Mark Wolfson had actually done two recordings, or even that she'd sent two grand to this guy. He wasn't *the* guy.

"I'm sorry. I think I mistook you for someone else," Annie said softly.

Mark looked alarmed. "You mean I didn't get the gig?"

There was really no way to explain.

"No, you got the gig. I sent you the money already. Really," she assured him.

"Hey," Michelle greeted them as she bounced her way up the path again.

"How were the blueberries?" Mark asked.

Michelle looked confused for a moment, then seemed to remember her cover story. "Oh, the *blueberries*. Wow, really good. But there weren't very many, so I couldn't bring you guys any." She gave Annie an expectant look. "But then, you two were probably too busy to even think about blueberries, right?"

"Wrong," Annie replied, with the heavy eye contact that meant there was much more to the story.

"There's a nice patch to the south, when you come to the twin oaks that overhang the trail, about two miles back," Mark said. "I can give you the GPS coordinates if you'd like."

"We'll find them," Annie assured him, as she got to her feet and slung her wet pack over her shoulders. Michelle was staring at her like she was crazy, but she couldn't very well explain now. "So, we have to catch up with someone," Annie told Mark. "It was nice to see you." She extended a hand toward Mark, ignoring her friend's look of shock. "It was really nice of you to stop. The money's waiting for you at home. Have a great hike." She put out her hand. When Mark shook it, she didn't feel anything except keen disappointment.

"Thanks," Mark told her. "Glad I could help. Hey, if you get a chance to see *Hairspray* when it opens at the Geary, I'll be in it."

Annie started backward up the trail "Will do. Come on,

Michelle." She motioned to her friend, who seemed frozen in place. "I *know* you want to find those blueberries."

Michelle caught up with Annie. "Are you *insane?*" she hissed.

"That's not him." She ducked under some low-hanging tree branches.

"Annie, it's him," Michelle insisted. "Mark Wolfson."

"Mark Wolfson, yes," Annie agreed. "But Mr. Vibrator, no. The names got screwed up somehow."

Michelle used her forearm to push some stray hair from her sweaty forehead. "So, wait. We came out here *for nothing?*"

Annie inhaled deeply. "Fresh air. Great for the constitution."

They traversed a rocky area. "You understand that I have to kill you, right?" Michelle asked.

"As soon as we get to Nancy, we'll have her call in that chopper and we're out of here," Annie promised. She swatted some giant flying thing on her arm, which left a liquid splat and a stray wing. She brushed it off with a shudder. "I should have known that the real Mr. Vibrator wouldn't consider swatting insects a good time."

Don't give up. Promise me you won't.

The voice.

Annie muttered under her breath softly enough for Michelle not to hear. "I won't. But you're driving me nuts."

twenty

I have to remember every detail to tell Michelle, Annie thought as she looked around the backstage greenroom on Jay Leno's set on the NBC studio lot in Los Angeles. The walls were covered by framed posters of the host, and there were two black leather couches and a number of inviting plush chairs. Near one wall, a long table covered in snowy linen held a buffet of cold cuts, cakes and cookies, and beverages. One nice touch was a pegboard of NBC-logo terry-cloth robes that guests could don as a safeguard against inadvertent spillage.

Food and drink for Annie, though, were out of the question. She was too nervous, knowing that millions of Americans were about to watch her.

Oh, my God. Millions of people.

"Miss Albright?"

The assistant who stepped into the room was astonishingly beautiful, in the cookie-cutter I'm-an-L.A.-babe-in-the-entertainment-business kind of way. Blunt-cut jet-black hair fell to her shoulders with that cool, chunky effect that Annie adored but could never get her own thin hair to do. Both skinny and busty, the assistant wore a cropped pink tweed jacket with size nothing designer jeans, and pink and black suede polka-dot heels that Annie recognized as Christian Louboutin only because Michelle owned three pairs and planned to buy more. These shoes went for mid three figures. How could the assistant afford them? Annie would never pay that much for—

Wait. She was rich now. She could buy five dozen pairs if she wanted. She'd thought of herself as struggling for so long that it was hard to make the transition to—

"Annie, darling." Her grandmother nudged her arm. "I think it's time."

Time? No, it couldn't be time. Panic washed over Annie like a sudden spring storm. What was she doing waiting in a room where the stars chilled before going out to shake Jay Leno's hand and then chat up their latest movie, TV series, and/or scandal? One by one, she'd seen them summoned to the set. Governor Schwarzenegger, Cameron Diaz plugging her picture, and a young singer named Lindsay Haun who had sung her hit "Broken" with the orchestra before sitting down with Jay. They'd all been nice to her, Haun especially. Now, she was the last to be summoned.

"Annie? I'm Chamomile," the assistant told her. "But please call me Cammie, only you spell it with an 'H' and one 'M'; Chami, okay? I'll be escorting you out to the set."

Annie gave her grandmother what she could sense was a deer-in-the-headlights look. "I—I —"

Doris patted Annie's arm. "You'll be fine, darling."

"We're so happy that you're here, Ms. Albright," Chami went on.

"You should be thrilled," Doris said, briskly crossing her perfect legs. She wore a silk kimono that swirled with jewel tones of red, purple, gold, and royal blue, and navy pants that she'd purchased from QVC and loved because they were so comfortable. "Do you know how many media requests my Annie has received in the past week?"

Chami nodded. "Oh, I'm sure. Everyone in America is talking about you. Jay is so excited that you picked his show."

Every big media outlet in the world had vied for Annie, because hers was a unique and amazing overnight success story. Via the modern wonder of the Internet, and the old-fashioned wonder of the church social hall, PTA, hair salon, and AYSO youth soccer sideline, friend had told friend, mother had told mother, and grandmother had told grandmother about their new playmate. In the last month, sales had exploded—upwards of half a million Mr. Vibrators had been sold in North America alone.

With Michelle leading the charge—the only reason she wasn't in the greenroom with Doris and Annie was that she'd flown to Taiwan to meet with the manufacturers—they had quickly taken the business international. Several foreign-language professors at UC-Berkeley helped them add French, Spanish, Russian, Chinese, Hindustani, and Arabic versions. Though the voices they'd found for these models didn't have the same visceral effect on her as the English-language version, the target audiences seemed to be responding well, via new language-specific Web sites. Combined international sales were quickly approaching the levels of those in the United States and Canada.

The most bizarre thing was that the business ran itself. The Taiwan production facility was now handling demand easily, and Annie had hired exactly one person to run the tiny office she'd opened in a small nondescript space just a few blocks from her grandmother's home—Doris herself. In fact, Doris had insisted that she be the one to handle the phones, filing, and correspondence, especially since her resignation from Funtime Industries. What gave her the most pleasure, though, other than Mr. Vibrator himself, was the giant check she'd been able to write to her synagogue for a new library—the Murray A. Rosen Memorial Library, named for her late husband, who had so loved a good book.

Ironically, it turned out that being the filthy-rich magnate of an international corporation gave Annie little to do. She would amuse herself by sitting at the computer and watching the sales roll up on her Web site, but after $55 million in worldwide sales, of which the vast majority was profit, even that started to feel like overkill.

She had to look for things to do to amuse herself. She increased the amount of time she volunteered at the senior center, but found her mind wandering as she helped the elderly with their craft projects. She'd taken her sketch pad to Fisherman's Wharf and sketched various people who caught her eye, but she found fault with all of her work. When she realized that she'd sketched a handsome man with a cartoon bubble coming out of his mouth containing the words "Would you like an aromatherapy massage?" she realized that she was, quite simply, obsessed.

That was when she decided to redouble her efforts at finding *him*. She went back to Echo Sound Studio and talked to Rocket, the space cadet recording engineer. He'd apologized for the amount of LSD he'd done in his youth and explained that the short-term memory was the first to go. So, honestly, he wasn't sure which guy had been *the* guy, or even if he had written down the guy's name at all.

After that, Annie realized that her pursuit was futile. So she did what countless women with a surfeit of money and time do for distraction. She went shopping.

The first thing she wanted was a new place to live. When she called the real estate agent that Michelle suggested, she made the mistake of saying that money was not a big issue, causing said agent to arrive at Annie's apartment building with a black stretch limousine twenty minutes later. For a day or two, it was flattering to be chauffeured around the City's wealthiest enclaves, as well as certain sections of Marin County, by eager-to-please Kris Perkins from Coldwell Banker, who assured Annie that she had sold more $5 million homes than any other Realtor in the Bay Area.

It turned out that $5 million hillside homes in Marin County didn't appeal to Annie. Neither did she see herself as a Pacific Heights mansion kind of girl. She did walk through an absolutely magnificent four-bedroom house in the Castro district, but decided that her love life was already challenging enough without living in a neighborhood that was ninety percent gay men.

Finally, sick of the fog in the Inner Sunset, yet loving that neighborhood's mix of races, ethnicities, and incomes, she decided to explore Potrero Hill, and she found her dream house merely by driving around with Michelle. It was a three-bedroom, two-and-a-half-bath Victorian on Connecticut Street, two stories, with huge east-facing bay windows and the original hardwood floors, which were in pristine condition. It was priced at $1.3 million. The owner, a small, balding man who was moving back to Michigan to help care for his gravely ill mother, was selling the place himself. He almost wept when Annie wrote a check for the entire amount and placed it in his hand.

After real estate came a new wardrobe. Annie spent three days visiting designer boutiques and high-end department stores. And she did buy some things, but she found that only when she mixed and matched them with her quirky thrift-store or flea-market finds did she feel truly at home in them.

Then there was makeover day, when she, Michelle, and Doris got streaks, glossing treatments, and haircuts at 77 Maiden Lane, followed by facials and makeup at Tru Spa. Then the three hot chicks (though Doris insisted it was two hot chicks and one colorful and still-hot hen) sashayed into a Lamborghini dealership prepared to pay cash for the Murcielago model, one of the ten most expensive cars in the world. In the end, though, Annie didn't feel like herself behind the wheel, so she opted for a hybrid Saturn and felt good about both buying American and saving the planet.

All of this was heady, fantastic fun, except for the one thing that was missing: his voice. It had disappeared the morning she went house hunting and stayed gone every moment that she was spending money. It wasn't until the spree was over—the house, the clothes, the new furniture, the car, the new La Perla lingerie she had on though there was no one to admire it but her—that he came back to her.

Don't give up on me, Annie.

Arghhh. It was maddening. When she couldn't think of any other way to find him, she'd decided to resort to national TV. Which was how she found herself in the backstage green-room of the Jay Leno show.

"Ms. Albright?"

Annie looked up at Chami, who still hovered in the doorway. "Yes?"

Chami moved closer and spoke confidentially. "I just wanted to tell you . . . I've been working on Jay's show for two years. We've had thousands of guests. Deepak Chopra. Tony Robbins. Lance Armstrong. Even Oprah. But no one has meant as much to me as you. I *mean* it."

"Thank you—"

"I just wanted to say . . . you changed my life. Before, I couldn't ever . . . you know. And I couldn't bring myself to buy a . . . you know . . . because it seemed so sleazy and icky. But Mr. V is sweet and fun and now I can . . ." A smile spread across her beautiful face.

"You're orgasmic? Congratulations!" Doris cried. "We're both so happy for you."

Chami nodded. "And I was able to show my boyfriend, Jason, how to . . . you know? So now I can . . . you know . . . with him, too. Plus, I had Jason listen to what Mr. Vibrator

says, and it helped him understand the kind of things I wish
he'd say."

"Fantastic," Annie told her, and meant it. It really was
very gratifying to know that she'd helped women of every
age, size, shape, and nationality achieve sexual satisfaction.

Chami got even closer to her and dropped her voice to a
bare whisper. "Please don't say this on the air, but I think that
Jay's wife just bought—"

A male voice came through the headset around Chami's
neck loud enough for Annie to hear. "Chami?"

The assistant quickly donned the headset. "Yes . . .
uhhuh . . . fine." She looked at Annie. "They just went to
commercial. It's time to escort you two to the set. But if you
could, quickly—" Out of her oversized black leather bag came
a Mr. Vibrator. Chami handed it and a permanent marker to
Annie. "It's a gift for my best friend's bachelorette party. Could
you autograph him?"

Annie quickly scribbled her name, hoping that the marker
was hygienic.

"Thanks." Chami dropped Mr. V back into her bag.
"Okay, ladies, follow me. It's showtime."

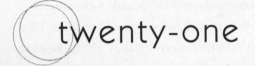# twenty-one

"You want sliced strawberries on that ice cream, Charlie?"

Charlie cupped his hands and called to his friend Patricia, who was in her kitchen fixing them a late-night snack. "Sure!" Then he plumped two pillows behind his head and reveled in the cool of her crisp white sheets.

As always, when he and Patricia found time to hook up, the sex had been robust fun. They'd been friends for years, having met by chance at the opening session of a California state teachers convention in Sacramento. The speaker had been Bill Cosby, whom they'd both enjoyed, but the dinner they'd shared afterward at La Scala, and the generous after-dinner sharing in Charlie's hotel room, had really been the highlights of the day.

It turned out that they both taught in the Bay Area. Patricia was a special-education instructor in the Pacifica school district and lived in an apartment near Lake Merced in the Outer Sunset. Since that time in Sacramento, they'd seen each other from time to time. One would call the other, and if both were inclined for pleasant conversation and sexual release, they'd rendezvous.

Patricia was girl-next-door cute, with chestnut hair she invariably wore in a ponytail, freckles on her pert nose, and equally pert breasts. That very first dinner in Sacramento, she had made it clear she wasn't interested in monogamy. Being a committed bisexual, she felt she could never get everything she wanted and needed from any one relationship. No reason to cause unnecessary heartache. This was more than fine with Charlie. He was able to enjoy Patricia's occasional companionship and the sexual smorgasbord that came with it without ever having to pick out the perfect kiss-off gift.

As Patricia puttered in the kitchen, Charlie closed his eyes and relaxed. The four weeks since his trip to Washington had been ridiculously hectic. Much to his chagrin, the secret that he was a contender for the High Summit Award didn't stay a secret very long, because two of the committee members, Lin Mei and Reginald Martinez, had made a site visit to evaluate Charlie's skills in the classroom firsthand.

Once the word was out, Mays-McCovey had done everything possible to support him. There was a special assembly where the distinguished guests spoke, his kids had been briefed on the importance of this visit, and—this was lucky—it happened to be an extremely interesting time in his classroom. Following his *Romeo and Juliet* theme, he'd assigned his kids to write their own short scene, inspired by Shakespeare but with characters of their own.

These scenes were read in class during the site visit. To

Charlie's pleasant astonishment, Jamal had written the best scene of all. Breaking every rule about writing what you know, he'd made the protagonists a Navajo Indian boy and a white girl in a dusty town in rural Arizona where there was tremendous tension between Indians and whites. At first Charlie was suspicious that Jamal might have plagiarized it— the writing and the idea were that good. But one day soon after that assignment, he'd stayed to grade papers after school, and since he was taking Jamal home, he'd asked Jamal to write a short story while he waited, just for fun. In an hour Jamal wrote something wildly creative and hysterically funny about space aliens who come to Earth and find out they're allergic to everything on the planet.

During the committee members' visit, Charlie had Jamal read his Arizona story for the class. Charlie didn't think he'd ever seen a smile as big as the one on Jamal's face— except for those on the two judges. After that, the judges wanted Charlie to take them back to the school's old building in Hunter's Point. There, because of the asbestos, they'd all donned protective gear and Principal Witherspoon guided them through the facility. The principal had spoken about the pedagogical challenges of the neighborhood, and the passion he and his staff had for serving the local youth. Charlie could tell that Lin and Reginald were impressed. He knew what idiocy it would be to get his hopes up, to think that he actually could win this award. But he couldn't help himself—he would visualize getting the call from the foundation, and then visualize his own call to Principal Witherspoon.

"I can save Mays-MacCovey," he would say. "The money from the High Summit Award? It's yours."

Patricia swung naked into the bedroom carrying a breakfast-in-bed tray. "French vanilla ice cream, sliced strawberries, cold apple cider, and biscotti. Should be enough to fuel us for another round."

"Sounds good." Charlie glanced at the clock. It was eleven forty-five now. He didn't have to be at school tomorrow until eleven because of a field trip the kids were taking to the Exploratorium, but he did have spelling tests to grade. If he stayed here until one thirty, he could be home by two, still wake up in time to do the grading. "I can stay until one thirty."

"Cool." She set the tray in Charlie's lap, then climbed back into bed next to him. "You like Leno?"

"Sure," he said easily, though to tell the truth he wasn't much of a late-night-talk-show fan. Movie stars pretending they were "just chatting" when really every little story, every cute anecdote, had been planned by whoever had the job of doing these things. Charlie really, truly, deeply hated fake. He bit into a biscotti.

"Leno's a hoot." Patricia found the remote, turned on her TV, and upped the volume. Charlie kept half an eye on the show and another on the tops of Patricia's breasts. The freckles really were so cute. It made him want to play dot-to-dot with his tongue.

"So we have two incredibly interesting guests with us tonight," Leno was saying. "Granddaughter and grandmother. You don't know them, but—and my wife can back me up on this—they are responsible for a product that the women in our audience know intimately. This is the best overnight success story I think I've ever heard. Ladies—I think you'll recognize their names. Annie Albright and her grandmother, Doris Rosen!"

Charlie chewed his biscotti as he watched the two women walk onto the set. The camera panned to the audience, where the women were giving them a standing ovation. The grandmother was fabulous, very well preserved, reminding him of a round-faced Shirley MacLaine. The granddaughter was petite and darling, with choppy blond hair and a sweetheart of a face. She wore gray trousers with a delicate blue silk blouse, and when the camera went to close-up, he saw that the blouse was the same shade as her cerulean eyes. She wasn't beautiful so much as she was . . . compelling. Endearing. Touching. He felt like putting his arms around her and protecting her from the world.

But that was crazy. It's not like he knew her. So why did he feel like he did?

Weird.

The younger woman sat next to Jay, the grandmother to her right. "Well, it's a pleasure to meet you, Annie and Doris," Jay said. "If I can call you that?"

"Sure," Annie replied. She sounded nervous. Her grandmother patted her leg.

"As the female half of our audience knows," Jay continued, "you created and marketed a certain adult product that's been sweeping the nation." Jay looked into the camera. "This might be a moment when you want to make sure the kids are in bed, mom and dad. It's called . . . Mr. Vibrator."

At the mention of the name Mr. Vibrator, there were more female whoops and cheers from the audience.

"I heard about this," Patricia exclaimed, then spooned some ice cream into her mouth. "Half the teachers at my school already own one."

"I see some of our audience has firsthand experience," Leno joked. "For the rest of us . . ." He reached into his drawer and took out a white vibrator that looked to Charlie like any other he'd ever seen. "Can you tell our audience, Annie, how you dreamt up this incredible product?"

"I'm not really sure," Annie told him. "It just sort of came to me."

"I'll say!" Leno cracked, which made this girl Annie blush. Charlie felt for her. Why'd she even come on the show? And what was the big deal with a vibrator, anyway?

"And you, Doris?" Jay asked.

"When Annie told me her idea, I knew it was genius," the grandmother said.

"She put up the original financing," Annie added.

"Well, you know what they say," Jay quipped. "The family that plays together." The audience laughed again. "Just in case you've been living on the moon for the last month and don't know how one of these works, let's let Annie demonstrate its unique qualities for you. With her clothes on." Leno handed the sex toy to Annie, who looked nervously at the camera.

"Well, Mr. Vibrator has two main features. One is, he's completely silent when you turn him on."

Jay raised his eyebrows. "Usually that's not considered a good thing. Some of us need feedback."

Annie blushed while the audience dissolved into gales of laughter again.

"And the other feature," Annie continued, "is that he, you know, talks."

She pressed a button on the base of the vibrator and held it near the tiny microphone that had been attached to the collar of her blouse. Out of the vibrator came a deep male voice.

"What you need is an aromatherapy massage and a pedicure."

Charlie jumped so high that the dessert tray tumbled off of him and onto the bed, spilling ice cream, fruit, and biscotti everywhere.

"What the hell—are you okay, Charlie?"

"You're perfect exactly as you are. Have another piece of chocolate cake."

Holy shit on a fucking shingle. It was *his* voice.

"Charlie?" Patricia called again. "Are you sick?"

"Fine!" Charlie yelped. "Just . . . a killer cramp." He grabbed at the bottom of a foot with his one hand and helped Patricia put the stuff back onto her tray with the other, all the while keeping his eyes glued to the TV.

"You are the most fantastic, gorgeous, sexy woman in the world."
Where—how the hell did they get my voice?

Then he remembered. That thing he'd gone to with Mark a couple of months ago, a voice-over for female affirmation tapes. Charlie recalled sharing a blunt with the stoned sound engineer and recording the lines with which every guy there had to audition. *This* was the female affirmation tape?

"Tell me everything. I'll listen," said Mr. Vibrator.

"Wow," Jay remarked to Annie. "How can us real guys compete with that?"

"You can't," Cameron Diaz quipped from the other end of the couch. "Sorry, honey!" she added, batting her eyes at the camera.

"Foot any better?" Patricia asked Charlie once all the food was back on the tray. "Let me take this back to the kitchen."

"Yeah, it's better," Charlie muttered as Patricia walked away. Meanwhile, all he could do was stare at the TV screen.

Jay leaned conspiratorially toward Annie. "So tell me this, Annie. Who's the voice that women all over the world are falling in love with?"

Oh no. Oh no. Charlie felt like barfing. And then he remembered: he'd written down Mark's name and address. Surely Annie was about to tell the world that the voice behind the member was a guy named Mark Wolfson. He held his breath.

Annie shrugged. "That's the problem. I don't know. I thought I knew, and I contacted the person I thought it was, but it turned out not to be him. There was some kind of weird mix-up at the recording studio. So I don't have his name."

Charlie fell back against the pillows and exhaled, wiping the flop sweat from his brow. Damn. That had been close. He would just imagine what adding "The Voice of Mr. Vibrator" to his résumé would do to his career in education. It would end it, that's what it would do.

"So we have a mystery voice, do we?" Jay asked Annie.

"We do," Annie agreed. "But it's a mystery I really, really want to solve. I just . . . I *need* to find him."

"Well, I can do something about that," Jay promised. He faced the camera and his audience. "Ladies and gentlemen, the *Tonight* show is hereby offering a reward of one hundred thousand dollars to the person who can correctly identify the man who fits the member!"

The audience went wild. Charlie buried his head in his hands.

Patricia put a hand on his shoulder. "Are you sick?"

He nodded. It was all he could manage. No one had ever been more thoroughly fucked without physical contact than he was right now. A hundred thou was a great motivator. Someone was going to figure out that the voice of Mr. Vibrator belonged to Charlie. Then the Summit Foundation would find out. And then, he could kiss his award, and his ass, good-bye.

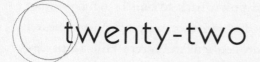# twenty-two

Whup-whup-whup.

Annie came slowly out of a dream, where she and the voice of Mr. Vibrator were running toward each other in slow motion across a crowded room; she couldn't see his face, but she knew it was him. When his arms finally wrapped around her, and he pressed his lips to hers for a perfect kiss, she felt electrified with joy. She looked down to realize that the red pumps she was wearing, à la Dorothy in *The Wizard of Oz*, had, quite literally, lit up.

Whup-whup-whup.

What was that annoying noise? She didn't want to stop dreaming, because at long last she was just about to get a good look at Mr. Vibrator's face, and—

Whup-whup-whup.

Damn.

She swam up from her dream, the last filmy edges dissolving, all because of some damn thing that was making some damn racket outside the window of her new house. Okay, so she couldn't go back to sleep. But she delayed getting up to see what the noise was, and instead lay in bed, remembering the night before.

She and Doris had flown back to San Francisco on Jay Leno's private jet immediately after the taping. A limo picked them up at SFO and drove them to Potrero Hill. Doris decided to spend the night at Annie's instead of going all the way out to the Richmond district, so that they could watch the show they'd just taped together, and so Doris could do some Shabbat shopping at the Ferry Building farmers market in the morning.

But as they'd hustled up the magnificent stone steps of Annie's new house—she was still having trouble coming to grips with the fact that she owned it and didn't even have to think about a mortgage—she found herself mortified by what she'd done. What had she been thinking, going on national TV to ask America to look for Him? It was nuts. Why hadn't her grandmother stopped her? Here she was, a monumentally successful businesswoman, obsessed with a voice in her head. At least, thank God, she hadn't confessed on Leno that she heard his voice talking to her personally, or her insane idea that somehow he was her destiny and she was his.

"Your mother is going to call, you know," Doris informed Annie, as they headed into the family room.

Oh, God, her mother. Annie felt humiliated all over again. She could just imagine what her proper, crepe-soled-shoes math professor mother would think of her sex toy, not to mention finding out that her daughter and her mother had gone on national TV to talk about it.

Her parents were in the middle of her dad's retirement cruise, a gift from twenty friends who had pooled their money for tickets for a six-week voyage. Her parents had started in Lisbon, gone around the Cape of Good Hope, and then headed back up the east coast of Africa.

"How can she possibly call?" Annie demanded. "They're on a cruise!"

"Annie, dear. You've never been on a cruise," Doris pointed out.

"So?"

"So satellite TV, darling," Doris explained. "Check your messages."

Annie called in to her voice mail. There were a few calls from friends and acquaintances back east where the show had already aired, congratulating her on her success and wishing her luck on her quest—one asked for money to open a boutique—but thankfully nothing from her parents.

"Well, I dodged that bullet," Annie announced. She sagged onto her rust and taupe couch.

"Temporarily," Doris said. She looked around the room, which was furnished in an eclectic combination of old furniture of Annie's with which she'd been unable to part and new furniture a decorator had chosen. "Where's the remote?"

"Look on top of the dolls." Annie had installed custom-made Plexiglas shelves at one end of the room to show off her collection, including two more nineteenth-century models she'd recently purchased from Ethereal.

"Got it," Doris announced, waving the remote around as she headed back to the couch. "Let's see how we look. Leno's about to come on."

Suddenly Annie couldn't bear the thought of seeing herself on TV. "Gramma, would you mind if we didn't watch after all?"

Doris sat next to Annie and smoothed some hair off her face. "You're having second thoughts about what we did?"

Annie nodded. "Suddenly I saw myself through Mom's eyes. And I cringed."

"My darling granddaughter," Doris said. "I love your mother with all my heart. She's a wonderful person. But between you and me, she's always been rather constipated. What she thinks about this? TS."

"Tough shit?" Annie translated, and giggled. She got an idea. "You know what I'd really like right now? Hot chocolate, and—"

"Battleship," her grandmother declared. "Definitely Battleship."

Annie smiled as her grandmother went off to the state-of-the-art kitchen to make her special hot chocolate—it involved milk and fresh cream and high-test melting chocolate. She followed a few minutes later, after checking her upstairs computer to see if there'd been a sales bump back east. There had been. Twenty thousand units sold in the last two hours.

For a while, as they played the same game they used to play when Annie was a girl, Annie forgot about mystery men, millions of dollars, and even appearing on a national TV show. But then, at about eleven forty-five, Annie's landline and cell rang simultaneously.

"We must be on the air," Doris observed. "B-2."

"Hit," Annie acknowledged, crossing the ship off her chart. Both phones kept ringing.

"Aren't you going to answer?" Doris asked.

Annie shook her head. The phones stopped, and immediately started again. She imagined the worst—crackpots and wackos, begging for a chance to prove that they were the voice of Mr. Vibrator. Ugh. She turned off the ringers, hugged her grandmother, and went upstairs to bed, imagining the endless and gross messages she'd have to pick up in the morning. Maybe she should let Doris screen the calls.

The last thing she remembered thinking before she finally dozed off: What had she been thinking?

"Annie?"

She opened her eyes and craned around. "Hi, Gramma."

Clad in the Betty Boop print pajamas Annie had lent her the night before, Doris crossed the room and handed Annie one of two mugs of coffee she was carrying. They were both designed in shaky squiggles, hearts and stars, painted during a crafts session by one of the residents at the senior center. Annie sat up and sipped gratefully, as the damned *whup-whup-whup* continued outside.

Did the Department of Public Works have to pick this particular morning to repave her street? Not that Annie recalled it needed repaving.

"You should keep more food in your house, Annele. There's no fresh fruit. I'll buy some when I go out."

"Thanks. Did last night really happen?"

"It did," her grandmother confirmed, sitting on the end of Annie's new king-size oak canopy bed. "And it worked. I checked sales this morning. Another forty thousand units ordered. Come downstairs, rich granddaughter. I'll make you a bagel. Those you've got frozen. I looked in your freezer." She rose and started toward the door, as the strange noise outside suddenly got louder.

"That's driving me nuts!" Annie exclaimed.

"When you get up, have a look outside, maybe you can tell them to be a little quieter," Doris said casually. She kissed Annie on the forehead and walked out. Annie took another minute with her coffee. The longer she could put off facing the barrage of phone messages she knew was waiting for her—including her mother's—the better.

Whup-whup-whup.

Dammit. She threw back her silk and eiderdown paisley quilt, marched over to the picture window, and peered out. And almost dropped her coffee cup. The street in front of her house was blocked off, and a substantial crowd was being kept away from her steps by a handful of uniformed cops. Out on the street itself were several television remote trucks and vans. Annie spotted the vehicles of *Entertainment Tonight!* and E!, plus a couple of local network affiliates. She heard the *whup-whup* again and looked skyward. A helicopter was circling a thousand feet over her house.

"Hey! There she is!"

Though her window was shut, she heard someone shout and then point—that was followed by more shouts and pointing. Photographers were raising cameras with telephoto lenses, and she saw the TV cameramen jockeying for position.

She snapped her curtains shut and staggered back toward her bed. Holy shit. She was at the center of a goddamn media circus. The worst of it was, she knew it was of her own making.

"Good morning," Doris called cheerfully when Annie, clad in jeans she'd had forever and a ratty old sweatshirt, skittered into the kitchen.

"Did you see outside?" she asked her grandmother, horrified.

"Of course. Sit and eat." Doris slid a toasted bagel in front of Annie. "You want more coffee, Miss Celebrity?"

Annie lifted the shade and peeked out the rear window, then heaved a sigh of relief. Evidently the police line was holding, and no one had been able to get into her—

"Annie! I have to talk to you!" a guy with long, stringy hair yelled as he made a mad dash for the back door. Annie watched in horror as a city policeman tackled him and then snapped on the handcuffs.

"Oh, my God, this is insane." She checked the dead bolt on the back door and then pulled the window curtains all the way shut.

"S.S. darling, S.S. Sex sells." Doris poured them both more coffee. "You're a brilliant girl, Annie. You must have known, somewhere in your great brain, that you'd wake up to *this*. So let's talk the R.R. about last night."

"Real reason," Annie translated.

How could she tell her grandmother that she'd fallen in love with a voice? The only one who knew the truth was Michelle, who had sworn she would take the secret to her grave or her wedding, whichever came first.

This was so hard to do.

"The voice, Gramma," Annie admitted. "The voice of Mr. Vibrator. I know this is stupid and juvenile . . . but I can't get it out of my head. I feel like I know him, or I'm supposed to know him. Or something. I know it sounds crazy."

"I've heard crazier," Doris said, then spread some salmon cream cheese on one of the bagels and put it on Annie's plate. "Did you know Bella fell in love with the milkman's son before she ever met him? Why? Because she smelled his cologne on a letter he wrote to another girl. And she married him six months later. Who knows about such things?"

"I've tried so hard to find him," Annie rushed on. "I've called and looked. And you know that time Michelle and I went camping back east?"

Doris nodded. "With no Chinese food delivery. I did think that was odd. So, go on, darling. What about it?"

Maybe if there hadn't been several dozen strangers and half a dozen media trucks parked on the street, Annie would have been less forthcoming. But faced with the choices of dealing with the media, listening to deviants on her voice mail, or confessing all to her grandmother, she opted for the confessional.

When she finally wound down, she eyed her grandmother over the coffee mug. "Do you think I need to see a shrink, Gramma?"

"For what you just told me? *Feh!*" Doris made a face. "I have a friend, Jeanne Hopson, from my yoga class; lovely woman, short, plump, maybe sixty-seven, sixty-eight. Not Jewish but all right, no one is perfect.

"Anyway, her husband, Robert, is movie-star handsome," Doris continued. "She tells me the story of how they met. It was her first day of high school, she was fourteen years old, short and plump even then, according to her. So she walks into the cafeteria and sees this tall, gorgeous boy she had never seen before, a senior, dating all the prettiest girls. Jeanne turns to her friend Charlotte—why I remember her name I don't know—and she says: 'See that handsome boy, Charlotte, over there surrounded by all the most popular girls? That is the boy I'm going to marry.' And she did. To this day, the man is still a looker, and he still adores Jeanne. So who knows?" She leaned toward Annie and put her hand over her granddaughter's hand. "Passion, Annie. She had a passion. She *had* to meet Robert."

"What if it didn't work out?" Annie asked.

"Eat your bagel, it's no good stale." Her grandmother shrugged. "Life is full of 'what if,' Annele. But some things are meant to be. Your Grandpa Murray was meant to come into the USO when I was on duty, which is why you are here today. Jeanne's Rob was meant to come to the cafeteria. Bella was meant to smell that cologne. And this man who is the voice of your creation? Maybe he was meant to do this recording, and you were meant to find him."

"Do you really believe that's possible?" Annie asked wistfully.

"My darling granddaughter. The question is—do *you* believe it?"

Annie nodded.

"Well, then! I wish for you a B.L., my darling. A Big Love."

Doris spread her arms wide and hugged Annie. When they let go, Annie saw tears in her grandmother's eyes.

"Ignore me," Doris said, and dabbed at the tears with a paper napkin. "You get very emotional after menopause. So you should listen to your phone messages. He might have seen Leno. He might be waiting for you to call him, right this minute."

"What if it's my mom? From the cruise ship."

"Annele, this is why God invented 'press three to delete, nine to save.'"

The metallic voice that greeted her carried a warning. "Your mailbox is full. To play your messages, press one-one." Annie found a small notebook and a pencil, and sat down to listen.

"Annie? It's . . ."

Static garbled the next several moments, but Annie recognized the voice immediately. Her mother, calling from the cruise ship. As best as Annie could make out through the static, she'd seen Leno on a satellite download while they were in port someplace in Mozambique.

"Vibrators, Annie? We sent you to college for—"

That was it. The call cut off. Well, at least that one was over with, though there was no doubt what her mother's opinion was on the whole business. Fortunately, she and her dad wouldn't be back in the States for two more weeks.

The rest of the messages were exactly as Annie had anticipated. Freaks, wackos, and nutcases, mixed in with dozens of additional interview offers, from *The View* to *Larry King Live* to Country Music Television (she couldn't figure that one out at all). Four people claimed to represent Howard Stern, and one of them sounded eerily like the shock jock himself. As for the freaks and wackos, Annie learned quickly that the sound of heavy breathing inevitably led to more heavy breathing, and to delete before the climactic climax, so to speak.

There were plenty of pretenders to the throne of Mr. Vibrator. Thirty-seven guys, in fact. Plus one girl.

Two and a half hours later, Annie had a splitting headache. But she'd also deleted every single message.

"So?" Doris asked, coming back into the kitchen. "I cleaned your upstairs bathroom. You should pour some Drano down those pipes. Or I'll call Roz's son-in-law. He's a plumber. So?"

"No Him," Annie reported.

Doris picked up the breakfast dishes, which were still on the table. "When it's meant to be, you'll find him. Meanwhile, I went outside to talk to the press."

"Why would you do that?"

"Because your car is parked on the street and you're going to drop me at the farmers market soon, and I thought if I did it now it would be better than later when I'm in a hurry. They were very nice. Maybe you should do it, too."

"God, no!" The idea of facing more cameras was horrifying.

"They're never going away unless you do," Doris pointed out. "Plus a very nice police captain who invited me out for coffee said that if you would just talk to them for five minutes, he'd get everyone to clear out."

"A policeman asked you to have coffee?" Annie was still back on a little thing Doris had slipped into the middle of her usual run-on sentence.

"Captain O'Brien. Widowed two years ago. His mother was Jewish, so he's Jewish. He's sixty-five but doesn't want to retire. I like that. Murray said he'd work until he couldn't anymore."

"Did you say yes?"

Doris shrugged. "Coffee never hurt anyone."

"Fine." Annie rose.

"Where are you going?"

"To talk to them." She headed toward the front door.

"You might want to comb your hair, Annele," Doris advised.

Annie shook her head. "Today, they can take me as I am."

"How come you don't know who the voice is?"

"Is this a publicity stunt?"

"Annie, is it true you're really gay?"

"How often do you use Mr. Vibrator yourself, Annie?"

Annie stood at the bottom of her steps, surrounded by cameras, bright lights, reporters, and gawkers, and waited patiently for the questions to peter out before she even considered saying anything.

"Thank you," she told the throng, once it had quieted down. "This is an actual neighborhood, and I'm happy to talk to you now if you promise to go home afterward." Dead silence greeted this proposal, which she interpreted as assent. "Okay, well . . ." She cleared her throat. "This is not a publicity stunt. Mr. Vibrator is a product that has brought pleasure to millions of women around the globe. The voice of Mr. Vibrator, through a series of strange events, is still unknown to me. If anyone out there can figure out who the voice is, I'll double the reward that Jay Leno offered last night on TV. That's two hundred thousand dollars," she added, just in case anyone didn't know the original figure.

"For that kind of money, everyone will claim to be him!" a reporter called out. "How will you know when it's the right guy?"

"I'll know," Annie insisted, because someplace deep inside herself told her that this was true. "Don't worry. I'll know."

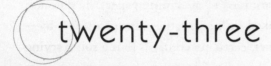 twenty-three

Mays-McCovey had relocated to the humanities building at USF, a campus that was going to be back in full swing with its full complement of college and graduate students in approximately three weeks. At that time, the charter school would have to find another new home. Meanwhile fund-raising to rehab the school's campus in Hunter's Point had stalled at the halfway mark, despite the best efforts of the principal, the faculty, and even the students.

As far as Charlie could see, the only shot they had was for him to win the High Summit Award. Strangely enough, the grants would be announced on the same day that the academy had to vacate USF. After the site visit from the foundation committee members, he'd been on the verge of confidence. After the Leno show, though, that confidence was in shambles. It didn't take a certified teacher skilled in the ways of No Child Left Behind to know that just as a Nobel Prize would not be awarded to a pornographer, the High Summit Award would not be awarded to the voice behind the world's most popular talking vibrator.

He'd left Patricia right after Leno, claiming a bizarre onslaught of idiopathic cramps that would distract from any extracurricular activities. Instead of grading papers, he'd done a shot of vodka, cranked up his favorite music to think by— classic Allman Brothers—and paced in his living room trying to concoct some kind of plan that would not result in his life and his school being completely ruined.

For a while he'd considered going directly to Joe Witherspoon first thing in the morning and telling the truth: that he'd been duped and recorded under false pretenses. After all, a female affirmation CD was not the same thing as a talking vibrator, and everything he had to say was G-rated in any case. There'd been no profanity, and nothing sexually explicit. Any parent could play his recording for their kids . . .

Well, not really. Not if you paid any attention to what it was being played *on*.

Then he dropped the idea. Witherspoon was having enough trouble just trying to keep his school afloat. If it got out that one of his teachers was the voice of America's hottest sex toy, he could turn into the laughingstock of the California educational community. Like *that* was going to get people to donate money. Also, while there were plenty of liberal parents who'd chosen to send their children to Mays-McCovey, there were plenty of conservative ones, too, and Charlie guessed that they would go ballistic.

Which would not just ruin his career, but it could ruin the school as well.

His only hope, he finally decided, was that not many people had watched Leno and that this big fear would turn out to be a non-fear. After all, Patricia had been right there next to him, and she hadn't put his voice together with the voice on TV. If she hadn't, maybe he didn't need to be so fearful. Somewhat comforted by this thought, he did one more shot of vodka, graded the spelling papers, and went to sleep.

The next day, he got to school at eleven thirty, an hour before the kids were due back from the Exploratorium. By the time he'd finished setting up a fresh pot of coffee in the teachers' lounge, he realized that his hopes of the night before were laughable and that he was, in fact, utterly and totally fucked.

"Girl, my best friend gave me one for my birthday last week. I thought I'd died and gone to heaven."

Over by the photocopy machine, Tonya Roosevelt, the middle-aged and middling zaftig science teacher, was expounding to two of the kindergarten aides. Charlie swallowed hard and hoped they were not talking about what he was afraid they were talking about. He dared a glance at the women, who were all nodding their agreement.

"If I'd have had a Mr. Vibrator when I was married to Terrance, we might never have gotten a divorce," Tonya concluded.

Shit. Then Greg Landis, the gay guidance counselor, looked up from where he was addressing envelopes. "Girls, I say buy one for every room in your flat. You never know when you'll experience an overwhelming need for his particular brand of solace."

The women all laughed. "You saw Leno?" Tonya asked.

"Are you kidding?" Greg grinned. "I ordered one for myself when it was over. That Annie Albright is the cutest thing. I'd almost go straight for her."

"I think she looks like Renee Zellweger when she was younger," Tonya decided.

"Are you talking about Mr. Vibrator?" Katie Unger, a cute midtwenties music teacher with a J.Lo kind of ass and a penchant for short skirts, sailed into the room. "It's so darling. And that voice! I ordered one right after the show. Charlie, can you bring me a cup of coffee when that's done?"

Charlie waved weakly.

"I was listening to KCBS on my way in," Katie went on. "He said Annie upped the reward for finding the voice this morning. Two hundred thousand dollars."

Charlie choked loudly on his coffee. Two hundred grand?

"You okay, Charlie?" Tonya asked.

Charlie pointed to his throat, hoping this would convey that his coffee had gone down the wrong pipe.

"Don't forget my coffee, Charlie," Katie reminded him. "So anyway, all these guys started calling in, and they all claimed to be the voice. Of course, none of them sounded like him, because the host keeps playing the real voice over and over."

"Yo, man, I'm that vibrator dude," Tonya intoned in a deep voice, imitating a Haight Street stoner, to the mirth of her friends.

"Actually, this one stoner did call in," Katie said. "He

said his name was Rocket, and that he was the sound engineer who recorded the voice. But he just couldn't remember
the guy's name. Charlie, you've got my coffee?"

Charlie realized there was no way to avoid the conversation any longer. He poured Katie a Styrofoam cupful—he
knew she took it black, that she was constantly on a diet, and
that her ex-boyfriend had made her feel self-conscious about
her ass—and brought it over to her.

"Thanks," she told him. "Did you see Leno last night by
any chance?"

On impulse, Charlie pointed to his own throat. "Laryngitis," he rasped.

Katie looked concerned. "Are you okay? Do you need to
see the nurse?"

"Just a cold," he whispered.

"Poor Charlie," Katie cooed. She'd flirted with him on
many occasions, and Charlie really did think she was very
cute. But it didn't seem wise to him to graze in his own pas-
ture, so to speak, so he never got involved with women with
whom he worked. She put a cool hand to his forehead and
gazed into his eyes. "I think you have a fever. You're really
very hot." Her significant eye contact put an interesting spin
on that.

He took a step backward and tried to make his whisper
even more pathetic. "Don't want to infect anyone."

"Honey, his head isn't what's burning," Tonya commented.

"Nurse. That's a good idea." Charlie decided it was a
good time to go to his classroom. To continue the ruse,

maybe he could borrow a megaphone from the cheer squad so his students could understand what he was saying. But what about tomorrow? And the day after tomorrow? What then? Short of some miracle disease that he could find on the Internet, Charlie knew he was fucked.

"Yeah, just some kind of cold bug," Charlie rasped into his phone. Patricia had called not long after he got home to see how his cramps were doing and whether he wanted to pick up where they'd left off the night before. But Charlie begged off on account of his *terrible cold,* one of the *worst colds* he'd ever had. So bad, in fact, that he was thinking of going to the *doctor.* His voice was *just about gone*, in fact. Patricia was appropriately sympathetic and proposed a rain check that Charlie accepted with no date certain.

He was just hanging up when he heard his doorbell ring. Damn. He'd have to play Charlie Has Laryngitis in person. Better to ignore it.

Bam-bam-bam! Whoever it was, they were now pounding their fist against the door. Then he heard a booming voice.

"It's Mark! I know you're in there, man. Your car's outside!" Mark. But he wasn't due back from the trail for another month, at least. "Come on, man! Open up! I'm not gonna nail you!"

He knew. Goddamn Mark knew.

Charlie opened the door for his friend.

"You know, Charlie, I never thought of you as a dick before." Mark smirked.

Charlie dead-eyed him. No need to fake laryngitis. "And the critics say you can't play comedy."

"Saw Leno last night in the emergency room in Roanoke, Virginia," Mark explained. "Which is where I was, doubled over in pain. Fucking kidney stone. I wasn't feeling right out on the trail the last few days, so I packed it in early. Passed it this morning, caught a plane home this afternoon, and here I am. You got a brew?"

"Anchor Steam or Coors?" Charlie asked over his shoulder as Mark followed him to the kitchen. "It's good to see you, man. I missed you." He gave his friend a spontaneous hug.

"I missed you too. Anchor Steam."

Charlie took two beers from the fridge, tossed one to his friend, and popped the other one open for himself. For someone ill enough to spend the evening in the emergency room, Mark looked really good. He'd lost at least twenty pounds since he'd hit the trail, his face was tanned, and there were sinewy muscles under his T-shirt. He looked more fit than he had in years. Still, he figured he should ask.

"Should you be drinking, Mark?"

"I pissed the little fucker out—it was the size of a small child. I wouldn't wish one on my worst enemy. But I'm good for now." Mark took a thirsty pull on his beer, then smiled at Charlie. "So you know, huh?"

"If anyone finds out it's me, I'm fucked, Mark. I mean it." Charlie settled down on one of his kitchen chairs.

Mark took another one. "You signed my name on your release form, I take it."

"It seemed harmless at the time."

"You were trying to do me a favor, man. I appreciate it."
Mark took the check from Turn Me On, Inc., out of the
pocket of his jeans and put it on the table. "You have a pen?
I'll sign it over to you. Two grand."

Charlie waved his hand. "Keep it. I've got a bigger problem. Like, a million-dollar problem. And damn me if I can
figure out what to do."

Mark raised his bushy eyebrows, and Charlie filled him
in as succinctly as he could on the events of the last six weeks.
"I really thought I had a chance at that award, Mark. But
now I think it's all over."

Mark whistled. "You've been busy. How'd you happen
to record your voice that day, anyway?"

Charlie tilted the beer back and drained it in one long
swallow. "What difference does it make? I never thought
they'd actually pick me." He gave Mark a bleak look. "Did
you know that Annie what's-her-name doubled the reward
to find me this morning?"

"I can go one better than that," Mark replied. "I actually
met her."

Charlie looked puzzled. "When? At the audition?"

"No. I know this is going to sound crazy, man, but it was
out on the AT."

"She's a hiker?" Charlie couldn't believe that the woman
he'd seen on TV had a penchant for backpacking.

"I don't know. But I rescued her backpack after she fell in
this stream, and she recognized me. She thought I was the

one who did the recording, told me she'd already sent me the check. Nice woman by the way. Sweet. Great ass. She had a cute friend with her."

For a moment there, Charlie had felt the briefest instant of hope. It gave way quickly to despair when he made the obvious logical connection. "She knew it wasn't you, then."

Mark shook his head. "Let's call a dick a dick, man. There's only one voice that's going to match the recording. That's yours."

"Maybe if I pretend I have this really bad cold and I don't talk for a week or two, the whole thing will blow over."

"Yeah, and I'm gonna start pissing diamonds instead of kidney stones." Mark sat forward, and waved off Charlie's offer of another Anchor Steam. "Listen to me, man, because I'm about to give you some excellent advice. Someone is going to out you, and I don't mean me—although for two hundred thousand dollars it's damned tempting. Do it yourself. Then at least you get the money, instead of some other asshole. You're taking the pain. You may as well get the gain."

Charlie stared out his kitchen window and thought this over. He'd wanted to believe that there was some smart way that he could ride out this storm, but his best friend was right. He'd seen it in the *Chronicle,* and heard it on afternoon talk radio as he drove Jamal home. He'd even had to change the station once the deejay started playing his voice recording. It seemed to be the only thing that anyone in San Francisco was talking about. It was only a matter of time before someone pointed the finger at him. Probably that stoner sound engineer. Hell, for all Charlie knew, there were security cameras at the sound studio, and someone was going to get the bright idea of checking them.

He felt like a mouse trapped in a maze, but at least at the end of it was two hundred thousand dollars worth of cheese. It wasn't the million Mays-McCovey needed, but he'd turn it over to Joe anyway.

And after that . . . he didn't have a clue.

twenty-four

"We found him!"

It was eight in the morning when one of Leno's producers, Reese Payton, called, her voice triumphant with certitude. Annie had just gotten out of the shower and wore nothing but pink fluffy slippers on her feet and hope on her sleeve. Her knees began to shake and she sat down on the edge of her bed.

"Are you sure?"

"He called us last night," Reese reported. "We had half a dozen different staffers listen to him, and we're all certain."

"That's . . . that's fantastic."

"No shit," Reese said. "He's from San Francisco, obviously, so I flew up with a camera crew first thing. We're out by Ocean Beach, and it's a beautiful morning. If we send a car, can you be ready in an hour to meet him? We'll film the meet and greet and confirmation, then we'll fly you on separate planes down to L.A. for the taping tonight. They're already promo-ing it on the *Today* show. Ratings will go through the roof. So, you good?"

Annie could feel herself starting to hyperventilate. The idea of meeting him was thrilling, yes. But it also filled her with dread. "Umm . . . couldn't he and I maybe meet privately first? Before you start, you know, filming?"

"Are you kidding? Millions of women will tune in to see that exact moment. They all feel like they're *you,* Annie. It's a total Cinderella story—we can't deprive our viewers of that. This is like *The Bachelor* on steroids. On NBC!"

Honestly, Annie didn't really care about the viewers. All she wanted to do was meet the voice. But she knew she would never have found him if it hadn't been for the exposure on Leno, and the original reward he'd offered. She owed him the payoff.

"Okay," she agreed. "An hour. What should I wear?"

"We'll do hair and makeup when you get to the beach. We're selling you as Every Girl, so dress casually. Think girl-next-door sexy—tight jeans—sell your assets—a tank top works, maybe a push-up bra. No prints, no dark colors. We good?"

"Yes. I guess, but—"

"Time's a-wasting, Annie. Go get ready."

"Hold on! At least tell me something about him," Annie pleaded. "What's his name? What does he do for a living?"

"Nuh-uh. We don't want to step on the natural surprise of the meet-cute. See you at the beach."

"Okay, Annie. He's going to run across the sand to meet you, carrying a picnic basket," Reese explained, as the makeup artist dusted loose powder across Annie's face. The producer was tall and large-boned, with an outsized nose and a receding chin, which made Annie think that she had to be very good at her job. Annie reckoned that people in show business in Los Angeles who didn't look fabulous were probably really good at their job, because they hadn't been hired as eye candy.

The shoot had been set up on the beach near the world-famous Cliff House, as far west as you could go and still be in San Francisco. A growing group of gawkers was being held back by red rope and various underlings in headsets. This being San Francisco, an enterprising mime was taking advantage of the crowd by doing his act in return for donations.

"But . . . would a guy really do that?" Annie asked hesitantly, as the makeup artist gave way to a balding guy who sprayed something on her hair. "I mean, run across a beach with a picnic basket? Heterosexual men don't even *own* picnic baskets."

Reese sighed. "It's *romantic,* Annie. It's television. So, look. He runs across the beach. He puts down the basket. Take a beat, look into each other's eyes, but don't make it look staged or anything. Don't worry. If it doesn't seem right, we can always go back and do it again."

"But—" Annie began. She couldn't finish her protest, though, because the makeup artist came back. A white girl with dreads down to her waist, she swiped pink lip gloss across Annie's lips. Meanwhile, Reese stepped away and spoke to someone over her headset, and then came back to Annie.

"Okay, Juana says the light is perfect right now. You good, Annie?"

"Um, yeah. I guess."

"Then let's go." Reese took Annie by the arm and led her over to a circle that had been drawn in the sand for the meet-cute. The closer Annie got to it, the more nervous she felt. What if he'd only come for the money? Back when she was poor, if someone had offered her two hundred grand just to show up and say "It's me!" she would have jumped at the chance.

"Where is he?" Annie asked Reese, as the gorgeous production assistant she remembered from the greenroom at the studio, Chami, joined them.

"They're keeping him in a little tent area they set up down the beach," Chami exclaimed. "God, I'm so excited, I feel like *I'm* the one meeting him!"

Annie eyed Chami's skinny body and lush curves, clad in low-cut black trousers and a pink tank top stretched tight over her gravity-defying breasts. No doubt the voice would prefer to be meeting Chami, or someone who looked like Chami. The best Annie could come up with this morning was a simple white T-shirt, ordinary jeans, and flat sandals that she hoped would work in the sand. She felt ordinary. And anxious. Ordinary and anxious were really not a good combination.

"Hey, she's that dildo chick!" a guy shouted from beyond the rope. Annie blushed furiously.

He was met by a chorus of female disapproval. "Shut up, asshole! We love you, Annie! Go for it, Annie!"

"You're a star now," Chami told her.

God, was that true? Annie shuddered. She'd never, ever wanted to be a star. All she'd wanted to do was meet the voice.

Reese peeled off, and Annie and Chami waited for three production assistants to lay down a colorful quilt, a bucket of ice with an open bottle of Taittinger's, and two crystal flutes. Evidently Mr. V would run in with all the other makings of a picnic in his basket.

"Uh-huh . . . uh-huh . . . got it," Chami said, responding to whatever was being said into her headset—Annie couldn't hear. "Reese says you should sit on the blanket and look wistfully out at the ocean. He'll run into the frame. You catch a glimpse of him out of the corner of your eye. You jump up. It's him! You're so happy. He'll drop the picnic basket and the two of you will embrace. Okay?"

Annie's mouth felt so dry she could hardly swallow. "What if we don't feel like embracing? I mean, what if that isn't natural?"

Chami chuckled. "Of course it isn't natural. It's television. Just make it *look* natural."

Look natural, Annie told herself. *Make it look natural.*

She sat on the blanket as two cameramen edged closer and two more stylists adjusted her hair and T-shirt. Then one of them clipped a wireless mike to the top of her shirt and ran the attached cord down her back.

"And Annie!"

Annie looked up—Chami was fairly glaring at her. "Never look at the goddamn camera. Forget we're even here!"

She made the okay sign with one hand, afraid to move lest she upset whatever primping had just been done.

A chubby guy in khaki shorts and a Hawaiian shirt plodded out into the sand carrying an electronic slate, which he held up to the nearest camera. Annie could read it: LENO #12,567. ANNIE GETS HER MAN. Then Annie heard the four most ominous words in the English language: "Take One . . . and . . . action!"

Look natural. Make it look natural.

Oh, God.

There he was. Down by the waterline. Running up the beach toward her. She got to her feet, and realized he was tall, wore baggy white cotton drawstring pants, a red T-shirt with a white heart painted at its center, and his long dark hair blew in the breeze as he ran. The picnic basket was tucked between both arms like a fullback determined not to fumble no matter how hard he was tackled.

As he got closer and closer, Annie realized that he wasn't just tall-tall, he was Big Bird tall, with intense, deep-set eyes, an Ichabod Crane nose, and a scraggly soul patch. Ten feet from her, he dropped the picnic basket to the sand. And then, she was in his arms. Her nose was plastered against the painted white heart on his shirt. That's how tall he was.

He pulled away and held her at arm's length so that he could look soulfully into her eyes. "Annie!" he cried.

Omigod. It was *the voice*. But how could she reciprocate when she didn't know his name?

"You!" she cried.

"Laredo. It's Laredo. I go by one name," he murmured. "I'm Laredo." He put both long, skinny hands over the heart on his T-shirt, then gestured outward. "This heart . . . is for you." Then he knelt in the sand, took one of her hands in both of his, and kissed it. "M'lady. 'I love your thighs.'"

Annie couldn't deny that he *sounded* like the voice of Mr. Vibrator. But something deep inside of her told her he *wasn't* the voice. What she felt was . . . nothing. But the cameras were rolling, and Laredo went back for the picnic basket, then set it on the blanket. When he sat down, she did too. The next thing she knew, he was pouring champagne.

"To us," he said, clinked his glass against hers, then entwined his arm around her arm and sipped the champagne. This was fine for him, since he had arms the length of Chile. But she could hardly get the flute to her lips, and she felt like an asshole.

"And . . . cut!"

The moment Annie heard the magic words, she edged away from Laredo. An instant later, Reese came bounding across the sand to them. "Okay, we need to do another take. We had a lighting issue."

"No prob," Laredo agreed. He reached for Annie's hand.

Actually, there was a *big* problem, and Annie couldn't pretend that there wasn't.

"Look, I don't want to hurt your feelings, Laredo"—she kept her voice low—"but we both know that you're not the right guy."

"I am the guy. I swear!" Laredo insisted.

"He's the guy, Annie," Reese said impatiently.

"No." Annie shook her head. "He has the voice. He probably has a lot of voices. Or else he's the luckiest man in America. He sounds like the guy. But he isn't Him."

Anxiety lines formed like twin exclamation marks between Reese's eyes. "Could I have a word with you, Annie? Laredo, follow Chami back to one, and we'll do another take."

"Will do. *À bientôt, ma chère.*" He kissed her forehead, leaving behind a gross, wet spit mark that she rubbed off as Reese knelt down to speak to her.

"Look, Annie. The show kicked ass to make your dream come true. My boss put a hundred grand on the line. The least you can do is cooperate."

Annie felt terrible. "I appreciate all of this, I really do. And I wish you had the right guy, but you don't. That guy, Laredo—he's an impostor."

"You've got to be kidding. Don't you think we know an imitation when we hear it? We kicked every impressionist in Vegas who swore they were the one. We had a goddamn ex-CIA voice analyst on standby."

"Well, what does this guy Laredo do?"

"He's a plumber. We had him say, 'I can snake your pipes.' It was hot."

"What was a plumber doing at a voice-over audition?" Annie asked plaintively. "You see, it doesn't make any sense."

"Yes, it does," Reese insisted. "*You're* the one who's not making sense. A lot of people do voice-overs in their spare

time. I'll tell you what's going on. I'm not a Hollywood
Barbie-doll type, so I should know. You made up this whole
romantic fantasy in your mind. You expected the guy to look
like—I don't know—Orlando Bloom. Because that's part of
your fantasy. No real guy could ever—excuse me a minute,
someone is buzzing me." She held her headset against one
ear. "Yes? . . . Oh, shit . . . Okay, thanks."

Off came the headphones. "Look, we gotta hurry. Somehow the media found out we're shooting here. It's gonna turn
into a zoo in about fifteen minutes. You've got to get it perfect on this take, Annie. Promise me."

Without waiting for an answer, Reese walked off, and
the makeup and props people swooped in with powder and
clean champagne glasses.

What if Reese was right? Maybe no real guy could live
up to her fantasy. But even as Annie tried to talk herself into
this point of view, she knew it wasn't true. So she rose and
walked away, ignoring the protests of the cameramen, looking for the producer again. She couldn't and wouldn't be a
part of this any longer.

There she was, over by the red rope, deep in conversation
with two guys. One wore jeans and a blue work shirt, the
other had on hiking boots and khaki shorts. She couldn't see
their faces, but it was clear from their body language that
they were upset about something, the guy in the work shirt
especially. Finally, Reese threw her hands in the air, lifted
the red rope, and motioned for the guys to duck underneath.

No way. Annie recognized one of them immediately,
though his beard was now gone and he was a good fifteen

pounds lighter than when she and Michelle had encountered him on the Appalachian Trail south of Damascus, Virginia. Mark Wolfson. The guy with him was tallish but not too tall, with dark hair that flopped boyishly onto his forehead and a sinewy V-cut physique that moved easily under his casual attire. Annie's breath caught. Before anyone told her, she knew.

"Hi," he said, in a voice she knew so well. "I'm Charlie. I think you're looking for me."

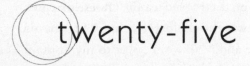# twenty-five

The proof was easy. Mark Wolfson showed the Leno staff his identification, Charlie told Reese the story about how he'd gone to the sound studio and recorded the affirmations as a lark, and then Mark pulled out the corporate check that Annie had sent him, signed by Annie herself. Reese tried to challenge them, as if she had something invested in her choice of Laredo, but when Charlie explained in the same voice as Mr. V that he'd filled out his friend's name on the release form, the producer admitted defeat.

"It looks like you're entitled to the reward, Charlie. We'll give it to you on the show tonight."

Charlie rubbed his chin. "Look, I've identified myself. She's met me. I really don't want to go on television."

"And I'm saying that for you to get the money, you're going on my boss's show tonight," Reese told him. "It was an implied part of the offer."

"Excuse me, but I don't want to go on TV either," Annie

said softly. She couldn't make eye contact with Charlie; it simply felt too personal with so many people standing around. Plus, he did not seem at all happy about admitting he was who he was, or at all interested in meeting her.

"You're both going on. End of discussion," Reese snapped. "And right now, I don't want you two interacting." She started issuing orders. "Charlie and Mark, walk over to my assistant director—she's the one with the Mohawk. Annie, go back to the blanket. We'll figure out some way to get you to Los Angeles on separate planes. Mark, I'm afraid you're on your own, but maybe we'll tape something now with you that we can plug in this evening. Okay. Charlie and Mark, follow me."

Without a word, or even a glance in her direction, Charlie followed the producer across the sand.

"Ladies and gentlemen." Jay Leno addressed his audience. "Normally, we'd tease the hell out of this next segment, and put it at the end of the show. But so many of you have tuned in to see it that I hate to keep you waiting just to make my advertisers happy!"

The studio audience laughed. Annie felt Chami take her arm. "Twenty seconds," the assistant whispered. "He's right across the way, on the other side. You'll come out at the same time. Feel free to hug."

It was so weird, to be back on Jay Leno's set. Annie had been flown down on a Southwest flight to Burbank—Charlie had been put on another plane—and whisked to this hotel to prepare for their taping. An African American dresser had shown up with four different outfits for Annie to try on, by

Chloe, Betsey Johnson, Armani, and Marc Jacobs. Ultimately, she'd decreed that Annie wear the Marc Jacobs citron sweater and low-slung tweed miniskirt combination, along with high, kicky boots and a matching newsboy cap, declaring the look to be young and hip and fresh.

The dresser had been followed by a makeup artist, who'd spent an hour on Annie's face, including the application of very long, very thick false eyelashes, which she characterized as the must-have look of the moment. The hairstylist worked magic with a flatiron, volumizer, and hot rollers. Annie caught a glimpse of herself in the full-length mirror and wanted to barf. She looked absolutely nothing like herself.

Chami showed up to drive Annie onto the NBC lot. Instead of holding her in the regular greenroom, they sequestered her in Reese's office, a surprisingly small cubicle with papers and newspaper clippings stacked high in all directions.

There was a monitor there, tuned to the local NBC affiliate, and Annie tried to distract herself by watching TV news coverage of a police pursuit, but it was impossible. All she could think was how she'd chided herself for coming on the Leno show the first time, and now she was going to do it again. She was a millionaire ten times over. She could go out with any guy she wanted. She'd even found Charlie, and knew his name. She could just find his number or just ask him out. Not that he showed any interest at all in going out with her, but still—

"When Annie Albright was last here," Jay was telling the audience, "I offered a hundred-thousand-dollar reward if the voice of Mr. Vibrator would come forward and come on the show. Now, you're going to get a chance to meet him. Let's welcome to the show for the first time the man behind the voice that is captivating half the species, Mr. Charlie Silver!" Jay beckoned to Annie and then turned to beckon to Charlie.

"Go for it," Chami hissed, and gave Annie a little push. To whoops and cheers that seemed even louder than for her last appearance, Annie crossed the set toward the famous couches. When she saw Charlie coming from the other direction, she was mildly surprised to see him wearing the same jeans/work shirt combination he'd worn that morning at the beach. They hadn't redone his wardrobe at all.

There was only the most perfunctory and awkward of hugs. Then Charlie went straight for the far end of the couch and crossed his legs, leaving Annie to sit closer to the host.

"Well, Annie," Leno said, "looks like we've found our man. I mean, your man. You happy?"

Annie nodded. Then she remembered that she'd been warned to respond audibly. "Yes, I am," she said, her voice sounding fake and too loud to her own ears.

"You happy, Charlie? Probably not as happy as you've made the women in our audience!"

The crowd whooped, and Charlie shrugged slightly.

"Well, here's something to make you happy, Charlie." Leno reached under his desk and took out one of those cardboard oversized checks. "A hundred thousand dollars!"

He offered the check to Charlie, who took it sheepishly as the audience cheered. Then he sat back down again.

"So what do you do when you're not making yourself the hundred-thousand-dollar man, Charlie?" Leno asked.

"Schoolteacher," Charlie answered tersely.

"And you're a man of few words outside the bedroom, I see," Jay joked, and the audience laughed again. "Popular with the PTA?"

"Doubtful."

"What grade do you teach?"

"Eighth."

"Been doing it long?" Leno pressed, trying to get more than a one-word answer out of him. He succeeded. He got two.

"Four years."

Annie felt ready to cry. This wasn't the way she'd pictured it at all. Charlie was supposed to have the same magical reaction to her that she had to him. Instead, he obviously wanted to be anywhere but where he was.

"Huh." Leno rubbed his formidable chin. Obviously, this wasn't going the way the host had expected, either. "So, Annie, I understand that you two haven't had a chance to get to know each other at all. I'm sure this is a little awkward. Is there anything you'd like to ask Charlie? Here's your chance."

"Hey, Annie! Ask him if he'll come home with me!" a chunky woman in the audience stood up and bellowed.

"I think you just did," Leno quipped to the woman, once the laughter died down. "Annie, anything for Charlie?"

Annie had so many things she wanted to ask. But not here. This was the wrong place and the wrong time. She shook her head.

"Nothing? Not even, 'Hey Charlie, do you have a girl-friend?'" Jay coaxed. Annie could see Reese just offstage, scowling at her. Reese mimed a talking puppet with her hand. But still Annie couldn't bring herself to say anything. She shook her head again.

"Then I'd say, this is a great time to go to a commercial. Hey, thanks, you two. Next up on the show, U2's Bono! Let's hear it for Annie Albright and Mr. Charlie Silver, the voice of Mr. Vibrator!"

To only the most moderate of applause, Jay shook hands with each of them. Then his band started to play, the lights came down, and the segment was over.

They walked offstage together. Reese was waiting for them, but instead of congratulations, she just pressed a check into Charlie's hand and waved them toward a corridor.

"Look the word 'ungrateful' up in the dictionary some-time," she snapped. "You're on the eight o'clock Southwest flight from Burbank to SFO. Wait in there for your cab."

No limo this time, Annie realized. And no private jet. How deflating. But no more deflating than the reality of meet-ing Charlie face-to-face. God. Maybe she did need therapy after all.

There was a tap on her shoulder. Annie turned.

"I just wanted to let you know," Charlie said, "you ru-ined my life."

Wow. He was really upset. Well, Annie could understand it. All this public notoriety that he hadn't planned on could be embarrassing. If she could just make him understand . . .

She found the check she'd made out to him for the

second hundred thousand dollars and handed it to him.
"You did something wonderful, Charlie. If you could see
the e-mails I get from women about how their lives have
been changed by—"

"Honestly? I'm way more concerned with changing the
lives of my students," Charlie snapped. "Of course, I'm not
going to get to do that anymore."

"Because—"

"Think, Annie," Charlie told her. "If you're a school
administrator, would you want the voice of Mr. Vibrator
teaching at your school? How many ways can you spell
F–I–R–E–D?"

Oh, God. He was right. She hadn't even thought about
that part.

"I'm sorry," she said sincerely. "I never meant to . . ."

"Forget it. I'm going to try to."

It felt unbearable to be standing there with Him, knowing that he hated her. "I think I'll . . . get a Diet Coke from
the greenroom. Want something?"

He shook his head.

She offered him what she hoped passed for a smile and
took a step forward at the same time. The heel on the stupid
designer boots turned, she pitched forward and went sprawl-
ing, the skirt hiked up to her crotch.

He helped her up. "You okay?"

Annie tugged her skirt down with one hand and pushed
a hunk of hair out of her eyes with the other, as Charlie
looked deeply into her eyes.

"You've got an eyelash on your cheek," he said.

Annie's hand flew to her right cheek and came away with one of the two huge false eyelashes, which looked like some kind of furry insect in her palm. The other one was still in place on her left eye; she could only imagine how strange she looked.

"Yours are really blond," Charlie observed. "Underneath all the gunk, I mean."

Annie sighed. "The makeup was their idea. So was the hair. And the outfit. I never look like this." She hesitated. "Are you really going to get fired because of this?"

"No doubt."

Annie hesitated. "I could help. Financially, I mean."

His voice turned cold. "I don't want your money."

Shit. She leaned back against the wall and stripped off the other eyelash, because what the hell. It was worse than she could have imagined. Not only had her magical connection with him been a figment of her overactive imagination, but she'd ruined the guy's life.

That's what you get, she told herself, *for listening to the voices in your head.*

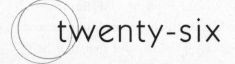# twenty-six

"It's a damn shame, Charlie," Joe Witherspoon told him. "If it were up to me, I'd keep you. You're one of the finest teachers I've got. But I just got the call from Sacramento. They want you on unpaid leave. Starting yesterday if they could figure out a way to do it."

"I'm fired," Charlie said. Saying it aloud made it seem that much worse.

"This school is history in three weeks anyway," Joe pointed out. He leaned his large head against the high-backed office chair. "I'm sick about the whole thing. Damn sanctimonious hypocrites. Probably every woman on that board bought one of those Mr. Vibrators. Hell, my wife bought one. I'm not a man who's threatened by that, by the way. A man's been married thirty-three years, he needs to add a little spice."

Charlie managed a smile, thinking this must be what it was like for a man on death row as zero hour approaches. He went to sleep the night before expecting that this would be his last day of teaching at Mays–McCovey, and awakened with the same thought. He'd picked up Jamal and arrived at school with the expectation that Joe would summon him to his temporary office in the basement of the USF humanities building even before the Pledge of Allegiance, and that was exactly what had happened. And then, word that that he'd been canned.

"Who's taking my class?" he asked.

"Mindy Patterson. Just graduated from Berkeley last spring. Starting at a middle school in the Richmond in September."

"A rookie?" Charlie shook his head ruefully. "They'll eat her alive."

"What difference does it make? We're shutting down in a couple of weeks. Anyway, I'll let you introduce her. Then you can read your kids the riot act," Witherspoon decided.

Charlie felt a lump form in his throat. "They're not my kids anymore." He swallowed hard. "You hear anything from any parents?"

Witherspoon rearranged a stack of papers on his desk that needed no rearranging. "Not from your class. A couple of elementary-school parents left messages for me, though. They weren't very complimentary."

"I'm not surprised."

"Well, at least this won't bankrupt you," Witherspoon observed. "What are you going to do with the money? How much is it? Two hundred grand?"

Charlie had already thought about this. He reached into

his pocket, took out the two checks—one from Jay Leno, the other from Annie—and put them on Witherspoon's crowded desk. "It's yours. I've endorsed them to Mays-McCovey. Add it to the fund."

The principal's eyes got wide. "Charlie, you're upset. You can't—"

"I just did." Charlie set his jaw.

"I'm not depositing these for a week," Witherspoon assured him. "Just in case you change your mind."

"I won't. If the fund doesn't reach its goal, Joe, find another way to use this money for my kids. Will you do that for me?"

"You have my word." Joe gave Charlie a sad smile. "I guess in some way they'll always be your kids, Charlie." He rose. "Come on. I'll walk you to your room."

Charlie looked out over his hushed classroom. His students had come dressed in costume today, as members of either the Montague or the Capulet family. They were supposed to be doing a dress rehearsal for a presentation they'd be making two nights hence, of scenes from *Romeo and Juliet*. All the Montagues gathered on the right side of the room, wearing variations on a theme in purple. Jamal, who was playing Romeo, wore a three-times-too-big purple T-shirt with a Nike logo. LaToya Jefferson had added purple yarn to her hair extensions, along with purple glitter false eyelashes.

The Capulets, who'd decided their color was orange, were clumped to the left. Toinette DeCarlo, a heavyset girl with the body of a very grown woman, would be Juliet. She wore orange leggings and orange lipstick. Frederick Bickford was to be her father, and he'd come in an oversized orange jacket. Manuel Jesus, who'd lobbied hard for the role of Juliet's nurse—and he was hysterical in the part—wore a hideous orange knit dress with balloons stuffed underneath for breasts. Manuel had asked to play the nurse after Charlie explained that back in Shakespearean times, men played all the roles, no matter what the sex of the character.

Charlie assessed the twin seas of orange and purple, and couldn't believe he was leaving them. These kids had come so far. They were working together, learning together, and they were excited about it. Adults had betrayed so many of them, like Jamal. Now, Charlie would just be another grown-up who had let them down.

Before he said anything, LaToya's hand shot into the air.

"LaToya?"

"Mistuh Silver, are you leaving school cuz you did a porno? 'Cause that's what I heard."

"No," Charlie insisted.

The new teacher, Ms. Patterson, waved the seating chart in her hand and called out from the back of the room, "LaToya, we don't say that kind of thing in class."

LaToya looked singularly unimpressed.

"Actually, Ms. Patterson, it's fine," Charlie corrected. "We call each other by our names, we don't use profanity, and we treat each other with respect. Which is exactly what LaToya just did with me."

LaToya beamed as Jamal raised his hand. "Why you quit, then?" he asked, scowling.

"I didn't quit. I would never do that. The school board isn't giving me any choice. But I'm going to talk to the drama coach about working with you guys on *Romeo and Juliet*, so that you can still do your show, and—"

"Know what? Fuck that," Jamal snapped, angry tears in his eyes. He grabbed his books from the desk.

"We don't use that language—" Ms. Patterson began.

"I'll handle this, Miss Patterson," Charlie interrupted, because while the young teacher meant well, she was exactly what his kids did *not* need right now.

"Come on, Jamal—" Charlie began. By the time he reached the word "Jamal," the boy was already bolting from the classroom. "Excuse me, guys," he told his students. "I'll come back to see you whenever I can. I mean it."

The hallway was empty, so Charlie checked the boys' john, the teachers' lounge, and even the building courtyard. No Jamal. Shit. He was still responsible for getting him back to the group home. He went out to the parking lot to see if Jamal was there. No. He'd have to report the missing kid to Joe and alert USF security. Damn.

Charlie trudged back into the building and went down the steps to Witherspoon's basement office. There was Jamal, sitting on the floor, knees drawn up to his chest, head tucked against his legs.

Witherspoon stuck his head out the door. "You looking for this guy?"

Charlie nodded and went to Jamal. But when he put a hand on the boy's shoulder, Jamal flinched away.

"Jamal demanded to talk to the person in charge who fired you," Joe explained. "I told him it wasn't me, but he's not listening."

"You a liar, man!" Jamal muttered into his thighs. "I *hate* you!"

Charlie sat next to Jamal. "He's not lying. It's not Mr. Witherspoon's fault."

"Oh, yeah, right," Jamal scoffed. "Ain't nothin' ever any damn adult's fault."

"Yeah, it is," Charlie said. "I know I let you down, Jamal. In this case, the fault is all mine. But you and I can still be friends, if it's okay with Mrs. Peabody. And I'll come to see you in *Romeo and Juliet*."

Jamal shrugged, and refused to look at Charlie.

Charlie's cell rang. He checked the number. Area code 202.

Great. He stood.

"Charlie Silver," he said into the phone.

"Charlie, Linda Fannin here. From the Summit Foundation."

Well, it wasn't like this was a shock.

"I'm with one of my students, Linda. Can we make this quick?"

"I'm so sorry to have to make this call, Charlie, but you've been eliminated from contention for the High Summit Award."

"Yeah, I understand the foundation's position."

"I know I shouldn't say this, Charlie," Linda continued

in her crisply accented English, "but I really do think you were a top contender. How could you . . . do what you did? You had to know how this would affect your career."

Charlie sighed. "It's a long story. Please tell the board of judges that I appreciate having been considered, and I wish them all the best. Good-bye, Linda."

He closed his phone and turned back to Jamal, answering Witherspoon's questioning look with a resigned nod.

"How can I help, Jamal?"

The boy shook his head. Suddenly Charlie got an idea.

"If you're worried about not coming to school anymore, I've got that covered," Charlie assured him. "If Mrs. Peabody gives permission, I'll still take you in the morning and bring you home in the afternoon. No matter where they have classes."

Suddenly the boy was on his feet. "I don't need no goddamn taxi driver," he spat.

As Charlie and Witherspoon watched in silence, Jamal walked down the corridor to the stairs—one little man who'd dared to trust, and whose heart had been broken again.

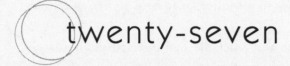# twenty-seven

"We could go shopping and spend ridiculous amounts of money on things we don't need," Michelle suggested. "That might cheer you up."

"It won't." Annie curled into a fetal position on her bed and shook her head. It was just past noon, but she was still unwashed, unbrushed, and in her pajamas. "How could I have been so wrong, Michelle? How could I have been so dumb? That's what I keep asking myself."

It was two days after Annie's appearance on Leno; she'd been in a funk for the whole forty-eight hours. It had never occurred to Annie that being chosen as the voice of Mr. Vibrator could ruin someone's career, but clearly it had. The day after the show, she'd tracked down the school where Charlie taught and called him to apologize again. But a brusque secretary told her that Mr. Silver no longer taught at Mays-McCovey, then hung up in Annie's ear.

So Charlie's instincts had been right. He'd gotten fired

because of her. Not to mention the whole mystical connection thing, about which she now felt incredibly humiliated. That voice she'd heard in her head had been nothing more than a flight of fancy, a romantic delusion. The last thing Charlie wanted was to meet her, or to be with her, or for her to find him at all.

Last night she and Michelle had gone through a large chicken Florentine pizza from Goat Hill, and a bottle and a half of Robert Young 2002 Scion Estate Red, which normally would have cheered her up for a week. Yet the carb/antioxidant overload had been only the most temporary of fixes, even when followed by a quart of vanilla with hot fudge from Tango Gelato. Not even a good session in her home office, watching orders for Mr. Vibrator pile up at roughly the same rate as the national debt, lifted her spirits. As for use of the vibrator itself, that was out of the question. One look at it made her slam it into her nightstand drawer.

Back in the days when Annie had spent all her time fantasizing about sex instead of making money from it, she would have been fantasizing about Charlie right, left, sideways, and tied to a four-poster bed. But now, post-Leno, she couldn't seem to fantasize about Charlie, or anyone else. The voice in her head was gone again, and this time it seemed permanent. Not even her doll collection brought her any solace, even when she positioned a vintage Barbie with white patent-leather go-go boots upside down atop the original G.I. Joe. No sparks. No fantasies. Nada.

Annie rolled over and stretched out. "He's a teacher, Michelle. He didn't want to be famous. He has such a good heart."

"He's also an eleven on the one-to-ten heat-o-meter," Michelle added. "Why don't you call him?"

"No!" Annie exclaimed. "He doesn't want anything to do with me."

"It's too bad, really. He's your neighbor."

"What?"

Michelle nodded. "He lives here on Potrero Hill."

"Great. I can run into him in the Safeway and he can stare daggers at me."

"You realize this is ridiculous," Michelle said. "The guy has two hundred thousand dollars burning a hole in his pocket. You know how long it takes a teacher to earn two hundred thousand dollars?" Michelle bopped Annie with an oversized pillow.

Annie grabbed the pillow before her friend could deliver a second blow. "But I don't think he cares about the money."

"*Everyone* cares about the money. Come on, get dressed," Michelle urged. "Have you seen my nails? I'm desperate for a manicure. Then we'll go to the Anchor Oyster Bar in the Castro for lunch, eat tons of fried oysters, and ogle the gay boys. And then we can go back to the Japanese spa and sweat it all off, or—I know! Hire a personal trainer." She snapped her fingers. "One of those guys who look like they just stepped off the cover of a romance novel? With the ridiculously long, flowing hair and rippling muscles? He'll get us in shape *and* you can fantasize about him—what's the downside?"

"It won't help Charlie," Annie declared.

Michelle smacked herself in the forehead. "I liked Annie with the deeply disturbed imagination a lot better than Saint Annie. So could you *please* give it a rest?"

Annie sighed. "Sorry."

Michelle stood and stretched. "Thank you. Enough of the pity party. It's just a little too self-indulgent for a twenty-nine-year-old overnight multimillionaireness. I'm going shopping. Are you coming or not?"

"Not." Annie said. "I would be crap company."

"Love ya mean it, and you're right," Michelle agreed. "I'll call you later. If you're not up, dressed, and ready to go clubbing, I'm bringing in a male escort for you. Empty, meaningless, but extremely vigorous sex with Sergio or Rock Hard or whoever shows up at your door is the cure for your ailment. And remember, no love without the glove—thus saith Dr. Michelle."

Annie could barely work up the energy to waggle her fingers in her friend's direction as Michelle strode out of the room.

Charlie poured a shot of Flagman into his black coffee. Then—what the hell—he added another one. He wasn't a man used to drinking for breakfast, nor was he a man who normally consumed said breakfast at two in the afternoon. The old Charlie would have been three-quarters into his teaching day at this hour. But yesterday, the new Charlie learned for whom the damn bell tolled, which meant that today he had neither a classroom nor a place to be. Worst of all, he'd blown the only chance of saving his school—his former school—by winning the High Summit grant. So why not drink breakfast? And why not drink it naked, the state in which he habitually slept?

He carried his fortified coffee into the living room, plopped onto the couch, and reached for the TV clicker. It was the usual assortment of game shows, soap operas, preachers, and QVC clones. He tarried momentarily on *As the World Turns* to watch a gorgeous blonde with pneumatic breasts seduce a much younger man, and then flipped to CNN. Why not? The state of the world was as fucked up as the state of his life. As if to confirm his assessment, the president was waving off reporters' questions as he hustled aboard Marine One for yet another long weekend at Camp David. Charlie rolled his eyes and took a long swallow of coffee.

Then he heard his doorbell. Who could that be? In the middle of the afternoon? The postman? Jehovah's Witnesses? Mormons? Mark? Nah. He'd have called first. Had to be one of the first three. Or . . . Jamal.

That thought made his heart sink. Charlie had called Mrs. Peabody the night he was fired, to offer to drive Jamal to and from school as long as Mays-McCovey was in business at USF. The housemother had nixed that notion right away. She was hired by the State of California to care for children, and she doubted that the state would want a teacher like *him* to be alone in a car with an eighth grader. Not that she was personally concerned, but she had her own job to worry about. Did Charlie understand?

Charlie said he did, and he offered to find another teacher who might be able to transport Jamal. But Mrs. Peabody said it didn't make no never mind, because Jamal now claimed to hate the school and everyone in it so much he didn't want to go there anyway. So Charlie mentally added *fucked up a really great kid's life* to his list of sins. Swell.

The doorbell kept ringing. If it was Jamal, Charlie didn't want him to leave, so he grabbed an afghan off the couch—made by a huggie-veggie-type girl he'd gotten to know very well on a weekend in the Bolinas—and wrapped it around his waist. He would just answer. If it was Jamal, the kid could wait while he dressed.

But it wasn't. It was a woman he'd never seen before. Beautiful, glossy dark hair that fell to her shoulders, full lips, a broad nose, and great, huge eyes. She was very attractive in a built-for-comfort-not-for-speed kind of way.

Her eyes flicked down to the afghan, then met Charlie's. "Nice outfit."

"Sorry. I thought you were—"

Charlie stopped. What difference did it make? He didn't know this woman, and his fortified coffee was waiting. "Whatever you're selling, I'm not interested."

The woman nodded. "Well, I'd say that if I were wearing an afghan, too. I'm not selling anything. I'm Annie Albright's friend Michelle."

Charlie stared at her blankly. Annie . . .

Ah. Annie Albright. The bane of his existence. What was her friend doing at his door?

"This is the part where you invite me in," Michelle added.

"Well, we seem to have gotten different scripts, Michelle.

Have a pleasant life." He started to close the door, but Michelle put her foot in it.

"Not so fast, bucko," she announced. "I have things to say."

"Great. Say 'em to someone else."

He tried to close the door again, but her foot didn't move. "Until recently I was a pushy and overbearing attorney for a major downtown firm, meaning I don't take 'no' for an answer," Michelle said sweetly. "Plus, I'm extremely litigious. My considered opinion would be you should invite me in."

Charlie so did not need this right now. But he made a dramatic show of ushering her inside to the living room, excusing himself briefly to his bedroom to put on some jeans. He returned, pulling a white T-shirt over his head and hoping against hope that she was gone. She wasn't. She was sitting in the easy chair opposite the couch. His coffee cup was in her hands.

"I have to drink when I watch CNN, too," she said, nudging her head toward the television. "How many shots are in this, anyway?"

Charlie sat on the couch, clicked off the TV, and took back his coffee cup. "What did you do, smell it or drink it?"

"If I did drink it, do you get cooties?"

Charlie was trying very hard to control his temper, but it wasn't easy. "Tell me, Michelle. Would you like some coffee or something stronger?" he asked. "You've got ten minutes."

"All I need is five," Michelle replied, crossing her legs. "I'm good, so let's just cut to the chase."

"Fine. Because I'm busy."

"No, you're not. You just got fired, and you're blaming it on my friend."

"That's your friend's fault."

Michelle leaned forward. "Let me ask you, Charlie. When you recorded your voice at the audition, did you give your own name?"

"No—"

"You didn't leave a phone number, or any kind of contact information. Correct?"

"Yes, but—"

"In fact," Michelle interrupted, "you used someone else's name and phone number—that would be your friend Mark. Do you know how many times Annie tried to call Mark, how many messages she left before she found out that he was somewhere on the Appalachian Trail? Do you realize she *went* to the Appalachian Trail to try and find the person who did the voice-over for our product?"

"Yes. Mark told me he met her there," Charlie admitted. "But your 'product,' as you so euphemistically call it, was already a done deal long before that."

Michelle's eyes narrowed. "Only because she didn't have your goddamn phone number. Let me tell you something, Charlie Silver. I have known Annie a long time. She is the type of person a mother dreams her daughter will turn out to be. She's kind and sweet and smart and funny and a much better person than I will ever be. If she had been able to reach you, and you had told her who you were and what you did, she never, ever, *ever* would have used your voice. But you didn't. So put the afghan back on and cry in your vodka, but from where I sit, you have no one to blame but yourself."

Whoa. Charlie felt as if he'd just been flattened by a steamroller with really great hair. Plus, as much as he didn't want to admit it . . .

"You have a point."

She shook her hair off her face. "Thank you. I was a fucking great litigator until Annie made me rich. You can add that to her list of attributes."

"You're her *partner*?"

"One of them," Michelle said. "So how'd it happen?"

"My voice? I was at the studio with my bud. Mark."

"The guy we met on the trail," Michelle acknowledged. "He's cute, or at least I think he would be without the whole bearded mountain-man thing going on."

"He's a hell of an actor, too. Well, I guess you know that." Charlie sipped his laced coffee. "Look, I've never done a voice-over in my life. I just happened to wander into the wrong room and there was the audio engineer and . . . Actors are always broke. So when I did the audition and gave Mark's info, I thought that if by some chance my voice got used—"

"Mark would get the money," Michelle filled in. She shifted uneasily. Charlie thought she looked a lot less sure of herself now. "That was really nice of you."

She scratched an itch on her cheek—Charlie noticed her nail polish was badly chipped—and then curled her fingers inward on her lap, as if to hide their ill-groomed state.

"Well, you have two hundred thousand dollars now," Michelle pointed out. "Split it with him."

"I can't. I gave it away. To my school. My former school."

"Why would you do that?" Michelle was bewildered.

"They needed it." He wasn't about to go into the details. Whining about what might have been really was not his style. "You sure you don't want that drink? Or we can both switch to straight coffee."

Michelle shook her head, tapped her watch, and rose. "Thanks for hearing me out. I have a feeling you really are a good guy, Charlie. If you're more than a good guy—if you're a great guy—you'll ask me for her address and phone number. She's your neighbor, you know."

Charlie smiled thinly. "So I understand. The helicopters circling over Connecticut Street were a dead giveaway."

"So? Are you feeling like a great guy?"

"I don't even know if I'm feeling like a good guy. But thanks anyway." He walked her to the door. "Enjoy your manicure," he added.

She looked startled. "How did you know—?"

He pointed. "Fingernails. Go with a red that veers toward orange. It'll suit the golden undertones in your skin."

She was still standing there, slack-jawed, when he gently closed the door.

twenty-eight

"I paint better than Grandma," Marci, a darling gap-toothed six-year-old, told Annie. "Lookit!"

"Very nice," Annie agreed. She helped the little girl clean her brush in a can of water so she could add another color to the ceramic plate she was painting with her great-grandmother, Estelle.

"Marci, did you know that your great-grandmother is a wonderful artist?" Doris asked. Annie knew that though Estelle was much older than Doris, the two women were old friends from synagogue and that Estelle's stroke of a year ago had left her with slurred speech and a deep palsy on her right side. Estelle had been an art teacher for forty-three years before she retired. How hard it must be for her to have a kindergartener granddaughter who could paint better than she could.

More and more, Annie found herself spending time at the BridgePoint Center, doing art projects with the residents.

She had plenty of time on her hands for volunteerism, and working at the assisted-living facility was one of the few things that brought her out of her funk. Today her grand-mother had decided to join her.

"Did you want the indigo, Estelle?" Doris asked, since the elderly woman seemed to be trying and failing to stab her paintbrush into the dark blue paint.

"Shlrr," Estelle mumbled.

"Sorry, I didn't catch that," Doris said.

"SHLRR!" Estelle gurgled even louder.

"Yes, I can understand that sentiment," Doris agreed. She took Estelle by the hand and eased the brush into the paint.

"All she does is baby-talk like my little brother." Marci gave a long-suffering sigh.

"I beg to differ, Marci," Doris said. "I heard her quite distinctly. She said 'shit.'" Doris guided Estelle's arm so that her brush touched the center of the plate.

Marci inhaled sharply. "I'm telling Mommy. Mrs. Rosen said a bad word!"

"Marci, didn't anyone tell you the rule?" Annie asked.

"What rule?"

"When you are over the age of ninety, you're allowed to say whatever you want."

Marci's brows knit together. "Is that she really that old? And is that really the rule?"

"Yes, dear," Doris said. "To both questions."

Annie thought she saw the functional side of Estelle's mouth curl into a smile.

They worked for another fifteen minutes before Marci's mother—Estelle's granddaughter—came to fetch the little girl. Annie promised to get Marci's plate into the new kiln she'd bought the center so it would be ready for Marci's next visit. Then an attendant wheeled Estelle back to her room. Annie checked the arts and crafts schedule. Mr. Faranghi—her Iranian friend—and Mrs. Rabinowitz were due in another hour, but Annie and Doris were free until then.

"You want to go for bagels on Noriega and Eighteenth?" Doris offered. "My treat." She said this with a smile, since each of them could take the entire city to lunch and not notice the dent in her bank account.

"I'm not really hungry," Annie admitted. She started cleaning up the brushes, paints, and drop cloths.

"So much mazel, Annele," Doris chided. "But you look like you lost your BF."

"Charlie wasn't my boyfriend, Gramma. I don't even know him."

"I didn't mean boyfriend, darling. I meant best friend. But now that you mention it—"

"He hates me," Annie declared. She took the brushes to the sink, rinsed them, and then dried them carefully.

"Like you said, he doesn't know you. So what's to hate?"

Annie shrugged. "I guess some things just aren't meant to be, because—"

"Annie? Is that you?"

Annie looked up. Elliot Wenner was in the doorway, pushing his grandmother in a wheelchair. He'd changed his hair since Annie had last seen him. It was shorter, but he still had the same dashing good looks atop the same lifts-in-his-Bruno-Maglis. As usual, he was dressed impeccably, in a gray suit, white shirt, and silver-and-black striped tie.

"Oy," Doris muttered. "Another country heard from." Meanwhile, Elliot asked an attendant to look after his grandmother, then stepped into the crafts room and enveloped Annie in a bear hug.

"Wow, it's so great to see you! Hey, Doris," he added politely, then turned back to Annie. "Damn. You look spectacular."

After how badly things had gone with Charlie, it felt good to be wanted and appreciated by someone. Even if the someone was Elliot. "How are you, Elliot?"

"I'm super."

"And I'm going to the ladies' room," Doris interjected. "Excuse me."

When she was gone, Elliot took Annie's hands. "Business is booming. I just bought a yellow Lamborghini Murcielago. I'd love to show it to you."

"Well . . ."

"I've missed you, Annie. Every single day, I've missed you."

Annie smiled. That was nice to hear.

"You stopped returning my calls," he went on. "You didn't really give me a chance to explain."

"Oh, you know, actions speak volumes . . ."

"Hey, maybe it's kismet that we're both here, who knows?" Elliot asked, brushing that comment aside. "Let me take you to dinner tonight."

"Umm . . . I kind of have plans with Doris."

"What the hell, I'll take you both out! Anyplace you want. You know money is no object."

Annie was cautious. Was it possible he didn't know about Mr. Vibrator?

"I kind of started a business venture," she said. "Maybe you heard about it."

"Yeah. It was kind of hard to miss." He leaned even closer. "Honestly, Annie? If you made a bundle off of horny women, more power to you. But you don't have to be one of those women . . ." He placed his lips softly on hers. Quickly, it turned into a full-throttle kiss, with lots of intensity and a little too much tongue.

"Ah." He leaned back, very proud of himself. "The old magic is still there," he said. "Was it good for you?"

Was it good for you? Same old Elliot.

"Sorry, Elliot," she told him. "But . . . no."

He looked surprised. "You don't mean that."

"I really do."

"Excuse me, you two." Doris was back in the doorway. "I saw that. Was I witnessing the end of a new beginning or the beginning of a new end?"

"The latter. 'Bye, Elliot. Good luck." Annie said.

"Your loss, Annie." He shook his head, then walked away.

Doris watched him leave, a thoughtful expression on her face. "Not that you asked me, and normally I wouldn't offer an opinion, but you made the right decision. So now what?"

"Remember when I was little, and the Moskowitzes lived

across the street from you, and I used to play with their daughter Hannah when we came for the high holidays?"

Doris nodded. "And?"

"And Hannah and I wanted Good Humor, but her mother said no, so Hannah and I stole the money from her mother's wallet—"

"And I caught you because Hannah wasn't allowed to have sweets—her mother was a nut, but that's beside the point. So?"

"So." Annie sat back down at the art table, lost in the memory. "You told me it wasn't enough for me to say I was sorry and pay Mrs. Moskowitz back. You said I had to do more. So I dug all the dandelions out of their lawn."

Doris smiled. "You were very angry with me when I asked you to do that."

"Yeah, I was." Annie nibbled on her lower lip. "I think the reason I feel so bad now is that I did something wrong to Charlie without even knowing I'd done it. I said I was sorry. And I gave him money. But . . . I guess it feels like I still haven't done enough."

Her grandmother smiled. "S.A.W.G., my Annie."

Annie searched her mind for what that could possibly stand for, but came up blank. "I got nothing, Gramma."

"Such a wonderful girl," Doris translated.

"I still don't know what to do."

Doris shrugged. "You're a brilliant girl. Look how Mr. Vibrator came right from your imagination. Use that mind of yours."

"That mind of mine is what got me in trouble. Look how wrong I was about Charlie and his voice."

"So, no one is perfect. But I have faith in you, Annie. You will F.I.O."

"Figure it out," Annie translated.

Doris hugged her granddaughter. "Like I said, a brilliant girl. Right now, your Grandpa Murray is smiling."

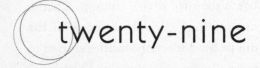# twenty-nine

Charlie stopped drinking and started running a few days after he was fired. He'd wake up, put on running shoes and clothes, and head down Potrero Hill toward the Mission or Market Street, just to see how far he could go without dying. Within a week, he had it up to five miles, which pleased him immensely, and he didn't even have to stop to walk on the return trip up the big hill. Then he'd come inside, shower, and settle down on his front porch to read the collected works of the Russian playwright Anton Chekhov, which he'd somehow missed in college. He had a crazy idea that maybe he could do with Chekhov what he'd tried in his classroom with Shakespeare, if he ever got another classroom. Plus, the idea of those great Russian sleighs plunging through the gloom of night toward the abyss pleased him in a mythic way.

Things had gotten complicated. He'd had to change his

phone number and his e-mail too, because every nutcase of
either sex who'd seen him on Leno wanted to have sex with
him, save his soul, or both. *Playgirl* and *Blueboy* had offered
him thousands of dollars for photo spreads. *Maxim* proposed
a ghostwritten "Dear Mr. Vibrator" advice column. Charlie
had zero interest in any of these things, or even in the
women who tracked him to his door. For a while he tried to
be polite when the doorbell rang. Eventually, he stopped
answering.

Mark kept pressing Charlie to go out with him, insisting that there was nothing like undressing a gorgeous new
woman to take one's mind off one's troubles. If Charlie had
been "the Man" in this department before Mr. Vibrator, think
about what it would be like now. But Charlie just couldn't
muster up the energy even for Irish coffee at the Buena Vista.
It was as if the pilot light of his essential Charlie-ness had
gone out.

Teaching had given him a place to be in this world, a joy
that went so much deeper than the transitory affections of his
latest conquest. He'd poured his heart and soul into the classroom. Without teaching, Charlie was at a loss. Mark assured
him that as a stockbroker, or an insurance salesman, or an
any-kind-of-salesman, the voice that had seduced half a nation could make him a not-so-small fortune, but all Charlie
wanted to do was teach.

On this particular Monday, Charlie was just returning
from a run when he saw the mailman at his front door. That
wasn't unusual—now that he was unemployed he knew the

mail usually arrived around eleven. What was unusual was the fact that the mail carrier had one of those plastic US MAIL bins at his feet and was ringing the doorbell incessantly.

"Hey, can I help you?" Charlie jogged up the walkway to him. He had a handlebar moustache, and Elvis-era sideburns. "You Charlie Silver?"

"Yeah." Charlie swiped a forearm across his sweaty brow. "What's up?"

"For you." He pointed to the box. "Just leave the bin outside tomorrow morning, I'll take it away. It's federal property, don't even think about stealing it."

"All *this* is mine?" Charlie was astonished. Though he was receiving eight or ten letters a day from America's loneliest women, he'd never gotten anything like this quantity of correspondence.

"Hey, this is only part of it. I've got two more just like it in my truck. I'll be right back with the other two. Weird, huh? No one gets snail mail anymore. Usually I'm just loaded down with bills and catalogs."

As the guy returned to his truck, Charlie untied his key from his running shoe, let himself in, and then brought in the mail bin. He picked up one of the envelopes at random from the pile—they were in every shape and color. Female handwriting for sure. No return address. He caught a whiff of perfume. Anais. He'd had a girlfriend in college who'd worn it.

Charlie tore open the envelope. There was nothing inside. No, wait. There was a personal check, folded into quarters. He unfolded it. Jesus. A hundred dollars, made out to

the Mays-McCovey School Fund, from a Mrs. Amanda Lor-
tell in Ada, Oklahoma. On the line at the bottom left, Mrs.
Lortell had written, in her same florid handwriting, "For
Pleasure Given."

What the hell? Charlie racked his brain. He didn't know
anyone named Amanda Lortell.

He tore open another envelope. Then another. And another. Inside each was a check, made out to the school fund.
Ten bucks. Fifty. Two *thousand*. He knew none of the senders,
but they were all notated identically. "For Pleasure Given."
Then, to his surprise, inside the fifth envelope, there was
more than a check. There was also a preprinted note card with
the logo of Turn Me On, Inc.

Turn Me On, Inc.

From the Office of the President, Annie Albright

Hello! If you're reading this note, you have just pur-
chased a Mr. Vibrator. For some time, the identity of the
voice on your Mr. Vibrator was unknown. Now we know
who it is—a schoolteacher at the Mays-McCovey Charter
School in San Francisco. His name is Charlie Silver. Un-
fortunately, the State of California doesn't understand the
value and joy that Charlie has brought to so many lives,
and it has relieved him of his teaching position because of the
work he did for Mr. Vibrator. While we lovers of his voice
cannot undo what's done, we can do something to make
Charlie happy by helping to support his wonderful but un-
derfunded school. I urge you to write a check today to the

*Mays-McCovey School Fund and send it to Charlie at the
address on the back of this card. Please note on your check
that it is being written "For Pleasure Given."*

Thank you very much.

> Annie Albright
> President, Turn Me On, Inc.

Whoa. This card had been inserted in Mr. Vibrator
boxes and—

There was a rap on his screen door. "Here's the rest."
The mailman dropped two more plastic bins on the porch.
"Hey, you ever see *Miracle on 34th Street*, where those bags of
mail get delivered to the guy who thinks he's Santa Claus?"

Charlie nodded, dazed.

"Well, Merry Christmas in August, Mr. Vibrator!" He
chortled, then whistled "Jingle Bells" on his way out the
door.

Charlie spent the morning opening envelopes, keeping a
running total on his calculator. When he was done, he had
approximately $111,000 for Mays-McCovey. The next day
brought double that. And the day after that, so much that
Charlie called in Mark and some of his actor friends to help
count. They were always up for free pizza and beer, plus they
loved a good story, and the story of all this money for an
inner-city charter school on its last legs was a gem.

On Thursday afternoon, Charlie filled one of the mail
bins with checks and drove it over to USF, then carried it
downstairs to Witherspoon's office. The principal was going
through his files, throwing things away, shutting down, in

the knowledge that the school was on its second-to-last day ever. Charlie saw there were dark circles beneath the principal's eyes.

He knocked gently on the doorframe. Witherspoon looked up, then smiled sadly. "Come to say good-bye, Charlie? We fought the good fight, man." He shook his head as he tossed another file folder into the trash. "What about these kids? That's what I keep asking myself. Half of 'em will end up in the military in four years, the other half'll drop out. Makes me sick to the bottom of my soul." Joe's eyes flitted to the mail bin. "Whatcha got there, Charlie?"

Charlie had never been so happy to deliver news to anyone in his life.

"Don't count Mays-McCovey down and out yet, Joe." He dumped the bin upside down onto Joe's bare desk—checks flew everywhere. "The cavalry has arrived."

On Friday morning Charlie was awakened by his phone at eight thirty, before he even got up for his morning run.

"Yeah?" He croaked, then cleared his throat. "Hello?"

"Wake up, man, it's a beautiful day outside!" Joe boomed in Charlie's ear.

That got Charlie's attention fast. "They're saving your school?"

"Some news shouldn't be given over the phone, Charlie. See you on campus in forty-five minutes, okay? Let's meet at the USF library."

"Why the—" Charlie began, but Joe had already hung up.

He showered quickly, pulled on some jeans and a T-shirt,

grabbed an apple, and ran out the door. The library was at the north end of campus, and he was lucky enough to find an empty spot in a faculty parking lot behind it. He checked his watch. Whew! He still had eight minutes. Principal Wither-spoon was nothing if not punctual. When he was still maybe fifty feet from the building, Jamal burst out the front doors, his skinny torso lost in an oversized Yung Joc T-shirt, the untied laces of his basketball shoes flopping onto the cement walkway.

"You early," Jamal declared.

Charlie was so happy to see that somehow, some way, the kid was actually here that it was everything he could do to keep from picking Jamal up in a huge bear hug. "Hey, little man. Glad to see you. How's it going?"

"I *said* you early." Jamal put his hands on his puny hips. "The man say ten, you be here at ten, you don't be here at no nine fifty."

"I take your point."

"'Cuz I was *supposed* to be the one to meet you at ten," Jamal continued. "So you *better* not be telling no one you got here first because that was *not* the plan."

"We're good," Charlie assured him. "I got here, you met me."

"All right, then," Jamal said. Then his face split with a grin so wide even his ears seemed to be smiling. "Right this way, Mr. Silver."

Jamal led Charlie into the library, down a corridor, and through the stage door of an auditorium. They snaked their way around cables, tables, and a lighting board.

"Where are we headed, Jamal?"

"We ain't 'heading,' Mr. Silver," Jamal said. "We there."

Jamal opened the curtains to the stage and stepped out—
Charlie followed him.

"Surprise!"

Jamal danced around the stage like a prizefighter as three
hundred and forty-seven kids, teachers, aides, and office personnel were on their feet and cheering. Then there was a
loud roar as Mr. Witherspoon bounded across the stage and
enveloped Charlie in the kind of bear hug that Charlie had
wanted to give Jamal. "A few good people wanted to thank
you for saving our school, Charlie," Joe whispered. "You
done good, man."

The principal went to a standing mike that had been set
up at the edge of the stage and held one arm high in the
air—the Mays-McCovey signal for everyone to pipe down,
which they finally did. "Today will be our last day of school
on the University of San Francisco campus," he announced.
"As of tomorrow, Mays-McCovey will be on a six-week
break—"

The students broke into loud cheers again. Charlie
laughed.

"During those six weeks, our school in Hunter's Point
will be cleaned up, spruced up, and made safe. School will
begin again on October 15. On behalf of all of us, we want to
thank you, Charlie, for making this possible."

"Yo, tell him the rest, Mr. Witherspoon!" Jamal yelled
from the lip of the stage.

Joe laughed. "All right, son, calm down. I'm getting to it.

Charlie, your students got up a petition to have you reinstated as a teacher. Last evening, that petition—signed by our entire faculty, almost all the students, a goodly number of parents and guardians—was driven to Sacramento and presented to the governor. He's overruled the school board—I knew there was a reason I voted for that man."

Joe motioned to Charlie and put his arm around his shoulder. "Will you come back to us, Charlie?" Joe asked.

Charlie found it hard to speak over the lump in his throat. "I *am* back, Joe."

For the next hour, Charlie was the guest of honor at a party without alcohol, hot-and-cold running babes, or rock and roll. The only entertainment was his students, reprising their roles as the Montagues and Capulets in a command performance just for him. It was the very best party of his life.

But even as he shared hugs, handshakes, and good cheer with the band of believers that made up their school, he knew that the person who really deserved the praise and gratitude wasn't there.

Charlie had to do something about that.

thirty

There was only one Michelle Garibaldi in the San Francisco phone book—Michelle Marie Garibaldi, to be exact. Charlie showed up at the front door of her flat on Sanchez Street in Noe Valley much the same way she had shown up at his front door only ten days before. She answered wearing red velour drawstring pants and an orange Syracuse University T-shirt—a dubious color combination—and carried a huge coffee mug that looked hand-painted.

"Charlie Silver. What a surprise. Get any good mail lately?"

That was when he knew for sure that she knew. "Can we talk?" Charlie asked.

"By all means."

She opened the door and ushered him inside. Her second-story flat was very spare, with the latest everything in chrome and white, including the furniture and fixtures in her kitchen.

"Want coffee? I just made a fresh pot." Michelle opened a cupboard door and pulled out another giant coffee mug. "I don't usually lace at one in the afternoon, but what the hell, I know you're into it." She poured him a mugful, topped off her own, and then added a healthy dollop of Bailey's. As she did, Charlie noticed her manicure—reddish-orange, with a sliver near the cuticle bare where it had grown out in the past ten days. He smiled.

"Why did she do it?" he asked.

Michelle leaned against the counter, fingers laced around the coffee mug. She shrugged. "Annie? Why does anyone do anything?"

"She saved my school. Do you know what an incredible thing that is?"

Michelle sipped her coffee. "Well, let's just say that you put one kind of smile on her face. Then, she put another kind of smile on your face. I'd call that an equitable offer."

"I wasn't very nice to her," Charlie admitted.

"You think?" Michelle asked, heavy on the sarcasm.

"So I need your help. I want to talk to her."

"So does every nut on the planet."

Charlie was sure that was true, since something similar had happened to him. Suddenly, the strangest feeling came over him, a kind of urgency that he only experienced when a kid or a friend was in trouble. It was almost like a voice calling to him from some deep place he couldn't even name.

"How about if you give me her number? I want to thank her, Michelle. Today. It really has to be today."

Michelle raised an eyebrow. "Well, aren't you the eager

beaver. Or whatever the male equivalent is of an eager beaver. Why today?"

"I don't know," Charlie said helplessly. "It's just a feeling . . ."

Michelle gave him the oddest look. "*She* says shit like that."

"She does?"

Michelle nodded. "She does. Well, how about tonight? She and I have plans. You can meet us."

"Yeah, great," Charlie agreed.

Michelle put down her coffee, got a pad and pen, and scribbled an address. She ripped off the page and handed it to Charlie. "Seven o'clock. Dress decently."

"Seven it is." Charlie put the paper in his wallet. Knowing he had it was comforting. It made that terrible anxious feeling dissipate. He hated to admit it, but he knew that there was a chance Michelle could have told him to fuck off.

"So, listen, I was with Annie on the Appalachian Trail," Michelle said. "It was a horrifying experience, by the by. I plan to hire a hypnotist to erase it from my memory." She took Charlie's mug and set it next to the sink. "But, anyway, I met your friend Mark out there . . ."

"Yeah. He told me."

She rinsed the mug, wiped her hands on a gleaming white dishtowel and turned back to him. "How about if you bring him along tonight?"

"How about if I do?" Charlie asked rhetorically.

"Really?"

Charlie noticed how quickly Michelle's tough veneer

melted away, how she sparkled like a little girl at her own birthday party.

"Yeah," he assured her. "Really."

"Great." She glanced at her wall clock. Charlie saw it was almost five. He'd need to get home, shower, and change in a hurry. "One last thing," Michelle added, just as he was going to thank her and say how much he looked forward to seeing both of them tonight.

"What's that?"

"If you hurt her, I will break your face."

thirty-one

". . . vitzivahnu, l'hadlik ner shel Shabbos."

Annie watched her grandmother give one more wave of her hands over the Shabbos candles on the dining room sideboard, and then open her eyes. "Good Shabbos, everyone," Doris told her friends.

She was met with a chorus of "good Shabbos" from the group—Bella, the short and tall Irmas, Roz, Ettie, and Marge, plus Annie and Michelle. Her grandmother had put in the large leaf, the one they'd always used for family holidays, so that the table took up practically the entire dining room.

Just then the doorbell rang.

"Who could that be?" Roz asked. "Anyone who knows you, Doris, knows not to ring your bell on Friday night."

"I'll get it," Annie volunteered. She hurried to the door. There stood Charlie Silver and Mark Wolfson, both in dress shirts and sports jackets. Charlie carried a bottle of red wine, and Mark a shopping bag from Whole Foods.

"I . . . I . . ." Annie stuttered.

"Nice girl, very inarticulate," Michelle said. She stepped into the hallway behind Annie. "Welcome."

"Does my grandmother know about this?" Annie hissed to Michelle.

"Why do you think she made so much brisket?"

"We're sorry we're a little late, Michelle," Charlie told her, as Michelle ushered them inside.

"Not to worry." Michelle eyed Mark. "You know, I almost didn't recognize you without a backpack and a beard. Mark, why don't you come with me into the dining room and meet Annie's grandmother and her friends? I think *your* friend wants to talk to *my* friend before we eat."

"Works for me. Hey, I brought you something." He handed Michelle the bag from Whole Foods. She opened it, and took out a huge container of fresh blueberries.

"Last time I saw you, you were looking for those," Mark reminded her.

Michelle laughed. "I *love* that you did that! Charlie, give me the wine."

Mark followed Michelle into the hallway, leaving Annie and Charlie alone in the foyer. Her grandmother's house was small, and Annie knew they could easily be overheard, so she stepped outside. When Charlie followed her, she closed the door behind them.

"I swear, I didn't know anything about this."

"I wanted to come, Annie. To thank you for what you did for my school."

Annie felt a lifting in her heart. "It worked, then?"

"Better than you could imagine."

"Well, don't thank me. Thank the women of America. And Canada."

"And England," Charlie added. "I got quite a bit of money from England. You—they—saved the school. Not to mention my job. I've been reinstated."

Annie grinned, because this was the best possible news. "I know you said you didn't want my money, Charlie. So I tried to find another way. If it hadn't worked, I would have funded the whole thing. No way would I let your school die. I guess I was hoping that this way, you'd see that what you did—what we did—is a good thing, for so many women. 'For pleasure given.'"

Charlie shook his head and a lock of dark hair fell onto his forehead. "How did you ever get the idea for it, anyway?"

"I kind of have a vivid imagination," Annie admitted, without going into detail.

Charlie chuckled. "Yeah, you do. Listen, the money is still coming in. I got two more bins of checks today. But the school has more than enough, so I'm not sure what you want me to do. Return the checks?"

"I was thinking maybe of a special fund," Annie mused aloud. "To expand your Shakespeare program. Like maybe we could do it at all the at-risk schools. And we could hire professional actors like Mark to come in and work with the kids—" Annie stopped midsentence and flushed. "Wait. I am so sorry. I didn't mean to say *we*. I meant *you*. Of course I meant *you*."

He looked at her cockeyed. "How did you even know about my Shakespeare program?"

Annie shrugged. "Research. If you're filthy rich, you have a lot of free time on your hands."

Charlie looked puzzled. "It's very odd, but . . . I kind of liked the 'we' thing."

Suddenly, Annie felt—of all things—shy. "You did?"

"This is even odder," Charlie went on, looking quite perplexed. "I feel like I could like it for an indefinite—as in very long—time."

Annie's eyes met his. "Why is it odd?"

His fingers brushed her shoulder. "I'll tell you another time. I think some people are waiting for us inside."

"You're right. And nothing is more important to them than food. Well, except maybe for your voice."

Charlie winced. "Really?"

Annie shrugged. "As my grandmother says, just because there's snow on the roof doesn't mean there's not still a fire in the hearth. But we can talk more later, if you want."

"To be continued after dinner, then?" Charlie asked. "At the location of your choice?"

"Anywhere you want. As long as it's Potrero Hill," Annie said.

She walked him back into the dining room. They were met with a spontaneous round of applause.

Charlie reddened. "I . . . guess you all know me better than I know you."

"Charlie, sit down and let my friends tell you how wonderful you are," Doris instructed. "Annie and Michelle, come help me in the kitchen, please. Then we'll make a kiddush and eat."

Michelle motioned Charlie to an empty chair next to Mark, and then she and Annie followed Doris into the kitchen. "Why did you two keep this from me?" Annie asked, taking the oven mitts from the drawer.

"Just because you're president of a company does not mean you know everything," Doris teased, as she put the small roasted potatoes in a serving dish. Then she started humming something under her breath. Annie noticed how pretty she looked; her cheeks were bright, and there was a new sparkle in her eye.

"What are you singing?" Annie asked.

"Was I? I didn't even realize." Doris sang a line. " 'Fairy tales can come true, it can happen to you . . . if you're young at heart.' I haven't thought of that song in years. Michelle, take the brisket out and put it on that serving plate. Annie, toss the salad."

"It's nice to see you so happy," Annie said. "If I didn't know better, Gramma, I'd say you were in love."

"Not love. I loved your grandfather. But like is also V.N.," Doris said, sprinkling some parsley atop the potatoes.

"Very nice," Annie translated. "What are you talking about?"

"You remember that police officer O'Brien I met in front of your house?" She reached for another serving bowl and began to fill it with carrots and peas. "He lost his wife about a year ago, too. He's a very nice man. Plus, your grandfather gave his blessing."

Annie knit her brow. "What do you mean, my—"

"It never occurred to you that the voices you hear might be inherited? Help me carry out the food."

The three of them brought the food to a buffet table that was already laden with good things to eat—roast chicken, a kugel and a challah under a special Shabbos napkin that Annie remembered crocheting for her grandmother twenty years ago at summer camp. Next to it was the kiddush cup already filled with wine, and the twin white candles that burned in their majestic silver candleholders.

"Finally we can eat!" short Irma exclaimed. "Charlie over there needs to keep up his strength!"

"Very funny," Ettie chortled. Annie noticed that her speech was nearly normal. Plus, she was in a regular chair and no longer had her Jamaican attendant.

"How are you feeling, Ettie?" Annie asked.

Ettie shrugged. "I'm here."

"Girls," Doris said, "one more thing. Go back in the kitchen and pour the wine. Bring out the glasses on the tray you'll see on the table. The bottles are there, too."

Annie and Michelle went back to the kitchen. On her old Formica kitchen table were six bottles of Chateau de la Tour Clos, already opened. "Gramma has upgraded since she became a multimillionaire," Annie noted.

"Good. Because if I'd had to drink one more glass of Mögen David in this house, I was going to set up a picket line."

"It's so funny," Annie mused as she poured the wine. "It wasn't very long ago that my grandmother brought me to Bella's house when she was doing her Funtime sex toy party. That was supposed to cheer me up."

"Widows in their seventies are not the cheeriest thing I can think of." Michelle emptied one bottle and reached for another.

"But in a strange way it—they—did cheer me up," Annie realized. "If it wasn't for that night, I probably never would have come up with Mr. Vibrator in the first place."

Michelle counted wineglasses. "We need two more."

"Under there." Annie pointed to a drawer below the cutting board where her grandmother kept the glasses that didn't match.

"Got 'em."

Annie leaned against the refrigerator, momentarily lost in thought. "Back then I was waiting for life to happen to me. Like . . . like something would come along and make me happy." She struggled to explain. "I don't feel that way anymore. I feel . . . happy."

Michelle took out the extra glasses and filled them. "A seven-figure bank account tends to do that."

"Yeah," Annie agreed. "But it's more than that. Remember when Doris told us—what did she call it? The secret to getting any guy?"

"Yeah—and?"

"And I think what she meant is . . . the secret is feeling that you're okay without one."

Michelle made a face. "That is way too evolved for me. Also a crock. Mr. V is fun and all that, but it does not replace the real thing. Come on."

When they got back to the table, they handed everyone a full glass. Doris waited for them to sit. Her gaze settled on each of her friends' faces, then it went to Michelle and Mark, and finally to Charlie and Annie. "Well, this is a very special Shabbos." She put both hands to her chest. "M.H.I.O."

Annie scrambled to decode. "My . . . house . . . ?"

"Heart," Doris corrected.

"My heart . . . is overflowing!" Annie exclaimed.

"Brilliant girl," Doris said. She lifted the ornate pewter cup from the sidebar. "Who's going to make our kiddush?"

"I'd be happy to do it if you like," Charlie offered.

The eyes of Doris and all her friends lit up like pinball machines. So did Annie's.

"You're a Jewish boy?" Doris asked carefully.

The room was absolutely silent. Charlie stood and took the kiddush cup from Doris. *"Va-ya-hi erev va-ya-hi boker, yom ha-shishi,"* he chanted.

"Just when I didn't think my heart could G.A.F.!" Doris cried.

"Get any fuller?" Charlie guessed.

"Exactly!" Doris said.

Charlie finished the kiddush, everyone wished each other *l'chaim*—to life—and then Annie did a quick blessing over the challah. After Annie broke off a chunk and passed it around for everyone to take a morsel, they all got in the buffet line for dinner.

Annie stood behind Roz, who was explaining in great detail to the two Irmas how she'd just booked herself a free cruise to Hawaii as a bridge instructor. Ahead of her, she saw Charlie serve Ettie some of the brisket. And the strangest thing happened. Annie imagined Charlie on his knees in her gorgeous new deluxe king-size bed, completely naked, undressing her with his teeth.

That was when he turned to her, with the most delicious and knowing look on his face. It was as if he was seeing exactly the same thing.

"So, Charlie," Ettie coaxed as he poured some gravy on the brisket. "Enough with the food. Ask me if I want an aromatherapy massage."

Everyone laughed.

"Also," Ettie continued, "I'm dreaming maybe you've got a widowed grandfather with a voice just like yours."

"You never know," Charlie joked. Then his eyes locked with Annie's. "Stranger things have happened."

And then, deep in Annie's head—and also in her heart— she heard Charlie add, *"Sometimes dreams really do come true."*

About the Author

Cherie Jeffrey is a pseudonym for a well-known writing team whose fiction has appeared on the *New York Times, USA Today,* and *Publishers Weekly* bestseller lists. They have also written for stage, film, and television. Learn more at the official Web site for *Turn Me On,* www.turnmeoninc.com.